TRITON'S CALL

TETRASPHERE - BOOK 2

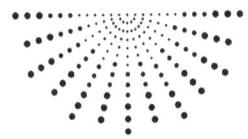

P.T.L. PERRIN

TRITON'S CALL

TetraSphere
Book Two

P.T.L. Perrin

Triton's Call – Tetrasphere Book Two

By P.T.L. Perrin

Cover by: Ewald Sutter, Azar, Trostberg, Germany

Cover Photos: Pax: © Olezzo | Dreamstime.com

Background: © Emavitale | Dreamstime.com

Edited by Lydia Moore and Mary Vallale

Copyright © 2016 by Patricia T.L. Perrin

Published in the United States of America

Worldwide Electronic & Digital Rights

Worldwide English Language Print Rights

Print ISBN: 978-1-950940-03-5

SeaQuill Press

Jupiter, FL 33458

❀ Formatted with Vellum

~

*For my Creator, who gives me the inspiration and ability to write,
and for my family and friends, whose love and enthusiasm keep the
creative flame burning.*

~

"Sunk! Sunk to the bottom of the sea, famous city on the sea! Power of the seas, you and your people, intimidating everyone who lived in your shadows. But now the islands are shaking at the sound of your crash, ocean islands in tremors from the impact of your fall." Ezekiel 26:18 (The Message)

~

"The secret sources of ocean are exposed, the hidden depths of earth lie uncovered the moment you roar in protest, let loose your hurricane anger." Psalm 18:15 (The Message)

1

JEWEL AMARYLLIS ADAMS

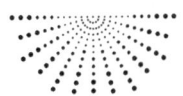

I still can't get used to how dull everything looks without my ability to see normally. How do the Dracans manage to block an ability that's part of my genetic makeup? It's one of the many frustrations defining my life now. No one has told me why they abducted me, and they're silent about the artifact, too. Marla has been a great help as far as teaching me how to survive here, I must admit, but she's as tight-lipped as the rest of them about what I really want to know.

Where is the artifact, and why did they take it? Why am I here? Where are my friends and family? Will the world end? Have we failed?

As far as I know, I've been here three and a half months, which puts us mid-January. The Dracans have treated me well, even though they won't allow me to return home, and I can't escape. I'm a captive living in luxury accommodations in a palace in the lost city of Atlantis at the bottom of the ocean.

I've tried to send a telepathic message to my family and friends, but my wristband won't work here. The one and only time I might have succeeded was two weeks ago when a breach in the force field protecting Atlantis gave the wristband just enough of an opening to form a connection. I felt it, but I'm not sure anyone received it, since there was no response. The wristband hasn't worked again. I'm afraid I'll be here forever, or at least until Earth destroys itself.

"Ready?" Marla asks, holding the door open. I smooth down the soft blue tunic I'm wearing over loose white pants and slip into sandals as I take one last look around the room. Confident I haven't forgotten anything, I follow her into the corridor.

We walk down a long hall on a solid sheet of marble, veined in swirls of gold, tan, and white on a mostly black background. Alabaster walls carved into filigree patterns meet a ceiling of inter-locking cedar planks soaring above our heads. We pass open arches leading into courtyards that take my breath away. Water flows from golden fountains in the center of intricately tiled floors, surrounded by lush greens and multi-hued flowers, with arches leading to more rooms beyond.

I've seen some of those rooms, with elaborate mosaics on the walls depicting epic battles or undersea scenes. I recognize some of the Greek or Roman gods, but I have never seen, nor imagined, many of the creatures in the mosaics. If they're beautiful in this dullness, how brilliant would they be with my full sight?

Marla leads me down several connected hallways and I'm soon hopelessly lost. She's taken me to visit some of the palace, but it's a vast maze, and I still haven't been able to map it in my mind. I wonder if it has anything to do with my ability being blocked. I normally have a keen sense of direction.

The warm, humid air reaches me before we arrive at our destination. The edge of my tunic stirs in the breeze, fragrant with greenery and flowers. I get a whiff of jasmine and honeysuckle and my knees nearly give way with sadness and longing.

We step into an impossible garden, one with no visible boundaries. The path leads over a vine-covered footbridge spanning a rushing creek. Green plants along the banks curl their branches above the water, and some, heavy with flowers, dip into it. Most are familiar to me, but the ones with meaty leaves and reticulated branches could be alien. It's the first time we've come here.

I breathe deeply and wish Pax and his sister Sky were here to see it.

And Storm, too, of course. Mom would love this garden, and Dad would want to know all about the technology making it work.

"How big is this place?" I ask. "How is this even possible? Aren't we at the bottom of the sea?"

"It's bigger than you can imagine. The Dracans have been able to replicate the full spectrum of sunlight and have created an atmosphere equal to the surface. You could say they experienced a Renaissance of their own after they were banished to the depths. Every one of their underground cities is magnificent."

"How long ago were they banished?"

"Twelve thousand years, give or take a few, after their war with the Allarans destroyed civilization. An entire continent was one of the casualties, along with the great city of Atlantis."

"Aren't we in Atlantis?" I ask.

"Yes, but not the original city. It would never have survived these depths."

"When was this one built?"

"Soon after the banishment. Dracan technology is very old, but effective. Humanity has suffered without it."

"What happened to the humans?" I ask, genuinely curious. This history isn't taught in our schools.

She says, "Eighty percent of humanity died in the war, and those who were left went back to survival mode. They lost all knowledge of the technology that made civilization into the thing of beauty it once was. Mankind has come a long way since then, but they still lack so much of what Dracans and Allarans have."

Most of our stories about those times are considered myths. Some Bible scholars believe people have only been around for six-thousand years, but others disagree, saying humans were here around forty-thousand years ago. The truth is, no scientist, religious or otherwise, can be certain how old our planet and its inhabitants are.

"Why didn't the Dracans and Allarans help the humans rebuild?"

Marla replies, "Creator made it clear they weren't allowed to interfere in humanity's development after the banishment. The Allarans were sent to live in their ships above Terra, and the Dracans were limited to living below the surface. They've had some interaction with humans, of course, but they've kept their existence mostly hidden."

"After all this time, do they consider Terra their home?" Since the Allarans call our planet by its name, I assume the Dracans also know it as Terra.

"Of course, they do," Marla says indignantly.

"Then why would they want to destroy this beautiful planet?

PAXTON HUNTER FLETCHER

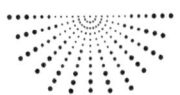

Shorts. Check. Sunglasses. Check. Everything is packed and ready for our trip to the Bahamas. Sky mumbles something about a delivery while she slams a drawer shut. She's projecting her impatient mood, and the calm I send her isn't helping.

I tap my wristband, a device Jewel's dad invented so we can communicate telepathically. We all have one: Storm, Jewel, Sky, me, and our folks. They're coded so we can open a communal line among the four of us or speak individually to each other. Our parents are linked to Sky and me and to the other adults. The problem is, Jewel's device isn't working for some reason, and we've only heard from her once since she was abducted, when she said, "Antiss."

What are you upset about? I ask.

She answers. *What if we don't find her?*

We will. We know the Dracans have her in Atlantis. The Allarans are sure it's somewhere in the Tongue of the Ocean off Andros Island. They're fully aware we can't fix any more of the artifacts without her, so they have a vested interest in helping us get to her.

I wish we'd never met any of the aliens. Her familiar fragrance precedes her when she comes into my room. My twin sister is a strong empath who can feel everyone's emotions and project her own to people around her. I'm like a bloodhound, with a nose sensitive enough to smell pheromones and scents too subtle for other humans to pick up. Thankfully, I can turn it off by raising a scent guard like a shield when I don't need it. I can also calm her down, usually.

It's worse for Storm, she says. *He was only ten when a Dracan ship killed his parents. And now this. It's no wonder he's angry all the time.*

Sky is in love with Storm, and he loves her, too, judging by his pheromones when he's around her. He won't acknowledge it, though, and I hate how it affects my sister. I figured it out the day he saved her after a Dracan ship caused her car to slide off the road into a ravine. His telekinesis kept her from dropping into the river far below.

All four of us have unique abilities, including Jewel, who sees millions of colors with her remarkable aquamarine eyes, multiple times more than any other human. She also sees through disguises and cloaking devices, which is how she's always been aware of her sentinel floating in the sky above her. I remember when she told us about the Allaran ships assigned to watch each of us. She thought they were here to protect us. Hers didn't do such a great job of it.

The doorbell rings and Sky goes back to her room while I open it. Sheriff Green stands outside, hat dusted with a thin layer of snow, red nose puffing steam with each breath. He stomps his boots on the ice-encrusted mat, steps in and hands me a small box.

"Found it on the doorstep. It's addressed to Sky. Are your mom and dad here?"

I take his heavy down jacket and hang it on the coat rack. "I wish you were coming with us, Sheriff."

"I do, too. There's a good chance my son is with Jewel. Your folks know how to contact me. If…when you find him, I'll drop everything and get there. Meanwhile, I'm needed here." His voice trails off and he heads toward the kitchen, where stairs lead from a door in the pantry down to my parents' office and the gym.

Max Green disappeared with Jewel when the reptilian Dracans invaded the cave where we'd just repaired the tetrahedron. It's one of many artifacts planted in different parts of the world to keep the planet in balance and in proper working order. They're failing, and we four are supposed to fix them, according to an ancient Cherokee prophecy. The Dracans took the artifact along with Jewel and Max.

"My bikini, and just in time," Sky exclaims, taking the package from my hand. "Now I'm ready for the Bahamas." She rushes off to stuff it with the rest of her clothes in the suitcase.

The pantry door shuts, and Dad shouts, "Time to go." He grabs his bag, Sheriff Green picks up Mom's, and we load up the back of Dad's SUV. We're going to meet the other families and the Allarans in the field in front of Jewel's house.

Dressed in her winter boots and jacket, Sky shivers next to me in the back seat. My nerves crawl with anticipation, and I shiver, too.

MY FOOT TOUCHES the sand in the circle of light from the open hatch, I find my balance and step away. The flat bottom of the Allaran ship hangs over my head, soundless and still. My sister floats down, followed by our parents, Dylan and Coral. Our luggage lands with a soft thump after they move out of the way. Dad and I grab the bags and set them down beside us.

Baran comes down last, his long white hair blowing in the sea-breeze. He stands in light that seems to spark off his silver skin. I tamp down my revulsion and wonder at the strength of it. He's been helpful, after all, and I can't blame him for anything other than his existence.

Maybe it's the dopey expression on Sky's face that bothers me so much. She seems to be completely taken in by the aliens, first Vega and now Baran. My gut reaction is the direct opposite of hers. I hate them, especially Vega. I can't forget Jewel's face the first time we met him outside the Cherokee sacred cave. I put aside thoughts of Jewel for now.

"We cannot take you closer, Star Children." His voice grates on my nerves, and I fight the urge to attack. My father, nose wrinkled in disgust, clenches his fists at his sides with the strain of holding himself back. Mom's face, on the other hand, is lit with a brilliant smile. It's a relief when the Allaran rises back into the ship and it turns invisible. A second ship replaces it.

The hatch opens and Storm descends, followed by his uncle Wolf and aunt Sequoia. This time Vega accompanies them, and Storm and Wolf fight the same visceral response Dad and I share. Sky says it has something to do with their voices, but it happens even when they don't speak.

"How will we find her?" Sequoia asks. There's a sweet lilt to her voice, and I can hear a low growl rumbling in Wolf's chest. "Thank you for bringing us here, but what now?"

"Charles is in touch with a marine archaeologist," Vega responds. "He does not know we exist, but he knows these waters and has the resources to help you find the city of Atlantis. For now, you must rely on human help. We will, as always, remain vigilant. We will do what we can when the time comes."

"What do you mean?" Wolf has a definite edge to his voice.

"We cannot invade the Dracans' city. We will watch and take any opportunity to help, unless it goes against Creator's mandate. It is the best I can offer."

Wolf and Dad nod, and Vega returns to his ship. When it disappears, a third vessel materializes. Jewel's parents, Analiese and Charles float down. I catch myself expecting Jewel, but a female Allaran drops down the shaft of light, instead. I drop my guard, and breathe in an unearthly forest fragrance, alien but not unpleasant.

Her white hair moves in the breeze, thick and wavy, and I long to run my hands through it. Her skin glows golden in the yellow light from the ship, unlike the silver skin of the males. When she smiles, my entire body grows warm, and when she speaks, I want to take her in my arms and guard her with my life.

"How wonderful to finally meet you, Star Children," she says, and I have the strangest impulse to wag my tail, as if I had one. What is wrong with me?

"My name is Chara, and I am the scientist whose DNA Carolina Sky shares." Storm steps toward her, and I assume the stance, eager to fight him for her, until I remind myself I am not an alpha dog, and

Jewel is the one I'm in love with. Is this the effect the male Allarans have over our women? No wonder they act like girls crushing on a rock star.

I glance at Sky and don't recognize the cold expression on her face. She's generally warm and friendly, but now her stance mirrors mine. We both hold black belts in karate, and even though Sky hates to spar and hasn't advanced, she's ready to attack the woman I'm determined to defend. I back down. The Allarans have far too much influence over us.

"We are watching, and when the time is right, we will help you. Jewel is safe for now," Chara's voice flows through me like a warm, slow love song.

"How do you know?" Jewel's mother sounds harsh. "Have you seen her? Have you spoken with her?"

The alien woman answers, honey on warm toast, "We are in contact with someone in the city. Not all Dracans are enemies, Analiese. Jewel is being cared for." When she turns toward me, the light sparks off her large blue eyes, the same shape and color as Sky's.

"You will find Jewel. You must. Our worlds depend on you." Chara turns and floats back into the ship. They're gone in an instant.

"Aren't there four ships?" Sky asks in her normal tone of voice. She's recovered from the Allarans' spells.

"Jewel has her own, the sentinel she's seen all her life. I hope we get to meet her DNA donor soon, especially if she's anything like Chara." I grin when she smacks me on the head.

While our eyes adjust to the night, I take a deep breath. Tropical plants smell softer than the woods in North Carolina, even with the heavy perfume of flowers and fruit permeating the air. The aroma of salt air and sand feels like home to me, like the beach in California.

Thanks to Storm's telekinetic ability, our luggage drifts behind us along a sandy path. Spiky grasses and palmettos brush our legs, and Sky stops now and then to swipe at something irritating her. I wonder about spiders and mosquitos.

We come to a clearing where three houses sit on pylons. Storm lowers the bags and we each grab one before we approach. It's too dark to get a good look at them, so we head toward the middle house, where a man waves in the dim glow of a light on the veranda.

"Welcome," he calls and comes downstairs to greet us. "I'm Tony Michaels, the property manager. My wife Meg and I live just down the beach. We're at your service."

He glances at my dad curiously. "I didn't hear you arrive. Did you take cabs from the airport?"

"We were dropped off and walked in," Dad explains, without giving anything away. "We needed the exercise."

His explanation seems to satisfy Tony, who directs each family to our respective houses. It's been a long day, and I'm grateful when he leaves, and we can finally settle in.

Our family gathers on the veranda after we've unpacked our clothes. The moon glints off softly undulating waves and lightens the sand on the beach we share with the others. Mom and Dad talk quietly at one end, while I find a lounge chair next to Sky and lie back to stare at the brilliant stars. Sky sends me comfort.

"We'll find her. According to the Allarans, she's nearby."

"Sure," I answer, wishing I could be more confident. "They seemed pretty sure of it, but I wish they could pinpoint Atlantis. If what Baran says is true, Dracan technology hides it from their instruments." Just saying his name leaves a bitter taste in my mouth. What is it about the aliens?

"For now, let's enjoy being in the Bahamas. It beats the ice and snow of home, doesn't it?" Sky sighs and folds her arms behind her head.

We fall silent, and I think about my beautiful Jewel. At least, I like to think of her as mine. As sad as Sky is, she sends love. We both miss our friend.

3
PAX

The morning air fills my lungs as I take deep cleansing breaths on the cool beach sand. Storm and I take our places and bow in salute. When Dad nods, I let my opponent get the first throw in. As I fall, my foot contacts his legs and sweeps them out from under him. We've been using both the Shotokan techniques Dad has taught Sky and me all our lives and the mixed martial arts moves Storm is familiar with. The combination is exhilarating.

"Enough," Dad calls, after what seems like an hour of sparring. We bow again and make a run for the water. Storm's a strong swimmer, but I outclass him, having grown up near the beach. He lived in Oklahoma before moving to the Cherokee reservation in Blue Mountain, North Carolina. No beaches in either location. We swim out a hundred yards to deep water when the mental link opens.

I'm beat. Heading in. Storm's thoughts are clear in my mind.

Right behind you, I say, then press the face of my wristband to close the connection before turning back to shore. He rarely uses the link anymore. Since the cavern, there hasn't been an urgent reason to. We're all dealing with anger and grief in our own way.

The sand has warmed up considerably by the time I reach it and collapse, leaving him floating on his back in the calm, shallow water. Jewel would love the color of the ocean here. It's the color of her eyes.

"Did you have a good workout?" My sister settles in the sand next to me and pretends to scan the horizon, but I know she's watching Storm. Her new green bikini accentuates her curves and sets off her crazy mane of red hair, making me want to wrap a towel around her. He's an idiot.

"Yeah. Where were you? You should have been practicing your forms."

"Mom and I went to visit Sequoia." She grabs a fistful of fine sand and lets it trickle through her fingers. "She isn't feeling well."

"Does she have a cold or something? She never gets sick." Storm's aunt is a Cherokee medicine woman who, I swear, knows magic. At least she knows a lot more about healing with herbs and natural ingredients than most modern doctors with their drugs and fancy equipment.

"No, she's just a little run down. No worries." Her answer along with the peace she sends my way calms me, and since Storm hasn't said anything, it must not be serious.

He wades out, shakes the water out of his ears and plops down on my other side, away from Sky. The cloudless, sun-bright atmosphere turns darker, and I realize my sister is projecting her unhappiness, fueling a rage burning in me since Jewel was taken. Burning deep inside, I stand up to leave. Let the two of them duke it out. I have enough to deal with.

From the deck, I glance back and see them still sitting in their spots. They don't seem to be talking, but at least they aren't running away from each other. I wish he would wise up. Pheromones don't lie. He's crazy about my sister. I ignore the fact I smell the same pheromones when he's around Jewel.

4

JEWEL

Marla's face registers shock. "Destroy the planet? They wouldn't! What makes you say that?"

"Why else would they steal the artifact after we healed it? Don't you know the artifacts keep Terra alive and balanced? If they sell them to buy passage back to their planet, they're dooming our earth to destruction." I watch for her reaction. She might not know any of what we learned from the Watchers.

"It's just crazy," she says. "Why would they need to go anywhere? Terra is our home. From what I've heard of their home world, none of us would survive there."

"What do you mean? What's wrong with their home world?"

"I'm sure Thuban can explain it to you better than I can. He's the leader of Atlantis and my mother's mate. If anyone knows what's going on with the artifacts, he does."

"You keep saying Thuban will explain, but it's been months. When will I get to meet him?"

"Soon," she promises, again.

"I also haven't seen your mother since the flood. Isn't she here with you?"

"They're away together, Jewel. I can't tell you any more," Marla answers. It's the same answer she's given me for most of my questions. She can't tell me.

She grows silent and we walk to a gazebo on the shore of a lake ringed by mountains. They must be holograms. Even if we're under an enormous dome, as I suspect, there's no way they'd fit mountains inside.

"Marla," I say as soon as we sit on a bench built along the inside wall of the gazebo, "won't you let me see you as you are? I know you're in disguise."

She sighs and the light around her ripples. I watch her shift and I'm surprised her appearance seems normal to me. Iridescent scales cover her skin and change color as she moves. Except for a slightly protruding snout and pointed teeth, her face closely resembles a human. Her round-shaped eyes remain the same, but her pupils have become vertical slits and the irises have gone from green to yellow, like the eyes of an anaconda. Her short sandy hair has become three golden ridges, like braids running from her forehead to the back of her neck.

"I've seen you this way a few times. You don't have to disguise yourself around me."

She snorts, and when she speaks, it's clear why her "s" sounds are somewhat drawn out. The shape of the teeth has something to do with it.

"I think I prefer to keep my human shape around you, at least for now," she says. When she ripples back, her eyes are different, warmer. In her human form, she's tall and shapely, moving with sinuous grace. Back home, the boys at school couldn't keep their eyes off her when she walked, and I could see their envy when she and Max were together. She's an attractive human, with her stylishly short blonde hair and green eyes, but she had a hardness about her in school. Her arrogant attitude didn't help. And yet during the flood, when we rescued her and her mother, she showed a lot of compassion helping the injured in the makeshift hospital in our house. I thought then we could become friends.

"It isn't a disguise, Jewel. I shift from one to the other. How did you know about my Dracan form, anyway? I've never told you."

"I'm a pentachromat, which means I can see millions of colors outside the normal range for most people. I also see auras, life forces, and through disguises. You were in your Dracan form every time I took my glasses off. My dad designed them so I could function at school without being overwhelmed by auras. If you're a shapeshifter, I must have seen your dominant shape."

"Why did you ask me to change, then, if you already see me as Dracan?"

"It seems I've lost my ability here. Something is blocking me, and I hate it."

She gets up and gazes out at the lake. "I know Storm has telekinetic abilities. I've seen him in action. What about your other friends? Do they have abilities, too?"

"Sky is an empath. She feels the emotions of everyone around her and can influence their emotions, but not yours." I join her at the railing and wonder how deep the water is, and how far it extends.

"Pax can detect subtle scents better than a bloodhound. Thankfully, he can turn his gift off unless he needs it, but it's useful. Sky told me when they lived in California, he smelled something odd coming from between two houses in their cul-de-sac. It wasn't human and it wasn't any animal he could identify. They didn't see what it was, but he smelled it again when you walked by in the lunchroom the first day of school. That's when he knew you were different."

Marla breaks in, "So Sky can't feel me, and my odor offends her brother. No wonder they weren't exactly friendly." She laughs. "I didn't intend to be friends, anyway. My assignment was to spy on them and identify you."

"What are you talking about?" I ask. "What assignment?"

"You'll understand later," she promises. "How long have you known I'm half-Dracan?"

"We suspected after you and Max took Storm to see the crystal grotto. He caught a glimpse of the real you in there."

"I must have been careless. Emotions can trigger a shift, or a partial one. I had to learn to control it as a young teenager. Apparently, I still don't have a complete handle on it." She laughs, and I smile. I like this Marla better than the girl I knew in North Carolina.

We stand in silence for a while and watch the lake. My head, as usual, is full of questions. How can trees grow more than a mile under water? They're real. I touched a few as we passed them on the garden path. How is it possible we aren't crushed by the ocean pressure? Is there an observation area, with windows to the outside? Is anything visible out there?

I open my mouth, about to ask, when I notice a strong ripple in the lake. Is there something in there? It's followed by another, and suddenly the lake is full of waves and the ground shakes violently. A beam in the gazebo comes loose and crashes behind us. The mountains in the distance flicker, and Marla grabs my hand and starts running back down the path.

5
PAX

"What makes you so sure we can find Atlantis from Andros?" Wolf voices my own uncertainty. We've gathered for lunch at Charles and Analiese's bungalow, where Tony and Meg had stocked the refrigerator with some basics, including frozen burgers and buns. We could do worse than a summer cookout on a winter day. Charles mans the grill, while we set the table with condiments and fresh lettuce and tomatoes. The smell of grilling meat has me salivating.

"There's conjecture the Bahamas are a part of the lost continent of Atlantis," Charles says. "A team of marine archaeologists led by my friend Dr. Julian Emery, recently sent a submersible to photograph a pyramid they found in the depths of a trench called the Tongue of the Ocean. It appears to be crystalline and we believe it may be part of an energy source for an undersea city built by the Dracans. It makes sense, if you consider the pyramids found all over the world were part of a complex energy grid in ancient times."

"I thought the glass pyramid story was debunked." I hope I'm wrong. Charles turns off the grill and brings the meat to the table. We grab the buns and dig in. I'm not the only one who's hungry.

"People should be skeptical," Charles explains. "If it isn't true, it should be debunked. However, authorities have been known to cover up more than a few discoveries. Dylan and I have been talking to Dr. Emery. He's assured us the pyramid is real and has sent us photos to corroborate his claims. I believe he's fascinated with the idea of extraterrestrials living under the ocean, and he's willing to work with us and let us use his equipment."

"Isn't Andros famous for bonefish and blue holes?" Storm pipes in.

"I've heard of the blue holes all over Andros," I add, "both in the ocean and on land. They lead to a vast labyrinth of caves under the island. They're a favorite with divers, but divers are usually limited to a certain depth, and they go much deeper. It would make a good hiding place for the artifact the Dracans stole."

"Is it possible the artifact is causing the problems we've been seeing on the news?" Analiese asks.

"Last week, Hurricane Alphonse was the earliest named storm in known history to form in the Atlantic," Mom says.

"There's no evidence of it on Andros because it started north of here, though still in the Bermuda Triangle. January third is far too early for a hurricane. Something is throwing the balance of the ocean off."

"Not to mention the poor dolphins and whales that have beached themselves and died recently," Sequoia adds.

"Just last week fifty bottlenose dolphins stranded themselves on Miami Beach. It's happened two other times since October, in north Florida and southern Georgia. Marine biologists think something is destroying their echolocation abilities."

"I wonder if the government is testing acoustical weapons," I comment, having done some research on government experiments when I first heard of marine mammals stranding themselves on beaches in California. It happened rarely until recently. Three times in three months can't be natural.

"It's possible." Dad stands up and stretches. "It's also possible the sounds interfering with their echolocation are made by an artifact."

That stops me cold. Did the Dracans break the one we fixed when they took it, or is there another one here? Are the animals dying because of an artifact?

"It seems like many factors point to this area as the most likely location for Atlantis," Dad says. "Wolf, Charles, and I are going into town to meet with Dr. Emery today. Analiese and Coral want to take one of the other jeeps to get some shopping done, and Sequoia has decided to stay here with you kids. You might as well enjoy the little bit of vacation you're likely to get."

Sky is delighted, and I can't wait for some downtime this afternoon, right after I eat another hamburger.

I sit back to savor the burger and daydream Jewel and I are exploring underwater caves and blue holes together. My sister and I have been scuba certified since we were twelve. If Jewel hasn't learned to scuba, I'll take her on her first dive.

I refuse to think of her as a prisoner. I imagine her walking the streets of an unimaginably beautiful city, immersed in a palette of millions of colors and, on impulse, I tap her code on my wristband.

Jewel, if you can hear me, know we'll find you. We need you and we love you. Heck, I love you. When I see you again, I'll say it to your face. Come back to us, Jewel.

I break the connection, even though I didn't sense her presence at all. I wonder if the Dracan technology blocking the link is also blocking her gift. I can't imagine Jewel in a life without colors.

6

CAROLINA SKY FLETCHER

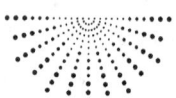

S and moves like silk under my bare feet in the shallows. Waving lines of sunlight dance in the ripples and reflect off the bottom, while glittering tropical fish dart here and there, followed by a slower silver bonefish intent on its prey. The colors revive my soul, which had gone gray and dull in winter's cold and my best friend's absence. I've waded quite a distance from shore, and the warm water in the calm lagoon soothes me.

I've always loved the ocean, and thankfully, I'm one of those few redheads whose skin tans without burning. As fair as my skin is in the winter, as soon as I'm in the sun for a few hours, my color deepens into a gold complementing the crazy colors of my hair. Thanks to my coloring and the liberal use of sunscreen, sunburn is one less thing I worry about.

I wish I could see the Sentinels the way Jewel does. I wonder why, if their futuristic technology can penetrate the depths, they can't rescue her. Couldn't they do it without invading the city? Didn't Vega say the skin of their ship allows them to move through air and water without resistance? If they can fly in the vacuum of space and with unimaginable speed through the atmosphere, why can't they skim through the depths of the ocean? I turn away, disgusted, and concentrate on the stained-glass blues and greens of the sea around me, while enjoying the warmth of the sun on my shoulders. I can't imagine how Jewel sees more colors than these.

Storm sits on top of his kayak, dangling his feet in the water. He's let his thick wavy hair grow long and keeps it tied in a tail with a leather thong. The sun has turned him golden brown and his amber eyes, fringed with long dark lashes, melt my heart when he looks at me, which is all too rarely. He's been avoiding my eyes since we kissed in the cave.

Pax went back to the house to do some research after a brisk swim. He can't relax while Jewel is missing. I wish he were still out here with us. He's a calming presence when my emotions begin to flare, like they're doing right now. I'm sorry for myself, and he knows how to break up a pity party.

We left Sequoia reading a book on her veranda. She's slowed down the last few weeks. I've caught her napping several times, and she doesn't seem to have much of an appetite. I've felt nothing but peace in her, but I wonder if I'd know if anything is wrong. I'm pretty sure she's an empath, too, better at keeping her emotions under tight rein than I am.

Storm is pensive, or maybe bored. He spent the last half hour fishing, tossing back every catch. Why hurt the poor fish if you aren't planning to eat them? He's unusually tranquil now, his rage under control.

"Are you okay?"

"Can't you tell? Don't you feel my emotions?" He sends a spike of annoyance and smiles.

"Oh, yeah. I felt it. Annoyance is better than nothing. What are you afraid of?"

He slips into the kayak and turns toward land. "I'm afraid we won't find Jewel. I'm afraid we won't find the artifact and the world will end. I'm not afraid of you, Sky."

He dips his paddle in the water and heads away from me. "Then why won't you let me in? Why do you have such a thick wall?" I direct my questions to his retreating back, and he doesn't answer. I'm tempted to slap him with my own annoyance, but what good would it do? I've lost him, if I ever had him in the first place.

I take my time wading back to shore. The three brightly painted houses we've rented perch on pylons that make me nervous. It seems a good tide could wash them out, despite their having withstood more than a few hurricanes. Ours is the middle house, painted aqua with white shutters. Pax and I each have a bedroom and bath in the left octagon, and my parents have the master bedroom and a fully equipped office in the right one. Picture windows along a wide veranda face the ocean. Each house resembles a dumbbell or an hourglass on its side.

Wolf and Sequoia are staying in the yellow house to the left, and Jewel's parents have the coral house on the right. A green jeep sits in a space under the Adams' house. A jeep for each house was included in the rent, along with kayaks, sunfish sailboats, and one speedboat we all share. If it weren't for the gravity of our mission, and if I could break through Storm's wall, this would be a wonderful vacation.

The tide is going out, and I push hard against it to get to shore. It's a slow process. I'm about twenty yards out when the sand heaves under my feet. There's no sign of Storm or his kayak. A wave slaps me from behind and knocks me into the water. Until now, the sea has been calm, with just small ripples moving with the tide. What's happening?

Another wave hits, and another follows, each one higher than the last. I struggle to my feet and shove one foot in front of the other, straining to reach the beach faster. It isn't helping. The force of the water vacuums the sand out from under me and pulls at my legs. A wave slams me from behind, sweeping me into the water. I flatten out and wait for the next one. I've surfed much higher waves in the Pacific Ocean. Instead of picking me up and taking me closer to shore, this one breaks over me and tumbles me like a load of laundry. This close to shore, the movement is unpredictable and violent. I'm a strong swimmer, but I'm no match for this.

"Sky!" His voice is faint through water that tosses and scrapes me along the sandy bottom. I have no control of my limbs and can barely hang on to my breath. Terror, not mine, washes over me as a hand grips my arm and pulls me up. I cough violently, and his arm wraps around my shoulders. Relief and warmth pour from him. His wall is down, and all I can think about is getting out of the maelstrom.

"Hold on. Here's another one." He pulls me to his chest and we both go down. Underwater, a low moan grows louder by the second.

When the wave recedes, we're still hanging on to each other. The moaning sound fills the air, and I'm grateful it isn't coming from him. We get to our feet and before I can scramble to shore, my feet lift out of the water and I realize he's floating us to safety. This time we make it and collapse on the sand, out of reach of the surf.

The sound comes from the ocean, and a sudden powerful jolt of intense grief washes over me. Pain slams my heart and rips the breath from my aching lungs. My throat closes and I can barely breathe. I curl up and wail, and don't hear Storm's voice battering at the gripping sorrow.

"What is it? What's wrong?"

The sound recedes, along with the anguish. With his eyes fearful and pleading and his face drained of color, Storm gathers me in his arms, his body trembling.

"Speak to me, Sky. What's happening?"

Still wracked with sobs, I turn away and see a dark shape just beyond the lagoon, where the reef ends, and deep ocean begins. A breaching whale. I wait for the telltale blow, but nothing happens.

"Is that a whale? Do whales make that sound?" I point to it and he stands up to get a better view.

The hump turns into two, then three, each one following the other. Finally, a long tail flips out of the water, as if one of the whales is about to dive, but there's no fluke on the end. The giant tail is forked. It disappears and the lagoon is once again still.

"It wasn't a whale," he says, still shaking. My emotions have settled, and I send a blast of calmness to him.

"I could tell by the forked tail. What do you think those humps were? And that sound? Seriously, I've never felt anything like it. It was unbearable."

He turns to me gravely. "It reminds me of the Loch Ness monster. I wonder if the locals know anything about this."

"I wonder if Sequoia heard it." I have an uneasy feeling and hurry toward the house. Storm runs past me, and I follow him up the stairs to the veranda where she'd been reading. Sequoia isn't there.

7

SKY

My brother pounds up the stairs behind us. He must have seen us running and sensed my distress. I grab the towel he hands me and wrap it around myself as we hurry to Sequoia's room, where she's on her bed, curled up with one arm over her head and the other bent protectively around her belly.

"Auntie, are you okay?" Storm sits next to her and gently pulls her arm away from her face. Tears burn my eyes at her grief and fear.

"I don't know what came over me." Her voice is thick, as if she's about to cry. "When the sound started, I was overcome with more sadness than I've ever experienced, even more than when I lost my sister." Storm helps her sit up and wraps his arms around her. She bows her head and covers her eyes with her hands. Her shoulders shake. "I'm so afraid for Jewel, and I'm afraid for my baby."

Baby? Of course. No wonder she's been feeling off. Love and joy fill me and flow out to her. She smiles through her tears, and Storm's eyes soften. He already knows. Why didn't he tell us? Sequoia reaches for me, and we hug and cry a little together. A baby! My brother wears a goofy grin.

We hear the crunch of gravel under the house before we have a chance to talk. "Please don't say anything," Sequoia pleads. "I'll tell everyone tonight."

Storm gives me one last glance and regretfully raises his wall again. Why is he doing this? I know he cares about me. Determination fills me. I'll break the wall down if it's the last thing I do.

Pax leads the way downstairs to greet Mom and Analiese. Storm is already floating bags of groceries into the kitchen, where we sort things out.

He taps on his wristband. *Don't say anything about the sea monster yet.* His voice is clear in my mind.

When? I ask.

After supper, when they've had a chance to rest and eat. That thing isn't going anywhere, and we could be wrong about it.

What thing? Pax asks.

The thing that made the sound. You heard it, didn't you?

I was asleep, he answers. *Something woke me up, but I don't remember hearing anything.*

We'll explain later, Storm says and closes the link.

Dad's jeep pulls in after the groceries have been sorted and put in the respective homes. He and the men don't say anything, but I notice the gleam in Dad's eyes and sense satisfaction coming from the three of them. They must have had a successful meeting with Dr. Emery.

We gather for supper at our house. Dad grills fresh mahi-mahi, and Mom serves it with mango salsa and coconut rice. I love this island life. After Storm clears the dishes, he tells them about our encounter with the sound and the overwhelming emotions. Sequoia says nothing, avoiding everyone's eyes.

"It was a sea monster," I pipe in, getting everyone's attention. I describe the humps I thought were whales, and when I mention the forked tail, Dad and Wolf exchange a worried look.

"I'll ask Julian if he can identify what it is," Charles says. "Julian, or Dr. Emery, heads up Oceanic Archaeological Research. OAR has been exploring these waters for years, and Dr. Emery has agreed to help us search for Jewel. In fact, you kids will meet him and his team tomorrow."

Pax grins, delighted. He's always loved the ocean and here's a chance to do some real exploring, and to find the city where Jewel is being held.

"There's one more thing we'd like to share with all of you," Wolf says. He stands behind Sequoia and puts his hands on her shoulders.

She smiles up at him and says to the rest of us, "We're going to be parents."

After the congratulations and hugs, they tell us the baby is due the third week in June.

The adults stay in the great room and talk quietly, while we sit on the veranda and enjoy the view of the moon rising over the water. How Jewel would love this, and how excited she'd be about Storm's little cousin.

"Do you realize Sequoia became pregnant right around the time the Dracans abducted her and Wolf?" I ask no one in particular, and no one answers. I form a mental picture of Marla Snow. We know she's a Dracan hybrid. Did they mess with the baby's DNA, like the Allarans did with ours, or would he or she literally be half-Dracan?

"Do you think the baby might be like Marla?" Pax voices my concern.

"I sure hope not," Storm replies. "Still, if my aunt was already pregnant, they might have done something to the baby's DNA."

I dread what he left unsaid. If the baby is half-Dracan, will Wolf accept the child? I remember the fear in Sequoia's eyes when Sheriff Green asked them about the abduction. Is this what frightened her?

The full moon shimmers and gentle waves sparkle through tears in my eyes. Even the sight of the Milky Way and pinpoints of starlight filling the heavens doesn't lift the sadness. I pray we find Jewel soon. I pray for Sequoia's innocent baby.

8

JEWEL

"It's a breach! Come on, Jewel, hurry!" Marla's voice is frantic, and we run faster. A railing on the bridge crumbles as we cross it. My chest burns like it's being crushed while deep gongs reverberate around us. My heart races and I have trouble sucking in air. She opens the first door to the right as we exit the garden, and slams it shut as soon as we run inside. She slaps her hand on a flashing light by the door, while the muscles in my legs give out and I sink to the floor with my back against the wall. My field of vision narrows.

"Stay with me! Take deep breaths. It'll be better in a moment." Marla pats my cheeks and when I breathe in, my vision clears. She's right. It is better.

"That was a big one," I gasp out. Is the floor trembling, or is it me?

"This is the worst one yet. What could be breaking the field? This doesn't happen!"

"What do you mean? It's happened a lot since I've been here."

The gonging stops and the light by the door turns off. Oh, no. My gut turns to ice when I realize I didn't try the wristband this time. How could I be so stupid?

"The last time the field cracked was during a violent earthquake seven years ago, and this one was as bad," she says. "I don't know what's causing these new cracks, and I'm worried. I wonder if we can see what did it."

Marla's face grows determined. "Come on," she commands.

I get up, heavy with disappointment in myself, and follow her into chaos as Dracans rush away from the garden, jostling and shoving each other. We hug the wall and join the mob, while uniformed soldiers push everyone aside to get to the garden. Did the breach happen there, while we were in the gazebo? Did it have anything to do with me?

"Where are we going?" I shout to be heard over the noise in the corridor.

"You'll see," she shouts back.

I'm once again confused by the twists and turns, until we reach a white marble door carved with swirls of palm fronds and flowers surrounding an Egyptian eye of Horus outlined in lapis lazuli with an onyx pupil. It's breathtaking, but she gives me little time to admire it. She presses her hand on the onyx and the door slides open without a sound, and just as quietly slides shut as soon as we walk through.

"What is this place?" Instead of marble and alabaster, white-tiled floors are flanked by plain beige walls. Hieroglyph friezes extend along each wall at a Dracan's eye-level, about a foot above mine. I recognize a few symbols, but don't know what they mean.

"I call this the heart of the palace," she says. "It's where everything is maintained, from housekeeping to mechanics. I'll show you one of my favorite rooms, but you can't tell Thuban you've been here."

We get to a plain brown door embossed with an owl hieroglyph. Dracans must be able to read the ancient Egyptian symbols. My room contains a library of their books, and they use the same alphabet we do. Marla says they pronounce words phonetically, but I've yet to learn the meaning of the words.

"Wait here, and don't make a sound." She cracks the door open and slips inside. I pray no one comes along this hallway. I'm fully exposed here, with nowhere to hide. In a couple of minutes, the door opens, and she waves me inside.

"Sit here," she says, pointing to a padded recliner with a series of controls on the armrests, and takes the seat next to me. "Don't touch anything."

As her fingers deftly manipulate her controls, the light dims and a humming sound comes from the screen. At first, there's nothing but inky blackness, but then my heart leaps. Strange creatures glowing with life force fill the screen. Or maybe it's simple bioluminescence? For a moment, I'd hoped my sight was back to normal.

"What are we looking for?"

"We have cameras all over the outside of the protective barrier. I'll see if I can find where the breach happened and maybe we'll see what caused it." The wall splits into multiple screens and I scan them, hoping to spot more of the luminous creatures. When my eyes adjust, the screens reveal monstrous fish with spikes for teeth in enormous mouths, terrifying sinuous snakes, and giant squid, to name a few. Every screen has them.

"When we were in the cavern, you said seeing in pitch darkness is one of your gifts," I remind her. "Can you see what's going on out there? I can't make out a thing, unless you count those creatures lit up with bioluminescence."

"They're flashing like crazy. I've seen this before. I think I know what might be disturbing them," she explains.

"I noticed the flashing, but they're all outlined in light," I tell her. "Most of them are various shades of red, but some dark blue and black ones are there, too."

"You can see them? Their whole bodies? How is it possible?"

"Maybe my gift works because the cameras are outside the city and not blocking my ability. I see their life force." My heart pounds with excitement. It's so good to see normally again, even if it's only through cameras. "Is this the only room where you can see outside?"

She smiles, reaches over, and taps my hand. "You haven't been to my room, yet. I'll show you my media setup. I think you'll be pleasantly surprised."

My eyes are still scanning when I spot them. "Wait, Marla. What is that?" I point to the one screen showing something I'd only read about. By now, nothing should surprise me, but this does.

She mumbles a number under her breath, jumps up and says, "Come quickly. We'll explore this in my room."

9
JEWEL

I can't believe how luxurious Marla's room is. I thought mine was palatial, with its enormous four-poster bed, thick carpets, couches, dining area, and library. Hers is an apartment, and she isn't kidding about her media setup. She has a room dedicated to multimedia, including theater seats, a wall-sized screen, and an impressive collection of movies and games.

"In North Carolina, you and your mom were living in a shack in a holler. Why? You seem to have everything you could want right here."

"It's a long story, Jewel, and when Thuban gives me permission, I'll share it with you. For now, let's see if those creatures are still there."

She motions me to sit in front of the screen and plops down next to me. These seats also have controls in the armrests and she immediately brings up the scene we witnessed in the observation room.

"Are those mermen?" I ask the obvious. What else would you call a creature who is somewhat human on top and has a fish tail?

"Apparently," she answers. "I've heard about them from some of our people who've seen them, but I imagined them differently. The question is, why are they here?"

Their upper torsos appear human, with two arms ending in webbed fingers, and they have the fish tails one would expect. One swims right up to the camera and grins, as if he knows what it is and is hamming it up for us.

It's obvious not all of him is scaled, just the tail. The skin of his torso shines like a dolphin's, with the same rubbery texture. He has wide-spaced glowing red eyes, and a flat nose in the middle of his face. I can't imagine what he uses a nose for since he's breathing through gills that fan out where our ears would be. His fish mouth is wider than it should be on the humanoid face. I shudder at the sight of his sharply pointed teeth and I get the impression his grin is not friendly. A tall red fin juts from a bony ridge in the center of his forehead and runs along the top of his head. When he turns, I can see it continues down his back and along the tail. Many of the creatures are holding barbed spears. I wonder why they've gathered there.

As we watch in fascination, something startles them, and they disappear in a flash of churned water. We wait, and the thing they ran from glides across the screen.

"That's impossible," I whisper. My mouth hangs open as an undulating mass of dinner-plate sized scales brush past the camera. I'm awed at the size of it. When it finally moves past and turns away, the last thing I see is a giant forked tail receding into the black distance.

"Did you see that?" Marla asks, her voice squeaky as if she can't quite push it beyond a lump in her throat that must match my own. "It's Triton! It has to be!"

"It can't be real. Dragons don't exist, do they?"

STORM DARROCK RYDER

The OAR research vessel Proteus is bigger than I expected, over a hundred feet long and towering several stories above the dock. Cranes heft boxes and crates on board, while shirtless crew-members unload. A uniformed man wearing a captain's cap leans on the railing close to the gangplank.

Another in a red batik shirt, sporting a deep tan with hair as black as mine, waves at Charles and shouts, "Welcome aboard."

"It's good to see you again, Julian," Charles calls back, as we make our way up the steep ramp. The two shake hands and slap each other on the shoulder. Charles introduces us to Dr. Emery.

He says, "I'm sorry about Jewel's disappearance, but intrigued by your theory she's being held captive somewhere below us." He leads us up one flight of stairs to the next deck and into a library where a conference table takes up most of the room, and introduces us to the two people already sitting there.

"These are my assistants, Dr. Isabella Andreas and Dr. Gabriel Williamson. They're both marine archaeologists and have been with our team for three years. They're very much interested in the possibility of an undersea civilization still in existence. Of course, they'll keep what we say here in the strictest confidence. I must say, if what you say is true, and I have no reason to doubt you believe it, then the world will want to know about this."

The two young scientists stand up and shake hands with Wolf, Dylan, and Charles, and Dr. Andreas gives us a little wave. Neither of them looks old enough to have a Ph.D., so it doesn't surprise me when Dr. Andreas says, "Just call me Izzy, and he's Gabe."

Izzy is a tawny-skinned, dark-eyed beauty with glossy black hair tied back in a ponytail. She's tall, with a toned body and long, shapely legs. Her white t-shirt shows a hint of red from a bikini top she's wearing underneath. Short cut-off jeans and flip-flops add to the impression she's not much older than we are.

A sharp jolt of pain hits me behind my eyes. Sky pushes past, throwing me a dirty look, and sweetly says to Izzy, "It's so nice to meet you and Gabe."

I tap her number on my wristband. *What was that? Did you just jab me?*

I don't know what you're talking about, she answers with a sly smile and turns her attention to Gabe. I don't like it. I know she senses my annoyance, and, for once, I don't put the wall up. I hope she's uncomfortable. Instead, she smiles wider while he checks her out in a way that makes me want to deck him. I break the link, instead.

Pax steps between them and shakes Gabe's hand. "I sure hope you guys can help us find Jewel." He glances at me and frowns, as if he knows there's something going on between Sky and me. She sits across from Gabe, and I take a seat next to her and across from Izzy. Pax settles on his sister's other side. She relaxes and I know he's doing his brother magic. I wish it worked on me. I'm tied up in knots.

Dr. Emery's team listens intently as Charles and Dylan, both highly respected scientists in their fields, tell them about the Allarans and Dracans. The archaeologists don't seem surprised to hear alien races are living on the planet.

"We've seen some USO activity in the Tongue of the Ocean recently," Gabe says. I remember USO stands for unidentified submerged objects.

"Our sonar has picked up objects moving much too rapidly to be large marine life or any kind of submarine we're aware of. The Navy runs acoustical tests in the Tongue, and they might have developed fast-moving subs. We haven't given them much thought. Are you saying they're actually aliens?"

"We've had close encounters with them, and the kids have been in an Allaran ship," Dylan replies. "The Allarans assured us the Dracans have taken Jewel to Atlantis. When we heard about the pyramid you've discovered, we hoped it would lead us to her."

Wolf is silent, until the conversation turns to the Watchers and the artifacts. He shares with them what the Cherokee believe about the artifacts and the prophecy concerning us.

"Creator placed the artifacts in the earth to act as organs, regulating and balancing the systems of Earth. It was prophesied, when they become unstable, four young people would be chosen to fix them and save the planet. It seems our kids are those four.

"The Watchers led them to the artifact in North Carolina, and they were somehow able to repair it. Then the Dracans took both the artifact and Jewel. We suspect it's hidden somewhere under Andros."

"What makes you think it's here?" Dr. Emery asks.

Dylan answers, "We've been watching water and weather patterns, like Hurricane Alphonse a few weeks ago, and changes in the currents, which I'm sure you've noticed. How many whales and dolphins have beached themselves along the Atlantic coast recently? What about all the strange anomalies of the Bermuda Triangle that have happened over the last century and before?"

Charles adds, "You've seen how violent storms, earthquakes, volcanic eruptions and other geological events have escalated in recent years. Once the artifact in North Carolina was repaired, those events in eastern North America seem to have calmed down considerably. Not so in the oceans and in other parts of the world. We don't know how many artifacts there are, but we do know many, if not all of them, are malfunctioning. These kids can and must find and repair them, but they can't do it without Jewel."

"Why have you decided on Andros, specifically?" Dr. Emery asks.

Charles answers, "We know the blue holes, inland and in the ocean, lead to a labyrinth of deep caves. The first artifact was hidden in a cave in the mountains. It's logical to assume this one is likewise hidden. Since the pyramid you found may indicate these islands were once part of Atlantis, we hope we're on the right track."

The young scientists inspect us with quite a bit more interest than they showed before.

"How can four teenagers be expected to fix the entire planet?" Gabe asks. I've been wondering the same thing. We fixed one artifact, but how many more are there? We can't do anything without Jewel, so first things first.

"We find Jewel," Pax answers, "before we think about fixing anything else. She's our priority. We know where she is, but not how to get there."

"You say she's in Atlantis, which you suspect is a Dracan city near the pyramid we found," Dr. Emery says.

"Yes," Charles answers. "It has to be near that pyramid. The Allarans told the kids about the energy grid covering the planet, and from the coordinates you sent me, your pyramid appears to be at the juncture of two of the energy lines. The city will be nearby."

Dr. Emery stands up and says, "We set sail tomorrow at noon. Bring your wives and pack for several days. We'll make cabins available. The boys will berth with Gabe, and Sky can share Izzy's cabin. We'll talk more tomorrow, but for now, we have preparations to make. It's great seeing you again and meeting your kids."

Gabe and Izzy escort us out to the deck. Sky hangs back as the men head down the gangplank, and I turn back to see why. I tap my wristband and open the link to her. *What's wrong?*

We should have reminded Charles to ask Dr. Emery about the sea monster. I wonder if these guys know anything about it.

"Have you two heard any legends about a local sea monster?" she asks aloud.

"I've heard of humanoids with webbed hands and fish faces," Gabe answers. "Why? Have you seen one?" He has a smirk on his face I'm itching to wipe off. A coil of rope begins to unravel next to his foot. Pax notices and lightly smacks me on the shoulder. I drop it, for now.

"The islanders talk about some sort of bird people, but I haven't heard anything about sea monsters," Izzy says. "Did you see something?" There's no hint of mockery on her face and I wonder if she believes the stories we shared about the aliens.

"Humps, like the backs of whales, but all in a row. You know how whales show their flukes when they dive? The last one raised a tail out of the water, but it was forked."

I added, "It made a sound full of sadness, and the surf churned up like crazy. When it disappeared, the sea settled back down."

"Plenty of creatures in the ocean haven't been seen nor catalogued before. It sounds like this might be a new discovery. I hope we get to see it when we dive tomorrow." Izzy gives Sky a short hug. "It'll be fun getting to know you. Tomorrow we take Theseus for a spin. One of you will get to ride along with Gabe and me."

Gabe winks at Sky and I'm tempted to wrap the coil of rope around him.

Don't. Pax has opened the link. *They don't know about our gifts, and now is not the time.*

The two scientists wave as we leave the ship. Sky is quite pleased with herself, so I turn and give Izzy one more wave. The disgusted expression on Sky's face is priceless. I've got to stop this. I can't leave myself open to her. I can't lose anyone else I care about.

11

JEWEL

"Thuban wants to talk to you," Marla announces before I'm fully awake. I yawn and stretch, recalling my nightmare of dragons and fish-faced people and spaceships shooting laser beams at me. I shudder, reluctant to get up, much less talk to a Dracan.

"He's back? Is your mother with him?"

She doesn't bother to answer, but pulls the cover off, grabs my hand and helps me to my feet. "I've laid out some clothes for you. You'll have time for a quick shower, but we can't keep him waiting."

She's in her Dracan form, scales gleaming in the light, and regal in an outfit I haven't seen before. A floor-length gauzy white skirt embroidered with gold vines and flowers flows from a high, brocade bodice. Diaphanous sleeves fall from her shoulders in a delicate wave, gathered at her wrists in a wide, adorned band. Gold sandals peek out from beneath the airy skirt.

I rehearse questions in my mind as I shower and dress, concerned I'll forget them all before I have a chance to ask Thuban. The clothes Marla has laid out for me are much fancier than the simple pants and tunics I've worn since I woke up here. My skirt, in shades of blue ranging from aqua to sapphire, falls from a plain blue bolero-styled top with short velvet sleeves. Silver sandals with straps wrapping around my feet and up my calves complete the outfit, and the image greeting me in the mirror is elegant and very much unlike me.

"You radiate," Marla says as she picks up a brush and runs it through my damp hair, which now reaches the middle of my back. When she's satisfied, she urges me out the door and quickly leads me along a maze of corridors until I'm hopelessly lost, again.

"Do you know what he wants to talk to me about?" My voice shakes a little with nerves.

"No, I don't, but relax. Just remember, the protocol is to keep your eyes lowered, and don't speak until he asks you to. He is the king, after all. You should be fine."

"You said he's the leader of Atlantis. Why didn't you mention he's a king?"

"Would it have made a difference?" Her pace picks up, and I'm glad for the straps holding these new sandals on my feet. We're practically running.

Marla doesn't say anything else, and soon we reach a golden door guarded by two Dracans dressed in Mongolian-style armor, with hieroglyphs covering their breastplates and layers of overlapping bronze plates covering the arms and around the skirts. Their peaked helmets with ear flaps and nose guards reflect the light of an enormous chandelier hanging from the center of the domed ceiling, thirty feet above.

One of the guards pushes the door open, and we enter a room lined with arches. A massive golden throne sits on a raised platform, next to a smaller one with an abalone back in the shape of a seashell. Clouds float across a painted sky, high overhead, and I admire the carvings of Greek and Egyptian deities surrounding each arch.

I glimpse a giant Dracan draped in a purple robe staring at us from the throne. A stunning human woman in a dress much like Marla's, is sitting next to him. This must be her mother. She bears no resemblance to the bedraggled person we saved during the flood, with the pain-pinched face and mop of scraggly, dirty hair. Granted, Marla didn't let any of us get near her, other than the doctors. She made sure she was the only one to feed and care for her until they were airlifted to a nearby hospital.

Marla pinches me and I quickly look at the floor. We stop below the platform. Are we supposed to bow? I follow her lead and simply stand, silent and with eyes lowered. The king snaps his fingers and two servants materialize from one of the arched doorways with two chairs, which they place behind us.

"Please sit," Thuban's voice rumbles in the cavernous room. We do, still gazing at the floor. He continues. "I know you have many questions, Jewel Adams. You must wonder why you are here and what happened to the artifact. Am I correct?"

I don't know if I'm supposed to speak when he asks a question, or just nod, but I can't keep quiet any longer. "Of course, I want to know why you abducted me. Why me, and not the others? And, yes, I'd like to know what you intend to do with the artifact, and where it is, and why you took it."

"Is there anything else, human?" he asks. Does he want all my questions at once, or is he brushing me off?

This time I stare right at him. "I'd like to know when I can go home, and what's wrong with your home world, and where Max is. Am I a prisoner here? Are there other humans imprisoned in Atlantis?"

1 2

JEWEL

A deep laugh rumbles from the chest of the giant reptilian. His yellow eyes narrow into vertical slits and his mouth flaps open in what seems to be a genuine belly laugh, revealing rows of pointed teeth. His sleeveless robe exposes muscular arms and a bare, flat chest. A wide gold belt circles his waist and loose gold pants cover his massive legs. Iridescent scales gleam over every inch of exposed skin.

The king stops laughing and spears me with his gaze. "I am Thuban. I am pleased you and my daughter have become friends. Are you not bothered by her Dracan beauty?" His voice is deep and rough, and I detect a more pronounced sibilance than Marla exhibits when she speaks.

I have no idea how to address a Dracan king, so I simply answer, "No, sir."

"You have spirit, for a human. I am impressed." He must not know many humans, other than the woman beside him. Her face is a mask, revealing nothing about her thoughts. She's beautiful, with long flowing blond hair and porcelain skin. Black eyeliner, or perhaps kohl, highlights the green of her eyes under delicate arching brows, and red lipstick shows off her full, generous mouth.

"You are here as our guest, at my daughter's request. Did she not tell you?"

I'm shocked and turn to glare at Marla, whose expression doesn't change as she stares at the floor. She requested me. Why didn't she tell me this? Why would she do this? She gives her head a tiny shake. Something doesn't add up.

"Let me reassure you," he says, but I'm anything but reassured by his gruff voice. "Your artifact is safe. We have not harmed it and, despite what our daughter says you have been told by the Allarans, we have no intention of selling it, or of traveling to our home world.

"In fact, Draconis, our planet of origin, has become inhospitable to our race. We have made Terra our home and intend to remain here."

"What's wrong with your planet?" I ask. If they can't go home, won't they try to take over Earth?

"Our sun has burned off much of the planet's atmosphere. Draconis can no longer sustain life, I'm afraid. We have no choice but to remain here.

"To answer another of your questions, you are here to prove to my fellow Royal Council members that humans have reached a point in their development where they are worth saving. I am known to favor humans, but many of my people have had no contact with your race, other than to mate with or experiment on them. If all goes well, you, my dear Jewel Adams, may become the first human ambassador to the Council."

Blood drains from my face and I'm suddenly dizzy. Marla reaches over and grabs my hand. Thuban grins as if he's just solved the world's problems.

"B-but why me?" I stammer. "Why not Pax, who has the temperament for it? Why choose any of us? What will happen to the earth if we can't fix the artifacts? Do you understand we four are the only ones who can heal them? If you split us up, you'll be dooming the planet you're living on."

"You see?" he roars. "This is why we chose you. You question everything. You've also shown kindness to our daughter, even now, while she's in her Dracan form. She has told us about your abilities, and about the others. Of the four, you were the first to reach out to her in friendship.

"If we can convince the Council your race is worth saving, then you will be reunited with the others, and we will aid you in your quest to repair the artifacts. If not, then I am afraid most of the Council is in favor of allowing Terra to put an end to humans."

"Won't Terra's destruction also kill the Dracans?"

"I believe so, but the others do not agree. They are convinced they can find a way to repair them before we, too, are destroyed. Our scientists are now examining the one you repaired."

"I wasn't the first to reach out to Marla. What about Max? He stayed with her even after he met the other Dracans, and they're far more impressive than Marla. Why not offer him the ambassadorship?" I know I'm grasping at straws. Max isn't the most courageous person I know, and he's certainly shown his lack of common sense and diplomacy often enough. In fact, his temper was always getting him into trouble, and he would usually turn tail and run when confronted. Marla shakes her head and frowns at the floor.

"Ah, yes. Max." Thuban sounds thoughtful, but I detect a hint of sarcasm. Can Dracans be sarcastic?

"I am afraid he would not be suitable for the task. The other humans are not being held prisoner, and neither are you. Do you know about the time and space anomalies in certain places on Terra? They were caused by the Allarans' unwise and liberal use of passageways you call wormholes to travel between planets.

"During the great war, most of those passageways were closed, but not all. Of those, most are unstable and appear at random, although clustered in certain areas like the Bermuda Triangle. A few have appeared near Atlantis and stayed for years, only to suddenly disappear. It's quite annoying. You will meet other humans here who were lost in the Triangle. The space and time distortion caused by the wormholes makes it impossible for most of them to return to the surface. The life they once knew is long gone. We have made them as comfortable as possible. You and Max have been here a short while, so we might have a chance to return you before the next major distortion makes it impossible.

"You must know, Jewel Adams, your friends and family are searching for you. You must hope they don't find you before we meet with the Council, or the anti-human faction may destroy them before we can intervene."

My stomach churns in fear. I can't communicate with any of them, so how can I tell them to stop searching? My throat has closed, and I can't squeak out another word.

A soldier rushes into the room and says something to Thuban in their language, and the floor under my feet begins to shake.

Thuban stands and says, "Daughter, answer any questions the human asks you. Now, go to safety. Hurry."

Marla abruptly stands, grabs my hand and pulls me to my feet. Thuban reaches for her mother's hand and they disappear through a door behind the throne.

"Come quickly," she cries. "Run! This one is bad." A sense of déjà vu hits me as we run into an archway to our right. Once again, we're in a small room and she shuts a heavy metal door, slams her hand on a flashing light and orders me to sit on the floor. A long moaning sound accompanies the warning gongs filling the air. I slap my hands over my ears and curl up in a ball. It sounds like the artifact's cry back home, shaking me to my core and filling me with fear. At least we had a chance to fix it when the four of us were together. Does this mean the end of our world? There's no chance I can save it without the others.

This time I remember to tap my wristband, and for a moment, the connection opens. *Stay away!* My mental shout carries my fear for them, and my longing to see them again. *Don't come after me!* The link is already closed. The sound dies off and the clanging stops. How I wish I could hear the mental voices of my friends right now. Will I ever see them again?

13

STORM

I've been elected to cram myself in the tiny capsule of the OAR submersible, Theseus, along with Gabe and Izzy. Sky and Pax convinced me I could use my ability to get us back to the surface if anything should go wrong. I reminded them, whether we're still breathing or not would depend on the scientists with me who are familiar with the vessel.

Gabe and Izzy busy themselves in the cramped space, toggling switches and checking instruments. They've placed me in the one spot where I'm unlikely to accidentally send us to the bottom. Izzy hands me a set of headphones, and I listen to a conversation with so many foreign words, I can barely understand what they're saying. Finally, Gabe says, "It's a go," and the sub jerks as it's lifted off the deck and hoisted over the water.

My stomach lurches when the crane lowers us to the surface. The engine kicks on, and I watch the ocean rise in the portholes until we're completely submerged. Then we dive and bubbles stream past the window for a few minutes. When they stop, I admire the way the sunlight glimmers through the water and catch glimpses of colorful reef fish. I'm grateful for the spotlights ringing the vessel when it grows increasingly darker. We're heading to a depth a mile below the surface.

"It should take us two hours to reach the pyramid," Izzy says, "which gives us plenty of time to get to know each other."

"Yeah," Gabe says, "Maybe you can enlighten us about a few things."

I don't like the sound of this. It's too much like an interrogation. I'm facing the porthole, so I tap on my wristband. *Do you hear this over the radio? I ask. What should I tell them?*

They've turned the mics off. Dr. Emery says he can monitor their vital signs and track Theseus, and if they need to report, they will. He's told our folks not to worry. I can hear Pax's concern in his thoughts. *He's sent us out on deck in the meantime.*

At least we can still hear you. Please keep the link open. Try to enhance it so we can see what you see and hear what you hear, Sky says. I open my mind the way we did when we called the Allarans after Jewel disappeared. A surge of energy pours through the link, and something else.

Stay away! Jewel's voice! *Don't...* It trails away and my heart drops.

Jewel! I shout, along with the others. My head explodes with all our voices shouting at once. Jewel has disappeared again. Fury rattles the bars of the prison I've created for it and roars, demanding to be let loose. Sky projects her pain, and Pax eases her emotions again. This must be especially hard for him. I can't imagine how I'd react if Sky went missing and called out to us. I'd want to rip everything apart to get to her. The thought stops me cold. Why Sky and not Jewel?

The rage retreats, for now, and I say, *I'm sorry. At least we know she's still alive. Why would she warn us away?*

I wish I knew. I hope you're with me in this, because I will never quit searching for her. Even if the world wasn't at stake, I'd risk everything to find her.

What makes you think I'd give up on my friend? Sky projects her annoyance at her brother.

Same here, I say. Sky's fearless spirit is one of the things I love about her. *We're a team, remember? We'll also need Gabe's and Izzy's help, if they're willing,* I answer. *How much should I tell them about us?*

It's your call, he responds. *If we want their help, you should probably tell them everything, except for our telepathic link, of course.*

"What's wrong, Storm?" Izzie's concern reminds me I haven't answered Gabe.

He suddenly laughs. "Sorry. We're only curious. Your story last night took us by surprise, and you must admit, it sounds far-fetched. Aliens and mysterious artifacts? We don't doubt you, don't get me wrong, but I'd like to know why you're so special."

"Do you want the long or short version?" I ask. "Believe me, I know how crazy it'll sound."

"You don't have to say anything," Izzy says, shooting a glance at Gabe. "We're used to secret missions and have completed many dives with people who can't reveal their purpose. Our research is funded by various agencies using Theseus, and since we're the pilots, we've done a lot of virtually silent dives."

"How about the short version, then," I say. Izzy puts me at ease, although I still want to throttle Gabe.

I felt that, Sky says, and she sends a flash of self-satisfaction. *You're jealous.*

"Each of us has genetically enhanced abilities that, when combined, give the artifacts what they need to heal."

"What do you mean by abilities?" Gabe asks, at the same time Izzy asks, "What do you mean by genetically enhanced?" They share a quick glance and laugh. I wonder if there's something between them.

"When our mothers were pregnant with us, they were abducted by the Allarans, who messed with our DNA to produce certain gifts. I'll show you."

I lift my headphones off my head, float them to Izzy, pull hers off her head and replace them with mine, all with my mind.

"Whoa," Gabe stares at the headphones. "Can you do that with anything? How much weight can you lift? Are you always that precise?"

I can't help laughing. "You have no idea. I picked up boulders and tore living trees out of the ground when I was attacked by a Dracan ship. Yet even so, I couldn't save my parents, and I couldn't stop those lizards from taking Jewel."

You saved my life. Waves of love and sympathy from Sky help calm me down, but the regret lingers, and my wall goes up. I gather she can hear my thoughts in this enhanced open link, but I won't let my hurt and rage affect her anymore.

Izzy's eyes soften. "I'm so sorry. We didn't know about your folks. Do you want to talk about it?"

"Let me tell you about the others first. Then I'll tell you what's happened until now."

I tell them about Jewel's ability to see auras and through disguises, and about how Pax's nose is like a bloodhound's. When I talk about Sky's empathy, I realize I'd let my wall drop again when Sky says, *I meant what I said in the cave.* She'd told me she loves me, and the memory nearly unhinges me. It's getting harder to block my feelings for her.

Izzy and Gabe ask a lot of questions, which reminds me of Jewel and her insatiable curiosity. Sky is projecting her sadness over our missing friend, and Pax chuckles in my head. I'm still not used to this telepathic link going beyond simple conversation, and it's a bit unnerving.

A sudden clanging on the skin of the submersible causes the scientists to spin around in their chairs and focus on the portholes and instruments in front of them. A circle of light stretches a few feet ahead of my viewport. Everything else is black, until a figure swims through the light. Suddenly, the sea around us comes alive with elongated shapes flashing yellow and green neon lights along the length of bodies that seem to be at least as big as our vessel. Is it an optical illusion?

"Cephalopod," Gabe says. "Giant squid. They won't bother us once they've tasted us. Theseus isn't appetizing to them." He laughs, while my heart races. I hope he knows what he's talking about.

"Wait, what is that?" asks Izzy. I can't see what she sees, but the tone of her voice worries me.

"What?" I need to know. I hope I can keep whatever it is away from our sub. A fish-faced, man-like creature with a finned tail flashes into view just outside my porthole, startling me. It hefts a spear and lets it fly at one of the squids, where it pierces the creature. The squid squirms and twists, spears jutting out all over its body before its lights fade out.

Did you see that? I ask.

I can't believe it, Pax answers. *Mermen are real? They're not like they're depicted in books.*

"Are these Dracans, by any chance?" Gabe asks.

"They're nothing like them. This is something else." I have no idea what they are, but they hunt in packs and use weapons, and they didn't attack us. I wonder why. They're obviously more intelligent than fish. "How close are we to the pyramid?"

"It's just ahead," Izzy answers. "Our lights will make it appear to be like glass, but we don't know what it's made of. We haven't been able to break off a sample. It's stronger than anything we've encountered undersea."

14

STORM

"Sonar is picking up a strange sound." Gabe flips a switch and says, "Julian, are you hearing this topside? Can you see anything up there?"

Dr. Emery replies, "We hear a thrumming sound, growing louder. The instruments show it coming from the vicinity of the pyramid. Record as much as you can and hightail it out of there."

"We haven't quite reached the destination. Just a few more minutes until we ascend," Izzy says, sounding perfectly calm. "We've had an encounter with cephalopods and mermen. Could they be causing the sound waves?"

"I doubt it," the chief scientist responds. "What we're hearing is big and coming closer to the surface."

"We see the sound on our instruments, and we're recording it outside, but we haven't heard anything in here."

That changes in minutes. My headphones do little to block the sudden roar filling the cabin. Theseus tosses and rolls in an ocean suddenly violent with waves and eddies a mile under the surface. Is it an underwater volcano? An eruption of gases from deep vents? Stories of the Bermuda Triangle flash through my mind in frightening clarity. I don't know if my panic is mine or coming from Sky.

I'm breaking the link, Pax shouts, and they leave me to face this alone. I'm glad. Sky shouldn't have to experience my fear. My hands grip the panel in front of me, holding on for dear life.

I concentrate on slowing the motion of our sub, trying to float it the way I float things in the air. It takes some time, but I get it under control. The sound recedes until we're surrounded by silence. I can't hear the hum of the engine, but I've experienced this before. Hearing will return shortly.

I tap on the wristband. *Is everyone okay up there?* I ask. *Please answer me.*

Intense sorrow slams into me, and the link cuts off again. I break out in a cold sweat. Something is terribly wrong. After a few agonizing moments, Pax reconnects, alone.

You're alive! Thank God. How is Izzy? Gabe?

Izzy is smacking her ear while Gabe checks over some instruments. *They're okay. Temporarily deaf, but otherwise fine. What's going on up there? Where's Sky? Who's hurt?*

The thing you and my sister described showed up. This time it raised its head out of the water, and you won't believe what it is. He sounds excited. He hasn't said anything about injuries, but what was its grief about?

Well? Spill it. I have no patience for guessing games.

It's a dragon. A real-life fire-breathing dragon!

That beats an old pyramid we didn't get to see any day. *Man, this keeps getting weirder.*

Pax's mental voice grows solemn. *The strangest thing is, the pain that knocked us off our feet after the sound deafened us was the creature's grief. Sky projected it to the rest of us. She's a sobbing mess, and so are our moms and Sequoia.*

Didn't the emotions fade when it dove back down? How can she feel it at all? She doesn't sense the Dracans or Allarans, or any other animal I've heard of. Sky's empathy works mostly around nearby people, except for her brother and me. She can sense us wherever we are. My wall is up not only to protect myself, but to protect her from me.

It didn't dive. The thing is following us.

How do you know it breathes fire? Why would a dragon need fire in the ocean? I can't believe I'm even thinking about what a dragon can or cannot do. Until now, they were myths.

It shot flames into the air from its nostrils at the peak of the noise. Sky says it's crying for someone it lost.

We should welcome it to the club.

My attempt at levity falls flat when Pax responds, *I've never felt such despair. The dragon has no hope, and Sky nearly broke trying to comfort it. She's gone to help Sequoia get some rest. Your aunt was affected as deeply as my sister, and everyone is worried about her and the baby.*

15

SKY

I join Analiese, my mother, and Sequoia in her cabin. I wish I hadn't projected the creature's grief, but it wasn't something I could control. Mom strokes Sequoia's hair as she lies curled on the bed, arms wrapped around her belly. I sit cross-legged on the floor in front of her and stroke her arm, while Jewel's mom plops down in one of the two chairs in the cabin, still sniffling.

I suddenly sense a fifth person in the room, one who's sending out powerful waves of contentment. I send back love and get an answering touch that bathes my emotions in a gentle warm rain. Every cell in my body fills with joy at a connection I've never experienced with anyone before, not even Pax.

Sequoia relaxes in sleep, and my mother and I share our wonder. "Do you feel that?"

She nods, speechless. I take in a deep breath. "All of it? The link?"

Analiese answers, "I've felt the baby's emotions a few times. At first, I thought it was you, but this is different. You send purposeful, deliberate waves, unless you're overcome like you were today and can't help what you project. This one is much more immature, like a child learning the basics of language or locomotion. Short bursts of pleasure or peace can quickly turn to discomfort, and when it happens, Sequoia gets up and moves around. What do you mean by link?"

"Is she aware her baby is an empath, and a strong one?" I ask.

"She is," Mom answers.

"I believe we've formed a bond of some sort, Mom. Time will tell, of course, but it's different from anything I have with anyone else."

"A bond?" Mom and Analiese ask at the same time. They smile at each other.

Mom asks, "Can you describe how it felt?" My mother has asked me to describe my emotions before, but I normally simply project them to her. I can't project this.

"It's like I was in a warm shower of love, with soft threads wrapping around my heart, tying it to the baby's. What will this mean after the baby is born, and as the little one grows up?"

Analiese's eyebrows draw together as she thinks.

"It remains to be seen," she says after a few moments. "Meanwhile, Sequoia has asked us not to say anything about the baby's empathy. We girls are the only ones who know, and we'd like to keep it that way for now."

I turn to my mother. "You know I can't keep this a secret from Pax."

"I know." She assures me. "If he specifically asks about it because he senses it, then of course share it with him. Can you keep it to yourself until then? At least, don't bring it up before he does."

How frustrating! I'm dying to share this discovery with Pax and Storm. I wish Jewel were here, for the millionth time. She'd be as thrilled as I am, then she'd ask the question that eats at me. Is Sequoia's baby half-Dracan?

I slip out while Sequoia naps and the others talk quietly about the dragon and the baby. I need Pax to calm me down. I spot him at the stern with Dad and the other men. Dr. Emery lifts binoculars to his eyes every few minutes.

"There you are," my brother says, while he swipes at a strand of hair sticking to the sweat on his face. He excuses himself and walks me around the deck. We find a spot in the shade, out of sight of the others. "Have you recovered enough to link up with us again?"

"Not yet." I know he's concerned and I give him a quick hug. I can't risk spilling anything about the baby's ability through the link. Not until I can control my reactions to it.

"Is Storm all right? What about Gabe and Izzy? Is the dragon still trailing us? I don't sense it."

He drapes an arm over my shoulders and I'm immediately less agitated.

"One question at a time, Sky. You're sounding like Jewel." He quickly suppresses his hurt. "They're fine. They're heading back to the surface and should be here in an hour or so. We haven't seen the dragon for a while, so it might have gone back into the deep. I hope the Theseus doesn't encounter it. That thing is massive."

"I'll say," Dr. Emery approaches, shaking his head. "I wouldn't have believed it if I hadn't seen it with my own eyes. We have security cameras running non-stop on Proteus while Theseus is in the water. If there's ever a problem, we can figure out what went wrong. Hasn't happened yet, but I'm very glad we're sticklers for protocol in this case. I can't wait to go over the footage. This is bigger than discovering a pyramid."

Didn't he suffer the creature's pain? Is he going to go public and exploit it?

"Does Theseus also have cameras on at all times?" Pax asks. "Something strange appeared down there, and it wasn't the dragon."

"How do you know?" Dr. Emery narrows his eyes suspiciously. "You weren't in there when Gabe reported in."

Oops. I wonder how he'll get out of this one. Apparently, our folks didn't say anything to the scientist about our telepathic communication. In fact, Charles has told us to keep it secret. The technology is too dangerous to be made public. I shudder when I think of how easily it could be weaponized for spying or mind control.

My brother thinks fast. "I overheard one of your crew members. It sounds like an exciting discovery." Dr. Emery is not happy about the information leak. I'm sorry for the crew.

"Theseus will dock shortly. I'm sure they'll tell us all about their sighting. We'll meet in the library once they're on board." He gives us a curt nod and walks toward the stairs to the upper deck.

Pax taps the code for me on his wristband. *That was too close.*

I nod. *We're not used to being around people who don't know about us. I wonder if our parents are planning to tell Dr. Emery.*

Storm told Gabe and Izzy about our abilities. Not about the link, though. We keep that to ourselves. He shudders.

We must also find and rescue our missing friend from a location that isn't supposed to exist, then find the missing artifact and a second one that needs fixing. All without the benefit of Watchers to lead the way. In addition, we have an emotional dragon to deal with, and a baby who could be half-alien, not to mention Storm and his issues. It reminds me of the "other than" game Jewel and I played when our problems seemed overwhelming. Other than all that, we have nothing to worry about. My heart aches for my friend.

16

JEWEL

I picture being flattened like a pancake under unimaginable pressure when the dome protecting Atlantis cracks open. I can see a tsunami crashing in, smashing the palace into glittering shards while fragments of bodies feed the creatures of the midnight depths. I hate my vivid imagination right now. My heart hurts with missing my friends. How badly I wish they were here to lift my spirits and loan me courage. Compared to this, finding and fixing the first artifact was a breeze. If the next breach doesn't destroy Atlantis, how can I convince hostile aliens humanity is worth saving, especially when they've decided they don't need us? I'm wearing a path in the carpet with my pacing.

Marla has gone to change after our meeting with Thuban, and to spend time with her mother. I've traded my fancy clothes for comfortable loose pants and a fresh blue tunic, which seems to be the only style available. It's fine with me. I have more to worry about than fashion choices.

A soft knock at the door is a welcome interruption, and I'm surprised to find Marla in her human form with her mother and Max beside her. Her mom leads the way into the room.

"Jewel, I'm so sorry I haven't yet introduced myself to you." She reaches out and touches my shoulder. "I'm Avery Snow, and I owe you a great debt of gratitude. Please call me Avery."

Her pleasant voice sets me at ease. She's taller than I remember, and graceful, but then, before the meeting with Thuban, I'd only seen her when she was injured and in a hospital bed at our house.

"I'm happy you're okay, Avery. You look wonderful." I turn to Max. "I'm glad you're okay, too, Max. Where've you been?"

He gives me the expected sullen face and says, "Around."

I roll my eyes at Marla, who grins and shakes her head. It seems Max hasn't changed a bit.

I gesture toward the couch and chairs placed around a low table in the seating area of my room. As they sit, the door opens to a girl pushing a cart with covered dishes and a pitcher of water. She's about my height and in human form, so she's either a true human close to my age or a Dracan hybrid. I knew someone had to bring the food and drink that appeared at mealtimes, but this is the first time I've seen her. There's something oddly familiar about her, but I can't put my finger on it. How did I miss her all this time?

The girl leaves without saying a word, and Avery graciously serves us a meal of fish in a lemony sauce and roasted vegetables. We dig in as if we hadn't eaten all day. Then I remember we haven't. I'm surprised I can eat with everything on my mind.

Avery lifts the lid off the last dish when we're finished, revealing pastries topped with mango and papaya. She's the first to break the silence as we bite into the desserts, and her comment surprises me.

"Jewel, I'm aware you need to get back to your friends. Thuban means well, but he has strong opposition, both in the Royal Council and here at home. His trusted advisor Shaula pretends to agree with him, but he is no friend to humans. You have reason to avoid him, if you can."

The name sounds familiar to me. He's the one Marla mentioned in the cavern.

"Is Shaula the one who stole the artifact? The one who abducted me? You were there with him."

"Yes," she affirms. "We were obeying Thuban's orders."

Max speaks up for the first time. "Yeah, he's dangerous, Jewel. Don't mess with him."

Of course, I have no intention of messing with him, and, in fact, sincerely hope I never get to meet him. I turn my attention to Max.

"You've been here as long as I have. Are you living in the palace, too? Why are you here?"

Marla answers for him, "Max lives in a section of the city with other humans. He's doing very well there. They appreciate him, don't they, Max?"

His upper lip curls in a sneer and I want to slap his face. What is wrong with this boy? What does she see in him? His answer surprises me. "I do maintenance work and teach mixed martial arts. Humans, Dracans, makes no difference to me. It's nothing. Keeps me busy."

"It's more than nothing," Avery adds. "Some people have been here for years, and although they've adjusted well to our way of life, Max provides them with some much-needed activity. I believe the ones taking the classes will be better prepared for coming challenges."

"Challenges?" I ask. "Like what?"

"You heard Thuban," Marla says. "If you don't reunite with your friends, there is no chance of repairing the artifact, unless he's right about Dracan scientists figuring out another way. It seems like a gamble to me, considering they can't get close enough to study it. We have to think of a way to get you back to the surface."

I did wonder if they had the technology to break through the force field the artifact spins around itself. Apparently not.

"Would Max come, too? And you, Marla?"

Avery stands, as if to leave, and we get to our feet, too. "It all remains to be seen," she says as she turns toward the door. "We'll work on a plan. It's best you don't know anything about it, especially when Shaula questions you. He will, you know. Since you've spoken with Thuban, Shaula is sure to want to meet with you. Tell him nothing about our conversation, Jewel, if you can avoid it."

They leave me. If I can avoid it? Does he plan to torture it out of me? I am not going to sleep tonight.

1 7

JEWEL

I wake up after a restless night to the smell of coffee and cinnamon. The same girl who delivered our food last night is just about to leave when I call out, "Don't go, please."

She hesitates, but then hurries out the door with the cart. Breakfast is on the table, and I pour the coffee and dip my cinnamon bun into it. When I'm full, I dress quickly and wait for Marla, who usually gets here before I wake up. She must be with her mom, and I don't blame her. When I get back to my parents, I may never leave their side, except to see my friends again. The familiar pain washes over me.

When the knock comes, I rush to the door and throw it open, ready to get out of the room and go anywhere with Marla, but it isn't Marla.

Shaula stands there, huge and menacing with his mouth full of pointed teeth stretched in a grin, his yellow eyes burning with intensity. He doesn't wait for an invitation, but marches through the door, his black sleeveless robe, belted with a wide silver sash, swinging open to reveal loose black pants. Don't Dracan males wear shirts? If anything, he's more muscular than the king, with darker, less iridescent scales. Maybe it's a trick of the light.

"They have put you in decent accommodations," he says, drawing out the "s" sounds.

"Yes, thank you," I answer, trying to hold the quaking in my voice to a minimum. Where I had no fear of Thuban, Shaula gives off a completely different vibe. Cold sweat breaks out between my shoulder blades and trickles down the middle of my back. My heart races and I fight the urge to blow on my ice-cold hands. My throat closes and I'm pretty sure I've lost the power of speech.

He strides to the seating area, chooses a large padded chair and sits down. "Please join me," he says, amused. He knows the effect he has on me. I obey and drop into a chair as far from him as I can, which, unfortunately, is just on the other side of the table. I grip the armrests to keep from melting into a quivering puddle of fear.

"I've taken the liberty of ordering some refreshments." His words seem normal, but my skin crawls, nevertheless. I wonder if he plans to poison me, or drug me with a truth serum. Avery's words echo in my brain, "He will question you."

The serving girl opens the door without knocking and pushes the cart in front of her. She keeps her eyes glued to her task and silently sets the table for tea and uncovers a platter of small cakes. Shaula's reptilian eyes are intent on me, completely ignoring her as if she doesn't exist. In my world, we don't treat people like that, and anger begins to push aside the fear. Strength flows back into my limbs, enough to enable me to cross my arms. Okay, it's still self-protective, but his attitude makes me mad. He's just another bully, and for all I know, she could be a prisoner like me. I watch her back as she takes the cart and leaves the room.

"May I ask why you've come to see me?" I ask, and my voice no longer quavers.

"Of course, Jewel Adams. Perhaps you can answer some questions for me."

Here it comes. The interrogation. Does he have instruments of torture hidden under his robe? Are there pockets full of pointy knives in those pants? Tears prickle behind my eyes, but I refuse to give him the satisfaction of seeing how afraid I am.

"What kind of questions?" I ask. "I can't promise I know the answers, but I'll do my best to tell you what you want to know."

"How very cooperative of you." He leans forward, narrows his eyes, then reaches for the teapot and pours the fragrant steaming liquid into two mugs. He lifts a mug to his mouth, stares at me and takes a long, slurping sip. Stalling tactics? I reach for the second one, hoping my hand doesn't tremble enough to spill the tea. The hot mug warms my hand. I take a sip because he's watching me. If it's spiked, there's nothing I can do about it anyway. I'm surprised at how good the sweet, spiced tea tastes.

"Now," his voice rumbles, "let us begin."

"Tell me about the artifact." Shaula reaches for one of the cakes and pops it into his mouth. I watch, fascinated, as he swallows it whole. I have the impulse to spill it all, the whole story in one rambling incoherent splash of words, but I pause to gather my thoughts.

"What about it?" I ask.

"How did you fix it?" He hasn't whipped out any knives or pliers, but that could change when he doesn't like my answer.

"I don't know for sure. The four of us put our hands on it. Each had a side, and we linked hands, and something happened, and it started spinning again."

"Please start from when you first saw it, Jewel Adams. Tell me, step-by-step, what you did. I know about your various abilities. Did you use them in the process? How?"

I'm suddenly struck by how much he reminds me of my Biology teacher, Mr. Abrams, who was a stickler for details. I shared his class with Sky. I'd give anything to be in school right now, yawning through boring classes with my friends.

There's no getting around this. Shaula knows about us and he has the artifact. I know he's fishing for information to help his scientists fix the others but withholding what I know wouldn't save the planet if my friends can't find me. I'm confident he knows nothing about our now-useless telepathic link, and I will not reveal it to him, no matter what he does.

"The artifact spins its own force-field, like an invisible hard shell," I tell him. "When we got to it, it was already dying, and the spin had slowed enough to cause it to wobble. We found a crack in its shell and broke in. Storm steadied it, and Sky knew what it needed us to do. We each laid a hand on one of the four faces then linked hands all around. Sky gathered the love we have for each other and sent it in a blast to the tetrahedron. That did the trick."

Shaula jumps to his feet. "A blast of love? Love?" His voice rises in volume with each word. "Do you know how ridiculous it sounds?"

He shouts the last question, and all I want to do is curl up in a ball and cower under the bed. Instead I freeze, trembling and fighting back tears. I told the truth. What more does he want?

He strides back and forth down the entire length of the room several times. It's a large room, about fifty feet from the door to the wall, and thirty feet or so in width. I'm estimating, of course, based upon counting my steps while I did my own pacing. The bed and furnishings take up a third of it and the seating area another third. The rest is open floor space, great for practicing my katas and, apparently, good for a pacing Dracan, too. I'm glad he isn't yelling at me anymore, but his silence is as unnerving.

Finally, he takes his seat again and speaks in his normal rumble. "Tell me how you used your gifts. How did you find the crack in its so-called 'shell'?"

"An amazing array of colors swirled around inside the shell. I'd never seen so many. Pax smelled something alien as we walked around it, and where the odor was strongest, colors leaked out. Sky sensed pain and confusion in that area, and we guessed it was broken. When Storm reached inside with his mind to open it further, it exploded and knocked us off our feet. The artifact's spin slowed to the point where it was about to fall to the floor. Storm cushioned it until we could touch it. I told you the rest."

He jumps to his feet again. He'll make me dizzy at this rate.

"Come," he commands, and grabs me by the elbow to lift me out of my chair. When he lets go, he whirls around and marches out the door. "Quickly," he says, and I follow.

18

JEWEL

I recognize the door with the eye of Horus, and we're back in the maintenance area. Shaula rushes past the door with the owl. I wonder whether this palace was designed to mimic the Minotaur's labyrinth in ancient Crete. It would be easy for me to wander around forever in here, trying to find a way out. Hostile Dracans can be just as scary as a half-man, half-bull. Worse, if I had an aversion to reptiles. My wandering thoughts are abruptly interrupted when we reach a heavy metal door with a symbol, a seven-pointed star on a stick with a curved canopy over it.

"What does it mean?" I ask Shaula, pointing to the door.

"It is the symbol for the Egyptian goddess Seshat, who, it is said, invented writing and mathematics. We are entering the science center of Atlantis."

My spirit suddenly lifts, and I wish my parents were here to see this. Dad is an astrophysicist and inventor, with an intense interest in anything related to science and engineering. Mom's area of expertise is genetics. They'd be beside themselves with excitement right now. I've inherited their curiosity and can hardly wait to meet the scientists, Dracan or otherwise.

Shaula leads me down intersecting hallways, past unmarked doors, until I'm lost again. Escape seems more impossible than ever. I hope Avery and Marla are working on a viable plan.

We finally reach our destination, and Shaula marches us into a room filled with tanks and lab equipment. When he stops to talk to a woman working at a table across the room, I take the opportunity to look around. My eyes are drawn to a creature floating in a tank the size of a small room. A perfectly preserved merman, complete with fish tail and humanoid upper body, floats with its eyes closed. I draw close to study it. A sense of wonder comes over me, and I place my hand on the glass. Big mistake.

The merman's eyes pop open and it rushes at me, lips drawn back in a menacing grimace. Naturally, I squeal and nearly trip over my own feet in my rush to get away from the thing. Then it laughs. I can't hear it, but the contortions of its body, the wide-open mouth and the way it's slapping the side of its tail, look unmistakably like a human enjoying a good joke at the expense of another.

I cross my arms and sneer, projecting my annoyance the same way I've done to Max a few times. It stops laughing and regards me with interest. At least, that's how I interpret it. It isn't human, so it's hard to tell what it might be thinking.

"We call him Cruiser," the woman calls from across the room. "He's the only one we've been able to capture alive. They said he was cruising along by himself and didn't dart away fast enough to miss the tractor beam." She chuckles and gestures for me to come closer. I give Cruiser one last glance and head over to where she and Shaula have been watching my antics.

"Do the females appear different from the males?" I ask. There's no obvious indication of the merman's gender, just as I can't tell a male from a female fish.

"Yes, of course," she replies, looking at me as if I'm too ignorant for words. It's enough to shut me up, and I study her, instead.

She's around my mother's age, somewhere between thirty-something and wrinkles, with smooth skin, a somber expression and keen intelligence in her brown eyes. I can tell she's intense about her work by her apparent disregard for her appearance. Wispy tendrils of long blond hair escape from a messy bun at the back of her neck and the front of her lab coat is splattered with slimy green stuff. I grimace at the goo, and she tries to brush it off, only smearing it more.

"Sorry," she says. "I'm working with some algae and it's a messy process."

Shaula clears his throat. At least I hope that's what the growl is, and says, "Jewel Adams, you will work with Dr. Jenkins and her team to discover a way we Dracans can repair other damaged tetrahedra."

"I'll do my best," I answer, knowing full well how impossible it is. When we discovered the Watchers had the same abilities we do, we asked them why they can't fix the artifact without our help. What will Shaula do to me when he discovers the artifacts will only respond to humans because we were created for Terra? If the Dracans succeed in penetrating the force field around a tetrahedron, they might destroy it. But fix it? The artifacts are sentient, and no matter how long they've lived on Earth, neither Dracans nor Allarans will ever be Terrans, no more than an old box in a garage will ever be a car. I am not going to be the one to reveal the truth to Shaula. I pray Avery and Marla have found a way for me to escape.

19

JEWEL

Shaula leaves me alone with Dr. Jenkins, after assuring me a guard would escort me back to my room in a few hours. I'm happy when the door shuts behind him and turn my attention back to Cruiser. If he were human, I'd say he's monumentally bored. Is he?

"Call me Ashley," Dr. Jenkins says from her perch at a high table. She's peering into a microscope. I wonder what's so interesting about microbes when she has a real live merman in the room. When I don't answer, she straightens, steps off her stool and comes to stand next to me at the tank.

"I'm sorry for him," she says, and my heart melts a little.

"Why do they keep him here? He's separated from his friends and family, with nothing to do. What does he eat? How do you feed him? Did you see him laugh? He has a personality."

"My, you're full of questions and judgments, Jewel. Let me show you around. You need to get familiar with the lab and our equipment. Then we'll talk about Cruiser."

She walks me around the laboratory, pointing out pieces of equipment and explaining their purpose, and I've tuned her out, my mind full of questions about the merman. We move into the next room, where more tanks line the walls, displaying creatures that live in the midnight level of the ocean, creating their own light with biolumi-nescence.

"How do they stay alive in there? Wouldn't the pressure differential kill them, or the light?"

"Ah, she speaks." Is that sarcasm? Coming from Ashley? I smile at her and get one in return. This might not be so bad after all.

"The tanks are pressurized. Except for Cruiser, none of the other animals can see the light in the lab. We observe them through a one-way mirror. We've been able to closely duplicate their environment, with naturally flowing sea water at the pressure they're used to, and even the feed dispensing system mimics the way they naturally feed. We use light in the red spectrum because they don't see it at all. They don't know they're enclosed in a tank."

"How do you get the sea water to flow into the tank?"

"The tanks are connected through reinforced tubes to the ocean. Each tube is made of the material protecting the city."

"Can they swim back out to sea?" It seems to me, if there's a way in, then there's a way out. I wonder if Cruiser can figure it out.

"I don't know," Ashley says. "I imagine the Dracans have a way of blocking them from exiting the tubes."

The few creatures on the media room screens gave me no indica-tion of the variety of nightmarish monsters swimming in the depths of the ocean. Ashley's tanks contain critters with names like bug-eyed hatchet fish, ogre fish, fang-tooth fish, viper fish, snakeheads, and dragon fish, each one uglier than the last. Some have mouths full of teeth like stalactites and stalagmites in terrifying caves that snap shut around their prey. I shudder at the strangeness of fish with transparent heads, with huge barrel-like eyes exposed and swiveling inside the bubble. A frilled shark swims in one of the largest tanks.

"This one is a living fossil. It's been on earth at least as long as the Dracans have been here." Ashley waves her hand toward the shark.

Its head has the shape of a giant rattlesnake with multiple rows of teeth lined up in furrows leading toward its throat like rows of spikes growing in a plowed field. Short fins jut out from behind its head, and grooves run the length of its gray body to the frilly fanned tail which gives it its name.

"Did you know around ninety-nine percent of Terra's biosphere is in the oceans?" Ashley asks. "In fact, the biggest biomass on the planet is composed of phytoplankton, the tiniest plants, which produce about half the oxygen in Terra's atmosphere. I've learned more about ocean life in the time I've spent here than most of mankind will ever know."

"How did you get here?" I'm curious. Did she come voluntarily, or was she also abducted?

"It's a long story. Let's just say I learned not to go fishing in the Bermuda Triangle." She says nothing more and leads me to a glass display case reaching from the floor to the ceiling. "Here's where we keep some of the interesting specimens after we've studied them. I glance at dry skeletons and jars of floating eyeballs and other fish parts, but my attention focuses on a stack of shiny black dinner-plate-sized objects.

"Please tell me about these," I ask, pointing to the plates. I don't want to let on I've seen a giant form covered in scales this size.

She opens the case and pulls one out. I notice how reverently she handles it, sliding her hand along the smooth curve of its top, running a finger along the edge. She hands it to me. It's slightly concave and grooved on the bottom. The top resembles a dark abalone shell, with hints of blue and green showing in the light. I miss my sight. I know the colors must be magnificent, if I could only see them.

"These are Triton's scales," she says, completely serious.

"Triton?" I repeat. "Wasn't he a god or something?"

"In Greek mythology, Triton was a son of Poseidon who carried both a trident like his father and a conch shell. He blew the conch to calm or raise the waves and scare sailors and fishermen. Sometimes he was depicted with legs, and other times with a fish tail, like a merman."

"Do you mean like Cruiser?"

"Cruiser's people have lived in the sea as long as humans have been on land, and humans have always known about them. It's only in recent history they've been regarded as mythical. Triton is another creature seen as mythical, and yet we know he isn't."

"So? What is he?"

"He's a dragon, the last of his kind, as far as we can tell. We call him Triton, but the Dracans believe he's the original Leviathan the Bible mentions several times. In fact, King David called him God's pet, and Isaiah prophesied that Creator will kill him in the end, like he did another dragon, Tannin. We think he bugles because Tannin was his mate, and he misses her."

I wonder if Pax read about this in the Bible. I had no idea it has stories like this. I'm still reluctant to tell her I've seen it. Now it seems I've also heard it.

"During the last breach, it sounded like someone keening over huge loudspeakers. I thought it was the call from another artifact, because the first one called us with a similar sound. Was that Triton?"

We turn at the same time when we hear a noise coming from the other room. Ashley takes off running, and I'm right behind her. It's Cruiser, banging on the glass of his prison. He's churning the water in agitation, and when he opens his mouth, he chatters faintly, like the sound a dolphin makes, only in a lower octave. Since I didn't hear him when he laughed at me, I assumed the glass is sound proof. I was wrong. He bangs on the glass with his fists, and glares at me, ignoring Ashley as she rushes to the door.

"Wait!" Her hand is raised to hit the smaller of the two alarm pads on the wall, but she stops and turns when I call. "He's trying to communicate. Help me figure out what he's saying."

The fin on his head starts to glow and becomes brighter every second. He rushes to the other side of the tank, turns back to me and the light from his fin reveals the opening of the tube above his head. He points upward then comes back to the glass. I'm riveted. He's miming. He undulates one arm in a wave-like motion, and with the same arm, smashes his hand against the glass. I shake my head. He does it again. When I don't get it the second time, he clicks madly, rushes to the tube, points up and comes back.

"He's telling us Triton is up there, and he's going to smash the barrier." Ashley can barely get the words out. Her face registers shock. Didn't she know a creature who plays a joke on another must be intelligent? I'm not at all surprised. Then it hits me. We're in imminent danger.

"Sound the alarm, Ashley! Now!" I shout, and scramble for the door, but she's already there, hits the larger alarm pad and the clanging begins. I hope she doesn't get in trouble. There's been no actual breach yet.

20

PAX

I take shallow breaths through my mouth as the excitement in the library, combined with Storm and the crew's brush with terror in their tightly enclosed space, ripen the air in the room. I'm very happy to keep my guard up. Even so, I'm sure we'll all be glad when the debriefing is over, and they can hit the showers.

I'd dropped my guard when they climbed out of the submersible and noticed Storm's pheromones spike when Sky ran to hug him. The pain in my heart spiked at the same time. Will I ever see Jewel again? When the scientists came out, I put it back up again, thankful I'd learned how as a child.

Izzy and Gabe give Dr. Emery the rundown on their experience, using jargon I'm not familiar with. My mind wanders and I think about Jewel, her brilliant eyes, straight black hair full of hidden rainbows, and her creamy smooth skin. I can almost feel my arms holding her body close to mine, and the softness of her lips when I kiss her. Sky pokes me with her elbow.

"I've been doing some research on mermaids and dragons," Dr. Emery is saying. "Most of it is garbage, legends and stories of mythical creatures, but I found a very interesting pattern."

He pauses until he has all our attention. "Mer-creatures have been seen all over the oceans. As recently as two years ago, two scientists in a submersible in arctic waters literally bumped into one and have, subsequently, publicized video evidence of their encounter. Others have reported sonar signatures that don't match the pods of dolphins and whales they were following, as if another species had joined the pod and was swimming along with them. Australian fishermen caught one in their nets. Once they raised it out of the water, it sliced the net with a stingray barb, escaped and left the barb tangled in the net. Deep-water fishermen often find spears tipped with the same kind of barbs in the fish they drag up.

"Ancient cave drawings depict men with fish tails either fighting against humans or with them against a common enemy. I can't imagine how this hasn't come across my radar until now, but we can no longer ignore them. It isn't my field of study, but I must admit curiosity about their physiology. How do they exist both in the depths and the shallows? Are they mammals? Do they have lungs, or just gills? It's all moot, of course, without a living specimen."

A surge of concern mixed with annoyance comes from my sister. "I hope no one ever captures one alive," she says with an edge to her voice. "They're obviously intelligent if they use spears, and I'd hate knowing someone calling himself a scientist is experimenting on one."

"Calm down, Sky." Dad shoots her a look I recognize as "Not now." Sky snaps her mouth shut, but her eyes spark and she narrows them at Dr. Emery. Her annoyance has turned to anger, and I send calmness her way. She isn't receiving it.

"As for the dragon." The scientist ignores the undercurrents. "Every culture in history has its version, from medieval fire-breathing monsters to snake-like Chinese dragons. The science community dismisses them as fairy tales, of course, but now I've seen one alive, I'm inclined to think this discovery might open new fields of study."

"Or a giant can of worms," Sky mutters. For once, she's allowing her unhappiness to affect the rest of us in the room. Izzy and Gabe are frowning. Wolf, Dad, and Charles have their arms folded, all leaning back in their chairs, and the women are glaring at Dr. Emery. I wonder if objects are going to start flying around the room. I grab Sky's hand

and squeeze. The atmosphere quickly lightens as she finally accepts the peace I'm sending her.

"Did you not experience the emotions the dragon was projecting?" She glares at each person in turn. "He's heartbroken and terrified. I didn't want to say anything because I've never experienced this before, but he sent me pictures and I know why he's grieving."

Mom and Dad jump up, nearly pushing their chairs over. "Why didn't you say anything?" Dad asks while Mom pulls her up in a strong hug. Good question. I'm sure everyone wants to know as badly as I do.

"It was too raw." Tears spring to her eyes and she covers her face with her hands. Analiese hands her a tissue, and she nods her thanks, wipes her eyes, and takes her seat again.

"He grieves for his mate. In his eyes, she was all golden light and rainbows of joy. Then it was dark, and my heart broke with his pain. Then he showed me an egg, shimmering in swirling colors. I watched as the colors began to fade and understood his terror. The egg is dying. He's the last. The egg is his only hope."

Something niggles at me. "How long has he nurtured the egg?"

"How would I know?" she answers. "I did get the impression, though, his mate has been gone a very long time."

"Sky," Storm says. "What if it isn't an egg at all? What if he has the artifact?"

21

PAX

Sky's revelation causes chaos in the room, but Dr. Emery sends everyone out and commands his young scientists to get a shower. Storm goes, too, leaving Sky and me alone on deck, watching the stars. I sniff at the delicious aroma of food cooking in the galley, and my stomach rumbles. An answering growl comes from my sister's and we both laugh.

"I'll be glad to get back," she says. "I don't believe we'll find Atlantis this way. Do you think the mermen deliberately showed themselves so Theseus would back off?"

Storm, freshly showered and shaven, joins us at the rail. "They weren't the reason we cut the trip short. It was like a volcano erupted around us while sound nearly deafened us. It took all the strength I had to stop the sub from shaking itself apart."

Sky moves over next to him and sends him love. "Thank God it was you who went with them. Pax couldn't have helped, and neither could I." His eyes are tender. Then I witness what bothers my sister so much. He straightens his spine, and his expression grows cold and hard. I have the impulse to deck him right here.

Instead, I wonder aloud, "If the dragon was keening up here, on the surface, how could you have heard it so loudly at that depth? You were a mile deep, weren't you?"

"We were about two thousand meters down, yes," he answers, "and I've wondered the same thing. Could there be another dragon?"

"No." Sky sounds very sure. "He's alone. He communicated with emotions and pictures, but the combination convinced me he is the last of his kind."

Storm asks, "Do his sound waves travel that far, that strongly, or is there another source?"

"What about the egg? If it's one of the artifacts, as I suspect, couldn't it have made the sound, like the one we fixed in North Carolina? It could be heard for miles in air, which carries sound waves with less efficiency than water." I'd been studying about the effects of sound waves since the dolphin beaching caught my interest and concern. I'm convinced the military is experimenting with acoustical weapons. Come to think of it, maybe that's what they heard.

"What about the Navy base on Andros?" I ask. "Maybe you were the victims of one of their tests."

"Or, maybe we were targeted," he says with a scowl, "but it's more likely the Dracans unleashed a sonic blast to drive us away than our being the target of some military test. The Navy knows Proteus is in these waters and Theseus was down there. Why would they target civilians?"

Storm's right. "Let's think about this. We know the artifact makes sound when it's in distress. So does the dragon. The military has sonic weapons and it's likely the Dracans do too. I say we eliminate the military as a threat, which leaves three possibilities."

"Is it possible all three are at play here?" Sky's question sends a shiver of ice down my spine. "The Dracans don't want us to find Jewel. Why else would she tell us to stay away? The artifact is dying. The Watchers said they're all sick. And the poor, poor dragon is in mourning. Our objective remains the same. Find and rescue Jewel and find and fix the artifact."

"That's all?" Storm sounds ready to explode. I drop my guard and smell the sharp stench of his anger.

"Don't forget the armed and dangerous mermen." He tightens his grip on the railing and clenches his jaw. "Finding Jewel in pitch-black crushing depths while under attack should be a breeze."

Sky sends him some peace, but it doesn't affect him.

"I made a connection with the dragon. If I can see him again and communicate, it's possible I can convince him to help us."

"I've never heard of anything so impossible," he says, and I can hear the bitterness in his voice. "But then, most people think alien occupation is impossible, not to mention invisible spaceships and huge underground cities."

"We're not most people," I say. "If anyone can convince a dragon to help us, it's Sky. She has to."

22

JEWEL

"I'm sorry, Jewel, but you've been confined to your room for now," Marla says, hunched over in the same chair Shaula occupied yesterday, before he led me to the science center to meet the unfortunate Dr. Jenkins. With her elbows on her knees and head in her hands, she's as dejected as I am.

"I understand. It's my fault, and I take full responsibility. Is Ashley all right?"

"I don't know. Shaula is furious, and there's no telling what he's done to her. Thuban threatened to banish him if he hurts you."

"Is it because I'm your friend?" I ask, hoping I'm right.

"Partly, I suppose," Marla answers. "He's still planning to bring you before the council to prove his point, and he also needs you to figure out the artifact."

I resume my pacing, and it dawns on me I'm walking in Shaula's footsteps. I stop and sit down across from her. "How were we supposed to know the merman was tricking us? How did his people know to force open the tube when the alarm went off?"

"Do you think the sea folk are telepathic? You figured out Cruiser is intelligent when he played a joke on you. His escape required cunning and planning. Just how sophisticated are they?" Marla gets up then and resumes wearing a path in the carpet where I left off.

"It makes me wonder if there's a way for us to communicate with them," I say, speculating. "What if they can help me escape, somehow?"

"It's too late now," Marla sounds discouraged. "He's gone, and you're unable to use your abilities here. And now you're more limited than ever."

"We should be thankful they didn't find a breach, Marla."

"True, but a false alarm causes everyone to mobilize, and they had to check every inch of the barrier when they couldn't find a point where it was compromised."

"They could think of it as a fire drill," I say, with little hope. "How do the Dracans travel from Atlantis to the surface?"

"Their ships are docked along the perimeter of the city." She leans over the table, moves the flowers in the center to the floor and draws an imaginary circle where the flower vase had been, a circle about three inches in diameter. With floor to ceiling bookshelves on one wall containing many volumes of books full of pages we could use to draw on, we still have nothing to write with. Marla draws her invisible diagram on the table.

"This is the palace. You haven't been outside it, so you don't know how large the city is. Imagine nine concentric rings, with the palace in the middle as the first circle, and each ring wider than the next as they extend to the perimeter. The second, fourth and sixth circles are fresh-water canals, where we raise most of the fish we eat and which we use to irrigate the crops in the seventh ring. A city this size needs plenty of fresh water, as you can imagine, and although all our water is from the ocean, it must be desalinated and purified. Six roads extend across all the rings, with beautiful bridges spanning the waters, like spokes on a wheel."

I picture a castle on a hill surrounded by a moat. I'd love to see it from the outside.

"Let me get this straight," I say, stopping her for a moment. "Here's the palace, and just beyond it is a canal, right?"

"Correct. We use the first canal for recreation. Parks run all along the banks, with lawns and trees and flowers, and we swim there. We also raise fish. The water is circulated through a purification system to meet all our needs."

"What's on the other side of the canal, across the bridges?"

"The third ring houses the marketplace, with fancy shops and restaurants closest to the palace, and food markets and trading booths just beyond. Within that ring are two circular roads with narrow connecting streets in addition to the six main roads."

"So, the second canal flows beyond that? And it's wider than the first one?"

"Yes. It's used mainly for fisheries and irrigation."

"What's next?"

"The fifth ring is housing for the upper classes. You'll find some beautiful mansions there, along with smaller elegant homes. The sixth ring is the widest band of water, irrigating the farms on the seventh ring. All our crops are grown there."

"Do the canals connect with each other?" I wonder if they use boats.

"Yes, they do," Marla says. Then she answers my unspoken question. "We use boats to transport fish and other food from ring to ring."

"Where do the lower classes of Dracans live? And the humans?"

"Dracan workers live in apartment houses on the inside section of the eighth ring. They live well, in spacious apartments they keep up to the highest standards."

"And the humans?" I repeat.

"They have adequate housing on the outside perimeter of the eighth ring. They also have their own marketplace, shops and entertainment."

"There's no water or farmland separating them from the ninth circle. What's on that circle?"

"It's where our armies are housed and trained. The power for the barrier is harnessed there, and our craft are docked on the outside, accessible only through the defensive ring."

"What would happen if the power goes out? Would we all be crushed?"

"We use an unlimited supply of electromagnetism for power. The energy is gathered in a giant pyramid located at a distance from the city, and we receive the power through obelisks scattered along our perimeter and inside Atlantis. Even if all the outside obelisks are destroyed at the same time, the power supply will not be interrupted."

"How do you know all this, Marla?"

She leans closer, with her elbows on the table, and says gravely, her voice so low I can barely hear her. "My mother and I have been trying to figure out a way for you to escape."

"Have you come up with a plan?" I whisper back, almost afraid to breathe. I certainly don't want to be paraded in front of a council of hostile aliens who want the planet for themselves. How can I make them think humans are worth saving?

"It's risky, and we can only do it with a lot of help, and only if nothing goes wrong."

What could possibly go wrong? Without warning, the door slams open and Shaula strides in. One glance at his face sucks all the air out of the room. I fight dizziness and stand to my feet. I won't go down without at least a show of the courage I don't have.

Marla also jumps to her feet and quickly masks her guilty expression. Did he hear us? How much does he know about our plans? Marla's plans. I don't have a clue what she and her mom have arranged.

"We leave for Council in the morning." Shaula's voice is deceptively quiet. His eyes speak much more loudly, snapping fire at me. I've never been this terrified.

He glares at Marla. "The king expects you to make sure the human is ready. You know the protocol and how she should dress. Soldiers will escort you to the transport after breakfast." She nods and stares at the ground.

The Dracan whirls and exits as quickly as he came in, slamming the door as he leaves. I exhale loudly. "Criminy. Do you think they know?" I suddenly realize I've used Sky's favorite expression when she's upset about something. If I allow my missing her to grow into full-fledged longing, I won't think clearly, and I push the thoughts back.

"All I know is, we can't wait. If the Council decides against you, I'm afraid your chances of survival are nil, and I won't be able to help you. We have to leave tonight."

23

JEWEL

A soft knock at the door alerts me it's time to go. I open it to Avery and Marla, dressed the same way I am, like servants in gray pants and matching tunics.

"Keep your head down and move quickly," Avery instructs me. "Do not raise your head or speak at all, do you understand?"

I nod and follow them down the deserted hallway. My heart races erratically, shaking my body with its uneven rhythm. We duck behind a statue of a Greek goddess and Avery pushes on the wall behind the figure, opening a hidden door. We enter a plain empty hallway and hurry toward another door in the distance. I hear a soft click and see an eye peeking out of the entrance to one of the rooms lining the passageway. The girl who brings my meals slides out and joins us, still mute. I wonder if she can speak. Avery notices her and nods. She must be in on the plan.

We slide through the unlocked exit to the outside of the palace. I wish I had time to enjoy the sweet-smelling fresh air. A breeze cools the sweat on my face and caresses my arms. Lights reflect off the water across the street, flowing and glowing beyond the stone railing. I wish Pax were here to enjoy this with me, but there's no time to waste. A vehicle, like a windowless van attached behind a bubble, pulls up, and Avery quickly opens the cargo doors in the back.

"Get in," she whispers. We don't need further encouragement. I scramble in. Avery gathers her daughter in a tight hug, then gives her a shove toward me.

"Aren't you coming?" I ask, also in a whisper. My insides turn to jelly when she shakes her head. It strikes me what she and Marla are doing might be considered treason. It makes sense if Avery is caught, there would be no one to plead our case to Thuban if things go south. I send a quick prayer to God for safety, thankful Marla knows the plan. The girl closes the doors from the outside, still without a word, and we're alone.

How did I not know Dracans have cars? It's odd I didn't ask how they get from circle to circle over land. Marla sees the question on my face and places a finger over her lips. Okay, we're still in silent mode. I really wish we had windows in here. At least the ride is smooth. Too smooth.

"Are we even moving?" I lean toward her and whisper in her ear. She nods and makes a flying motion with her hand. "No wheels?" I ask, annoying her. There's the finger again. I get the message and shut up.

After what seems like a long ride, the vehicle glides to a stop. We wait, and my stomach churns. Have we been discovered? Are they waiting for guards to pick us up, to pick us off?

The door opens and it's our quiet friend again. "Follow me." Her voice is soft and warm, as I imagined it would be. I'm glad she finally spoke.

"What's your name?" I ask her. I can't keep calling her "silent girl," especially now that she isn't any longer.

"Juliana," she says. Then she hurries ahead. Our transport is parked in an alley between two stone walls towering several stories above us. We could be in an American city, except the walls are unbroken by fire escapes, or even windows. Juliana leads us down a flight of stairs and through a solid metal basement door. When the door closes behind us, it's too dark to see my hand in front of my face. After a few minutes, when the lights I expect do not come on, Marla grabs my hand. It's like we're back in the tunnel in the cavern, where she led the way to the artifact chamber. That's when I discovered she can see in pitch darkness.

Is everything in Atlantis built like a maze? It seems like we're wandering forever, turning down one hallway and another. I imagine the unthinkable pressure of the ocean just on the other side of the barrier. We must be heading to the wall. To the barrier. To the sea and, quite possibly, to our deaths.

Someone ahead of me taps a pattern on a hollow-sounding wall. A sliver of light grows and momentarily blinds me as a door swings open from the other side. I follow Marla into a dimly lit utility room, full of machines and strange equipment. I'm surprised to see Max waiting at a door across the room.

Marla runs to him and he grabs her and holds her tightly. He bends his head, and she raises her lips to his for a long kiss.

Juliana interrupts their embrace and says, "Quickly, Max. Which bay have you prepared for us?"

He opens the door, checks to see if the coast is clear and gestures for us to follow. He leads us down yet another hallway to a wide metal door with an ibis engraved in the middle.

Just then, a tall Dracan guard lumbers around the corner. His eyes go wide when he spots us, as startled as we are. He shouts something in his language, and heavy pounding boots send echoes reverberating in the hall. In seconds, we're surrounded by soldiers. My stomach drops and my legs go weak. Claws scrape my arms, yanking them behind my back and cuffs close tightly around my wrists. Marla, also cuffed, stands next to me, held securely by another guard. Max and Juliana are on the ground, hands tied behind their backs, faces to the ground. Max moans, but no sound comes from Juliana.

The first Dracan speaks into some sort of radio resembling a walkie-talkie shaped to fit his large clawed hands. He barks an order to the others. Juliana remains slumped over while a soldier roughly hauls her to her feet. Her expression is empty, eyes downcast as if her spirit has fled her body. I don't know what's in store for any of us, but I imagine she'll get the worst of it. In Dracans' eyes, she's merely a servant.

Another guard savagely kicks Max before yanking him to his feet. His face is bone-white, his eyes wide and frightened. Then, when he catches Marla's eye, he straightens up and an unexpected transformation happens. It seems Max Green has a backbone after all.

24
SKY

I'm still reeling from the dragon's emotions. Pax's ability to calm me has helped, but the ache lingers and grows like a sinkhole in my heart, merging with the pain of missing my best friend, crumbling away my composure moment by moment. I don't know how much longer I can hold myself together.

Wolf and Sequoia join us on deck, and she envelopes me in a strong hug. A contented purr transfers to me from the little one growing in her.

The rest of our folks gather with us and Wolf announces, "The Navy has ordered Dr. Emery to return to Andros to restock. Then he must leave the region."

"What's the reason?" Charles asks. "Do you think it has anything to do with the dragon?"

"He didn't say," Wolf replies, "No one was around the area when the dragon paid us a visit. They might not know anything about it, although I tend to think they have us under constant surveillance here in the Tongue. It is their territory. Unofficially, anyway."

"It's for the best," Sequoia says. "We should be home by midnight, and we'll spend the next few days just relaxing. Storm, it seems you'll need to learn to scuba dive."

He laughs. "There's no way I'm going into deep water around here. Too many strange creatures live in these waters. Besides, Atlantis is inaccessible without a deep-sea submersible."

Wolf says, "We'll get together tomorrow to discuss our next steps. For now, let's get something to eat and pack our gear. We'll be docking in a few hours."

~

IT'S strange how I sensed the rocking motion of the boat all night, while in my bed on Andros. I hope it wasn't the island rocking. The early morning breeze blowing from the ocean smells fresh and salty. I want to breathe it in and pretend we're on vacation, but a strong sense of urgency tickles the edges of the void left by Jewel's abduction, as if I can tell she's in danger. I send up a prayer for her safety.

"Enjoying the view?" Pax joins me at the rail and hands me a cup of steaming coffee. Our veranda faces the beach we share with the other two families, and in this light, the sea is a glass mosaic in varying shades of aqua and blue. I desperately want to lose myself in its calm waters and to soak in the soothing peace.

"Are you going to train with Dad this morning?"

"No. He's giving us the day off. Storm has to study the online portion of his scuba certification today, poor guy." He grins as he says it, and I know he's relishing Storm's confinement to his computer screen. Scuba certification requires a written test followed by open water training.

"Who's the dive master?"

"It turns out there are two of them, our property managers Tony and Meg Michaels," he replies. "They have all the equipment we'll need, and they know the blue holes around here."

"I can't wait to dive the blue holes, but we can only go down so far. What good will it do, as far as finding Jewel and the artifact?"

"I'm not sure, but Dad, Charles, and Wolf seem to think clues in the underwater caverns might lead us to the artifact. Tony and Meg say the island is riddled with caves, many of them dry but only accessible from underwater. They've seen cave paintings they want to show us. It can't hurt. We need to cover all our bases."

"How long before he's ready to dive with us?" I worry his lack of experience might get him into trouble, until I remember his gift. It's best to have him with us in case we get into trouble.

"Three or four days, tops," he says. "He'll get the written stuff out of the way today. We can do the open water training in the lagoon out there, if the weather holds."

Pax and I each grab a kayak, paddle, snorkels, and fishing gear and head out into the lagoon. I want to paddle out to where the aquamarine gives way to the indigo of the trench, but he insists we stay in the shallows. I sense the pull of the dragon. If he's nearby, he might try to communicate with me again. I want to know if I can send him pictures like he sends me. If we establish a bond, will he help us find Jewel? He needs to know the four of us can save his "egg."

My fishing rod stays untouched in the kayak while I swim and play in the shallows. Pax soon tires of catching and releasing the poor fish with little holes in their mouths from the barbed hooks, and we head closer to the reef and put on fins and snorkels for my favorite pastime. I love being underwater.

The pristine reef glows with color and life. Jewel would love this. Pax's emotions go all soft and warm, encased in a shell of hurt as he thinks of her. Seeing the colors would remind him, as it does me, that our girl is out there somewhere, needing us. I wish Storm would let himself go all mushy, but he's not ready to let go yet. I'm patient, to a point.

I make up my mind to relax and enjoy the beauty of the barrier reef. A neon blue and yellow queen angelfish darts between branches of fire coral. A silver bonefish chases a banded coral shrimp under a spreading pink fan of lace. Sea fans wave in the lazy current, along with sea plumes bobbing like feathers adorning a church lady's hat. I spot a spiny lobster scuttling along the bottom heading for a cluster of brain corals, and a spotted moray eel peeks out from a rough coral wall. Motion and brilliant flashes of color are happening everywhere. A green sea turtle swims slowly by, as if he's enjoying the sights as much as I am. A pair of bottlenose dolphins swim a circle around me, chuckling in their high-pitched voices before darting off, only to leap out of sight into the air. I don't see where they land. For this little while, I forget about our quest.

Pax tugs on my arm, and I flip to my back to blow water out of my snorkel.

"It's time to go in," he says. "We have to eat, and I want to check on our parents."

"Why?" I know I sound whiny, but he did interrupt the magic.

"Oh, I don't know," he says. "Maybe because we need food and water?"

"No, I mean, why do you want to check on our parents?" I don't sense any anxiety, and assume everyone is resting, except for Storm, who should be studying. The sooner he gets his certification, the quicker we can explore the caves under the island.

"Come on," he urges, sniffing the air.

"What do you smell?"

"Smoke."

2 5

SKY

I don't smell any smoke, but I trust his sniffer, and without another word, we swim to our kayaks anchored to the shallow bottom and stow our fins and masks. I hop in with a little help from my brother, and as soon as he's settled in his, we paddle for shore. We drag our kayaks above the high tide line and hurry to the house.

"Pax, Sky, come in here," Dad calls out. He's in his office listening to a police radio Tony loaned him. "There's a fire in Red Bays, on the northwestern shore of Andros, and they're calling for volunteers to help. Think you're up to it?"

Footsteps pound up the stairs to the veranda, and Storm and Wolf come in.

"We'll help," Storm says eagerly. Too eagerly. Who wants to study on a beautiful day like this, when fighting fires is so much more fun? How exasperating.

"Isn't that the Black Seminole settlement?" Wolf asks.

"It is," Dad responds. "Do you think Sequoia would like to come along? Charles is talking to Analiese now, and I couldn't keep Coral away if I wanted to."

In the end, it's decided all of us will go. We gather as many supplies as we can find, blankets and first aid supplies, water and food packed in coolers. If this turns out to be anything like the flood back home, people will need whatever help we can give them. We pile into the three jeeps and start the long drive up the island.

Storm drives ours. "It's too bad we don't have a hotline to the Allarans," he says. "They'd get us there in no time."

"True, but this way we get to see more of Andros," Pax answers. I sit in the back and enjoy the breeze through the open windows. Queen's Highway turns inland, and we lose sight of the ocean. We pass a few homes and settlements, and the drone of the engine soon lulls me to sleep.

Acrid smoke snaps me out of a sweet dream involving Storm. He pulls over behind Dad's car, and Charles stops behind us. The men join a group of rangers and firefighters gathered around a tanker truck, while Mom, Analiese, and Sequoia help me get sandwiches and water out of one of the coolers. When the men return, they quickly eat, and we pile back in the jeeps and head west.

Pax drives while Storm relates what the rescue workers told them. "The fire swept around the village, missing most of it. No one was hurt there, but several families haven't been accounted for in the outlying areas. Search and rescue are in there now, and I know we can help if anyone is trapped. Does the smoke interfere with your ability to track?"

"If there are people alive in there, I can track them," Pax says with confidence.

"I'll know if anyone is distressed," I add, "and you can move mountains to get them out, Storm."

A little hero worship never hurts.

"We'll team up with some of the rescuers. They can hose things down for us while we do our thing." Storm seems sure of himself, but I wonder how they'll receive us. We brought the boots we wore from home when we first arrived. Other than footwear, we aren't exactly dressed for the job, and they don't know what we can do.

"Work your magic on them, Sky," my brother suggests. "They won't resist a good dose of feminine manipulation."

Storm frowns and I get a flash of jealousy from him. It makes me glad. One of these days, he'll realize he can't live without me.

26

JEWEL

I thought the comfortable room they kept me in these last few months was a prison, but I was wrong. My cell contains a narrow cot, a sink and a toilet. The bars spanning the front of the cell remind me of jails in western movies. They leave me no privacy. The thin blanket on the bunk will have to be enough for a bit of modesty. A narrow hallway separates the cell from a blank gray wall. I hold on to the bars and pray we won't be in here long.

A moan comes from the cell to my left. "Who's there?" I call out, and I'm answered by another moan.

"Jewel?" Max's voice sounds weak and thin.

"Max, what did they do to you? Are you all right?"

Silence. I wonder if they beat him or tortured him. If I yell, will anyone answer? Will I get the same treatment, or will they hurt Max even more? I decide to remain silent for now. The lights dim, and I'm growing sleepy. I crawl into the bunk, cover myself with the blanket, and remember nothing until morning.

"WAKE UP!" The gravelly voice wrenches me from a sound sleep. I sit up and rub my eyes. "Out of bed, now!" I recognize the Dracan barking orders and resist the impulse to cover my head with the blanket. What good would it do?

"What do you want, Shaula?" I ask, trying to control my shaking voice. This reptilian terrifies me. My stomach is tied in knots, and I swallow hard to control rising nausea. I stand up and pray he leaves soon. The trembling in my body isn't helping me control my full bladder.

"Ah, she's awake." His voice sandpapers my nerves. His grin sends shivers down my spine and I shudder at his bared teeth. Does he eat humans? I break out in a cold sweat as a picture forms in my mind that seems all too real. His claws, digging into my shoulders, his mouth opening, his hot breath as fangs sink into the back of my neck. It was a nightmare. It had to be. My stomach lurches and I force down nausea.

"Thuban commands you to dress and be ready for transport in an hour. His daughter will be here momentarily with appropriate clothing. I advise you not to waste time." He stares, the grin back on his face.

I don't know where the courage comes from, but I answer him, "The sooner you leave, the quicker I can get ready."

"Ah, yes," he answers. "Perhaps you can convince some on the Council of your worth. I am not convinced, however, and I have more influence with the others than the king of Atlantis suspects. Oh, and I would not repeat that to him, if I were you. Your days are numbered, as is. You may not want your life to end with a prolonged and painful death."

He turns and leaves me with that lovely thought. No one has ever repulsed me more.

Marla comes, accompanied by two Dracan guards, just as I finish washing up in the sink. Juliana is with her, again pushing a cart. The smell of coffee starts me salivating. I want to find out what happened to her, but she doesn't raise her head and I can't read her.

Marla holds a bundle of clothes in her arms. She's in her Dracan form and dressed much like she was when we had our audience with her father, only this time in shades of green. There's some commotion coming from Max's cell.

I point and raise an eyebrow.

"He's coming, too," she says. I pull the blanket off the cot and she lays the clothes down. She holds the blanket up to wall me off from the guards' eyes. I guess they don't care much about privacy.

The soft pants are a thin, gauzy material with flowing shades of green ranging from aquamarine to jade. The tunic, a solid shamrock green, is trimmed in gold along the neck and around the wide cuffs of the sleeves. A gold sash around my waist and matching sandals complete the outfit. The colors will complement my aqua eyes, and, hopefully, help me make a good impression on the other Dracan kings. I take a deep breath, pray quickly, and center myself. There's no getting around this crucial meeting.

After we eat a quick breakfast of coffee and pastries, Juliana clears up and takes the cart down the hall. A guard gestures for us to leave the cell. Marla leads the way and we meet Max in the hallway. I can't believe how good he looks dressed like a Dracan, with light green pants and a dark green floor-length robe, cinched by a wide brown belt around his waist. He's wearing no shirt under it, a fact I notice when he turns to follow the guards ahead of us, and his robe momentarily gapes open to reveal a well-muscled chest. His nose is red and slightly swollen, as are his lips, probably from his face-plant when we were caught.

"Why are we all wearing green?" I ask her.

She links arms with me, trying to help me keep up with the long strides of the guards. "Green is the royal color of Atlantis. Each city has its own color."

"Why is Max coming?" I ask her quietly, so he won't overhear.

"The two of you are under my protection. I have certain privileges as King Thuban's daughter."

"Is that why Juliana is still serving and not being tortured some-where? Aren't you in trouble for your role in the escape plan?" She holds a finger to her lips. We can't discuss it here.

We climb several flights of stairs and emerge into a room where

Thuban, Avery and several more guards are waiting. With crossed arms, the yellow glare he fixes me with might have left me a blubbering mess if I hadn't seen another side of him. Still, I cower and quickly lower my eyes. His stare burns through me, but he says nothing, and whirls toward a metal door. This room is like the one where we met Max last night, only empty of equipment, and I'm not surprised when we're in the same hallway, standing at the door with the ibis.

This time, a guard pushes it open and we're facing one of the Dracan ships. It's exactly like the one I saw attacking our house in Blue Mountain, a triangle at least fifty feet across and made of some pitted, non-reflective metal like a stealth fighter. The front of the ship slopes up to a set of viewports, and beyond that to a cluster of turrets at the peak, where the three sides meet. Nozzles and a series of lights line its edge. I wonder if the interior is anything like the Allaran ships. I'm about to find out.

JEWEL

A ramp drops out of the side of the craft and Max is escorted in first, with me right behind him. We're taken to a room with no interesting viewports, and no instant bubble seats. It's what I would expect of a military transport, utilitarian, with canvas seats bolted to the wall. It's not at all like an Allaran vessel. The king and his entourage leave the three of us alone in the room and shut the door. I suspect it's locked.

"Now we can talk," Marla says, "but quickly. It won't take long to arrive at our destination."

I have so many questions, I don't know where to start, and Max jumps in, "Where is this Council, and why am I here?"

She answers, "You're here because I made it clear I would not go along peacefully without you. You're my escort, and I expect you to behave like a gentleman." Her yellow-eyed glare is as impressive as her father's.

"Marla," I ask, "If you and your mom are royalty, then why were you living in a tiny cabin on the Cherokee reservation?"

She regards me oddly. "This might be the last day of your life, and you want to talk about an insignificant part of your past?"

"What I want is to escape and meet up with my friends, but it isn't going to happen today. I've been wondering about you and what you were doing in Blue Mountain. Please tell me. It'll keep my mind off everything else."

"Wild Bill invited us." Wow. That came out of left field.

"Wild Bill Stern?" I ask. He's the owner of the general store on the reservation, and the head of one of the Cherokee clans. Why would he invite the Dracans?

"He's my mother's brother, and the cabin belonged to their mother. When Mom disappeared from the reservation eight years ago your time, he didn't know she'd been abducted."

"My time? Around the same time Storm's family was killed? Did Thuban do that, too?" I ask, my blood heating up. Was Marla's father complicit in Salali and Tom's death?

"Her disappearance was not related to the incident that left Storm alone. Thuban's ship brought her to Atlantis. The other ship belonged to a different king."

That's better. I'm beginning to like Thuban.

"My mother has been in Atlantis nearly twenty years, Atlantis time. Remember what Thuban said about time anomalies? During this one, only one year passed on Terra for approximately every two and a half years in the city. He and Mom fell in love and I was born two years later. According to North Carolina time, I'd be a little over seven years old."

Max is having as much trouble wrapping his head around it as I am.

"I'm cradle-robbing?" He sounds shocked, and I laugh, until it dawns on me.

"Is time still accelerated? We've been here a few months. Has less time passed topside?"

"No, the anomaly ended a few months back, but there's no telling when another rogue wormhole will show up and mess things up again. Usually, our time slows down while it seems to move very quickly on the surface. It's why people who went missing decades ago in the Triangle are still here and relatively young, and why they can't be returned."

"So, how did Wild Bill find out about you?" I ask.

"Mom contacted him and said she's bringing her adopted daughter. He wouldn't have believed I'm his actual niece. In fact, he still doesn't know about her involvement with the Dracans. It was the ideal cover for us while I spied on you and she helped them find places to dig their tunnels."

"Just before the mountain slide caused the earthquake, he was on his computer at the store and seemed upset. Was he on to you? Did he figure it out?"

Max answers, "I mentioned something to him after I heard Avery's voice in the tunnel we were investigating. I knew he was Marla's uncle, but didn't know his sister was involved with the Dracans. I thought she was in trouble."

"No wonder he was upset," I say. "He was worried about you and his sister." I turn back to Marla. "Why were you spying on us?"

"The Allaran surveillance tipped off Thuban and some of the others. They noticed it when you four were young children. You must understand, the rivalry between the two races is ancient, and they watch us as closely as we watch them. Dracans are familiar with Allaran movement and what they're interested in. You four changed things. They haven't assigned ships to guard single humans since the time of the Roman occupation of Jerusalem. From the time you were born, four of their ships only moved when you did, and it was unusual enough to arouse suspicion something was up."

"That explains the Dracan in the park when I was three," I tell her. "To my mom, she was a middle-aged woman. When I told her the woman didn't have an aura and looked like a giant lizard, no offense, it frightened her so much, we went to live near my grandparents in Asheville. My parents homeschooled me until we moved to Blue Mountain last summer. I'd never been to school before the day I met you."

She nods. "Mom and I moved there in January, and you came in the summer. By then, Storm and the twins were already living in Blue Mountain, and so were their Allaran spy ships." I don't correct her misconception. They were guarding us, not spying.

"When yours joined theirs, we knew for sure something about you four was different and important to them. My job was to find out what your secret was."

"And did you? Find out?" I ask.

"I told her," Max says. "I told her everything Pastor John told me about the aliens and the artifact and how you and your friends were supposed to fix it. I didn't tell her about your gifts because I thought she already knew. I nearly peed my pants when she told me who she is and shifted right in front of me." He and Marla exchange an affectionate glance.

I realize this is the first time I've heard him speak without animosity and in complete sentences. I'm fascinated at the difference in him.

He glanced at Marla and looked at the floor. "When the quake took down the store, I was terrified Marla had been hurt. I would have stayed to help dig people out, but she left during the quake and I had to find her first. By the time I did, she was on her way back to her mom at the cabin, and I helped get her around the landslide and back home."

"You weren't there when we rescued them," I say. "Where were you?"

"I went back into town to join the search and rescue team. During the flood, I was with the same guys searching for people who needed help. I didn't know Marla and Avery were in trouble. I'm glad you got them out before their cabin broke apart."

Who is this guy? The Max I knew was a belligerent bully and coward. I can't believe I was so wrong about him. I want to ask why he behaved so badly with his gang of "lost boys," as Sky called them, but our conversation is rudely interrupted when the door opens.

28

JEWEL

A guard escorts us down the ramp to a platform where Thuban and Avery are waiting. As soon as they see us, they start for the large double doors leading out of the bay, and we enter a cavernous room teeming with Dracans rushing everywhere. The guards form a tight circle around us and push their way through the crowd. It reminds me of a busy airport, or Grand Central Station in New York.

The room is a huge dome, with walkways spiraling up toward a cupola ringed with lighted windows. I wonder if they're outside windows or just made to appear so. The Dracans at the top of the spiral seem tiny, giving me a sense of the massive size of this one room. Some of the Dracans are heading into arches lining the cupola. I pray we don't have to climb all the way up there. The sound of the crowd echoes everywhere.

"Where are we?"

I shout to be heard, and Marla shouts back, "Australia."

She's full of surprises today. When we're alone, if we're left alone again, I'll ask her for more details. For now, we march in silence and I try to see as much as I can. Thankfully, the door we exit is on this level. The more I think about the Council and what I'm supposed to say or do there, the more my legs turn to rubber and butterflies battle it out in my stomach. I wouldn't have made it up one of those ramps.

I admire the Aboriginal art lining the red stone walls of a hallway that seems to go on forever. We finally reach a dark paneled door covered in symbols I've never seen anywhere. I wonder if this is alien writing of some kind. I only have time for a glimpse when we're ushered into a room, much smaller than the other, but more opulent. The guard says something in his language, salutes, and leads the rest of the soldiers out, closing the door behind them. We're left in a room more like an Arabian palace than something in the Australian outback.

"Marla, take Jewel and Max to their rooms," Avery says. It's the first I've heard her speak since our debacle the night before. She and Thuban disappear through a door in the wall, covered by a gauzy curtain edged with gold beads.

We exit through another door, also hidden by a curtain, to a hallway with three arched doorways. Marla quickly ushers us into the middle room.

"This one is mine," she says. "Jewel, you're in the one on the right and Max is on the left. We won't meet with the Council until tonight, so there's time to relax. I'll have lunch served in here."

An enormous four-poster bed sits on a platform in the middle of the floor. The posts are thick columns carved with climbing vines. A deep green silken canopy drapes into curtains tied back at each column. Clusters of cushions and pillows dot the floor around it, with one arrangement on a window seat next to a bay window. The curved expanse invites me to sit and gaze at what should be a breathtaking view of a multicolored desert bathed in red and violet light. To me, it's dull, muted, and I know it isn't real.

Pain pierces my heart and my mind floods with all my losses, including my family, my friends, Pax, and my ability to see every sparkle, every nuance of color. I ache for Sky with her wildly fluid aura that blends so well with her equally wild red hair, Pax's blue and yellow aura, peaceful and warm and loving, and even Storm's black and red streaked aura full of a rage he keeps under tight control most of the time. Tears spring to my eyes and flow down my cheeks.

Marla's arm drapes across my shoulders and she hands me a scrap of linen edged in lace and says, "I'm sorry we don't have tissues here."

I start to laugh. I'm sure I've surprised her when she steps back with a shocked expression, and I laugh harder.

"What's so funny? I thought you were crying, and I just wanted to help."

I turn and hug her, still laughing. "Tissues? You're sorry about tissues?"

Max starts laughing then, too, seeing the irony, which is yet another surprise. When she gets it, we end up in a heap of pillows on the floor, laughing hysterically. I finally gasp for air, and it hits me. I'm in an impossible situation. My life could end tomorrow. Then the world will end because the Dracans will never fix the artifacts. My friends and family don't know where I am and may not know I'm even alive. And yet, I'm not alone. I have two new friends, as unlikely as they are, and we can still find humor in the darkness. It could be worse.

29

PAX

I shouldn't have been so cocky about my ability to track people in this smoky hell. It's all I can do not to choke on the noxious fumes making it nearly impossible to breathe. Storm and Sky have their faces covered with bandanas, and I'm going to need one, too.

"Feel anything, Sky?" I ask, after a bout of coughing racks my chest and throat.

"Nothing," she says, while we make our way around another burned out cabin. Storm lifts fragments of roof off walls, tosses them aside, and lifts the walls. There are no human remains, although the smoldering remains of a few animals is bad enough.

We helped with search and rescue during the floods in Blue Mountain, and I'll never forget the smell of human death. It's different from dead animals, and much more disturbing. I pray we don't find any bodies in this mess.

My feet are cooking in boots overheated by the hot ash and embers on the ground. I take a swig of water from a canteen one of the searchers gave me. Sky and Storm have their own, and, like me, they're conserving water. We shuffle through ashes and stumble over tree roots until we reach the next cabin.

"I feel someone," Sky shouts. "Is anyone there?"

Now I smell it, the faint odor of fear under the pall of ash and smoke. "Ryder, over there." I point to the source and watch as a cloud of ash explodes into the air, pushed up by a floating wall falling flat in the blaze.

"Help," a faint croak leads us to a shallow hole under what was once the floor of the house. A boy, ghostly in ash and covered in grime, with muddy tear tracks running from his eyes to his mouth, holds the limp hand of a woman lying next to him. "My mama won't wake up."

I sniff. She's still alive and I nod at Storm. He lays two fingers on her carotid artery and says, "She's breathing, and her pulse is strong. She doesn't need CPR, so let's get the two of them out of here."

Sky runs over to the boy and picks him up. He's skinny and half as tall as she is, and he tightly wraps his thin brown arms and legs around her. His eyes go wide as Storm gently lifts the woman, careful to keep her neck and back straight.

"Is there anyone else here?" Sky asks him. He shakes his head, still staring at his floating mother.

"Can you climb up on my back?" I ask, prying him off Sky. He nods and clambers up, and I notice how strong he is despite his small size.

We retrace our steps and safely get the woman and her son to the triage center. The boy isn't the only one surprised by Storm's gift. As soon as he lowers her, we're surrounded by the grinning faces of village women, many reaching out to touch us. Sequoia pushes her way through.

"Give them air, please," she pleads. "They can't breathe." The women back off, wonder still written on their faces.

Wolf and the men return with their team of searchers while we're refilling our canteens. They've brought two people back on stretchers, and three women wearing Emergency Medic vests rush over. I silently thank God the people are alive. Dad spots us and he and the others come over, dragging their feet in the dust and ash. Some of the women insist the rescuers sit at a table and eat. When someone lights torches around us, I realize how dark it's gotten.

"We're done searching for the night," Charles says. "There's nothing more we can do today. We'll have to find a place to bed down until first light."

We haven't discussed where we're going to sleep, but I should have figured the women would have it covered. Two of them lead us to a small church where cots have been set up. There are no showers available, but we'll get just as filthy tomorrow. I splash my face and rinse my mouth in the small bathroom sink, fall into a cot and lose consciousness.

～

MORNING LIGHT and bustling activity wakes me. I make my way to the bathroom and wait in line, Storm right behind me.

"We got word the fire's under control. Ten people are still missing, but some may have escaped by boat," he tells me.

"How much area still needs to be searched?" I ask.

"Not much. We'll get our assignment after breakfast." He yawns and stretches. My eyes are ready for more sleep. I really want a cup of coffee.

Sky joins us after we eat, and we head to the staging area to receive our assignment. We're surrounded by sleepy dark-skinned men, some with grim faces, but most of them nodding or smiling at us. Historically, the Seminole tribes in Florida had taken in many escaped slaves and allowed them to fully integrate into their culture. These are descendants of the Black Seminoles who escaped being sold back into slavery when they fled Florida during the Seminole wars in the eighteen-hundreds.

The boy we rescued yesterday breaks away from one of the men and runs to hug Sky. He's wearing clean blue jeans held up by a short length of rope, and a blue batik shirt a size too big for him. His boots fit him, and he has a backpack on with a canteen attached.

"How's your mom?" she asks.

"My mama is okay," he answers, a huge grin lighting up his milk chocolate face. "I'll help you today."

Storm shakes his head. "Sorry, but it's too dangerous out there," he says. He reaches out to put his arm around the boy's shoulder, but the kid shakes it off and glares at him defiantly.

"I know the woods. I know where the cabins are. My mama flew, and I know you did it."

"What's your name and how old are you?" I ask. Maybe it would be better to keep him with us. The whole community knows about his floating mother by now.

"I'm Adonis Conner, and I'm eight. Call me Donny. My mother is Lucaya, the healer."

"Donny," Sky says, "promise you'll stay close to us and do what we tell you, okay?"

He nods his head and runs to a tall man in uniform. The police officer nods at us, and Donny comes running back. We head out along a trail leading past a small general store and into the smoldering woods. My shield does little to dampen the sharp odor of smoke hanging like fog over everything. I wonder how long it'll take for the forest to recover.

Donny moves silently while we crunch and stumble our way through the burn. He scampers ahead and waits for us to catch up. "Speed up! You move like a coconut crab."

By mid-day, we've checked out three empty cabins.

"I'm hungry," Donny grumbles. We're all hungry and tired, so we head back to the village, where the boy runs to find his mother.

"They seem to have things under control," Storm says. "I'm going to find Sequoia. She must be exhausted, and all this smoke can't be good for her baby."

"I'm going, too." Sky's worried, so I tag along.

We find Sequoia in the church, deep in animated conversation with Donny's mother, who seems to be all right. A beige band aid plastered above her left eye sits in stark contrast with her dark skin, darker than her son's. An orange bandana holds her cloud of curly black hair off her face, some of the ends singed in the fire. I thank God the wall covered the two of them, or they'd have been toast.

As soon as she spots us, Lucaya stands and opens her arms. Sky is the first to hug her. After Storm and I take our turns, he hugs Sequoia and we sit on one of the cots.

"Your medicine woman has been telling me of your quest to find your friend. She tells me you've seen our dragon, Lusca, and I understand that you, Storm, have seen the sea dwellers. We've witnessed strange craft flying out of the sea and diving into it. These are things we don't talk about with anyone outside the tribe, but you are exceptional. You proved it by the way you found Adonis and me, and how you transported me to town."

"Lusca?" I ask.

"It is our name for him," she explains.

"It's our pleasure, Lucaya," Sky assures her. "Donny told us you're the healer here, much like Sequoia is for us."

"Yes," she answers. "Healer, medicine woman, resident shaman, whatever you'd like to call me." Her laugh is deep and loud and full of mirth, and we can't help but laugh with her. Sky is delighted.

"And now, my young heroes, my people and I are determined to help you find your Jewel. We don't know how, mind you, but we will give you access no one else has in order to help you solve this mystery. You can count on it."

30

JEWEL

The Council chamber is a circular room with thirteen thrones arranged on a platform in a semi-circle along the far wall, eight on a higher tier in the back and five below them. The other hemisphere is arranged in a similar fashion to one of our courtrooms, with a judge's bench towering to our right, a long table in front of the dais and chairs facing the thrones. Avery stands to my left at the table, and Marla to my right. Max is behind Marla in the first row of what appears to be a viewer's gallery. We remain standing as the kings take their thrones.

A massive Dracan dressed in solid black enters and takes his seat at the judge's bench, and I gratefully take my seat as well. I'm not sure how much longer my rubbery legs would have held me up. I hold my shaking hands in my lap as each of the kings announces his name in a roll call.

Four and a half months ago, I would have sworn they all look alike, but I would have been dead wrong. Each has scales that are unique in color, even to my dulled vision. Their faces are as distinguishable as our human faces, and they vary in size and shape. Each king is from a different continent or ocean, except for Asia, which the Dracans consider two continents, North and South Asia. The rulers of continents are seated in the upper thrones. Thuban, as king over Atlantis, but also of the entire Atlantic Ocean, sits facing us in the center of the five ocean rulers. I'm glad Marla took the time this afternoon to fill me in on the hierarchy and what to expect during the Council. My stomach churns and I wish I hadn't eaten the delicious lunch in Marla's room. I breathe deeply to control the nausea.

It appears there are other items on the agenda because the kings take turns discussing them, all in their own language. If I understood them, it might have held my interest, but my nerves grow tighter with every passing moment. Marla reaches under the table and grabs my hand. I'm grateful for the touch. It calms me and reminds me of Sky. I try to think of other things, afraid I'll burst into tears.

Cruiser. I wonder if he's happy with his family again. Longing for my own family nearly crushes me. Ashley. Dr. Jenkins. Did Shaula punish her for pulling the alarm that allowed Cruiser to escape? I send up a short prayer for her. I like her and hope I'll get to see her again. I hope I'll get to see everyone again.

My nerves jump when Thuban calls my name.

"Stand up," Marla whispers, and I jump to my feet, knocking over my chair. I can't control the trembling in my legs, and it gets worse when a few of the kings laugh at my clumsiness. I can't do this. I have the strongest need to run as fast and as far from here as I can. Deep breaths. There's nowhere to go, and my nearly liquid legs wouldn't carry me, anyway.

"Jewel Adams," Thuban says, his voice projecting as if he had a microphone. "Please tell us how you and your friends repaired the arti-fact we have in our possession." He studies the others as he says, "our possession." Some of them bare their teeth. Oh, God. How can I do this?

"Your majesties," I manage to squeak out. Again, a few of them laugh.

"Speak up," Thuban says, his voice gentling. "You are here under my protection, and no harm will come to you. Please explain how you four, with your gifts, were called and were able to repair it. Leave nothing out."

I begin with the mysterious sounds that emanated from the Cherokee reservation, and how our families were drawn together there. My voice grows stronger as I lose myself in the memories. I tell them about our gifts, and when I get to Storm's telekinesis, two of the kings glance at each other. Are they responsible for killing his parents and later attacking him? When I realize how disastrous it might have been if Storm were here instead of me, I'm glad they abducted me instead. Of course, I wish they'd left all of us alone.

"How did you find the artifact?" The question comes from a king in the back row, one of the rulers of continents.

"The Watchers led us to it after the final call," I answer. I know they know who the Watchers are because they attacked them. The next question confirms it.

"After we disabled the Watchers, how did you then find the artifact?" Another king asks. I suspect he's one of the two who had something to do with Storm's family.

Marla squirms on the seat next to me. I force myself to look straight ahead, afraid I might implicate her if I glance her way.

"We used our gifts to find it," I answer, leaving Marla and Max out of it. They led us directly to the artifact's chamber, but I'll never share that with the Dracans. She lets out her breath in a soft huff.

"Tell us how you repaired it," Thuban urges. I wonder if he knows about his daughter's involvement.

"We used our gifts." I explain how we found the crack in the force field, how Storm blew it apart and held the tetrahedron suspended while we all laid hands on it.

One of the oceanic kings asked, "What happened when you touched it?"

"We sent it love, amplified when we all touched it at the same time with joined hands."

Laughter roars through the room. They don't believe me any more than Shaula did when I told him the same story.

"What happened then?" Thuban shouts, and the kings quiet down.

"It sent back gratitude and started spinning again. I watched it build its protective shield back up. Then we were attacked. I lost consciousness at some point and don't know what happened to the artifact afterwards."

"It sent back what?" The incredulous question comes from the other king I suspect attacked Storm or his parents.

"Gratitude. The tetrahedron is sentient."

Pandemonium explodes in the room, with kings shouting at each other in their own language. My legs give way and Marla eases me back into my chair. Thuban nods at me and joins the verbal fray. From the sound of the escalating voices in the room, I seriously doubt I'll make it out of here alive.

JEWEL

"**L**et's go." Marla's voice breaks through the fear and confusion in my head while the Dracan kings seem ready to come to blows over my fate.

"Really?" I ask, a tiny flicker of hope jumps in my heart. "We can leave?"

She nods, and gestures for the guardsman standing against the wall opposite the judge. He comes over to us and waits while we gather ourselves, then leads us through the same door we came in. Max and Avery follow us into the hall.

"We'll rest and refresh ourselves in our rooms," Avery explains. "There may be no solution until tomorrow, but we need to be ready to leave at a moment's notice in any case, whether it's to return here or to go back to Atlantis."

I'm surprised at the hunger gnawing at my empty belly. Butterflies and crawly worms in my gut made the thought of food nauseating during the proceedings, but not any longer. I need to eat.

A delicious aroma hits me as soon as the doors open to our suite, where covered dishes, fresh fruit, and pastries cover a table near a set of open French doors. With Marla next to her, Avery takes the seat to the right of the head, which is where Thuban would have sat if he were here. Max and I sit across from them, facing the open window and a view of a desert sunset. It is, of course, nothing more than a dull hologram.

A golden samovar inlaid with abalone in the shape of a phoenix dominates the center of the table. I can almost see tendrils of spiced tea waving seductively under my nose, drawing me in, and my thoughts turn to Pax. If he's trying to find me, he's in danger. They all are. The lid of control I've been holding tightly over the pain of loss begins to crack, and a black void threatens to suck me in.

Avery pulls me out of it with a simple request, "Jewel, would you offer thanks, please?"

I respond with a simple prayer my mother taught me as a child, "God is great, God is good, let us thank him for this food. Amen."

We eat silently, each of us lost in our own thoughts. I pour a cup of chai and sit back, satisfied in body, if not in spirit. Avery watches me, a solemn expression on her face.

"Aren't you curious about our location, Jewel? You're normally so full of questions. It seems odd you're so quiet."

She's right. I've allowed the glum circumstances to dull my curiosity. Maybe she can rekindle it. It will keep my mind occupied, in any case.

"Sure, Avery. Marla said we're in Australia, but I've never been here and don't know much about it."

"Then you haven't heard the legends of Uluru?"

"Do you mean Ayer's Rock? I've seen photos of it and have always thought there was something mysterious about it." I remember it as a bare, red mountain rising out of a bleak desert. The photos in an old geography book struck me as something alien, giving me an odd hollow feeling. I've shied away from any mention of it since, but now I wish I'd studied it.

"That's what modern Australians call it, but Uluru is its Aboriginal name. Uluru is the name of a Dreamtime ancestor who was reptilian. To protect its sacred origin, they now claim it's simply a place name," she explains. I might have been right in thinking the mountain is something alien.

"The Aboriginals' story of Dreamtime is one of the few ancient legends remaining close to the truth after many thousands of years of oral tradition. If you research Uluru online, you'll see a lot of fascinating information, but you won't find much about what I'm going to share with you."

I'm all ears. Marla pours herself a cup of tea, and Max is munching on a pastry. We focus our attention on Avery.

"Dreamtime began with the arrival of Allarans and Dracans to Terra, and ended at the conclusion of the great war.

"While early humans were learning to survive outside the Garden, Creator allowed the two extraterrestrial races to interact with them and help them advance. He oversaw the genetic experiments that resulted in modern man and gave both the Dracans and Allarans permission to exchange their DNA with humans. Don't forget, Creator made them, as well. The Bible speaks of the Nephilim and other giants that came of those unions. Over time, people forgot about Creator and all races turned to their baser instincts. Eventually, Creator had enough and sent the flood to cover the earth."

"What happened to the extraterrestrials during the flood?" Max asks. I'm wondering the same thing. Weren't there giants afterwards, too? I vaguely remember a story about a boy named David slaying a giant with a stone and a slingshot.

"They temporarily fled the planet, the Allarans through their wormholes and the Dracans with their starships. They returned after the waters receded, although much of the planet was still covered in water, including this desert. In fact, some of the rock art in the region depicts something ancient Aboriginals might never have seen. Boats and fish. "

"Rock art?" I ask. I'd love to see it. How did the ancient people depict their world?

"Yes. Some of the rock paintings show humanoids covered in scales. They obviously knew the Dracans. Other paintings show tall humans in flowing robes rising into a light, possibly the Allarans. According to the Aboriginals, the Dreaming was a time when giant semi-human beings roamed the earth and built huge stone monuments.

They made everything the people needed to live and established secular and sacred laws for the tribes. We know, of course, who those beings were."

"Did Creator give them permission to be up to their old tricks again?" I ask. "I thought he ended civilization with the flood."

"No, he paused it. He cleansed it of the worst of the genetic experiments, but he never considered Dracans or Allarans to be mistakes, nor did he forbid them access to humans, at least not then."

3 2

JEWEL

Avery stands up and stretches. She walks over to the fake window and stares at the holographic desert. I take the opportunity to stretch too, and the others stand as well. We join her in silence for a few moments, then she motions us to sit on the cushioned window seat and resumes talking.

"With the aid of the two alien races, humanity again became civilized. Waters continued to recede, and mankind learned to harness global energy through the electromagnetic grid threaded throughout the planet.

"When this sea evaporated and left a vast desert, Dracans taught the humans how to find water and food. The people native to this region had no interest in energy and growth. They were, and still are, a simple folk, very much in tune with nature. Unlike the more aggressive civilized peoples, their population remained small, so their needs did not outpace their progress."

I interrupt Avery's story. "The Watchers told us about a great war between Allarans and Dracans. How did it affect the Aboriginals?"

"This desert became the final battleground in the war between the two interplanetary races. They had already destroyed the wonders of India and Egypt. Atlantis had drowned, and the Aztecs and Incas left their great cities. These "gods" who brought civilization to the inhabitants of Terra, had also destroyed it, and this is where they fought for the last time."

"Our history books never mention this. As epic as it must have been, why don't we know about it?"

"Men have intentionally changed historical records, Jewel, and the practice continues today. They re-write history to benefit the ruling class in power at the time. The records have become so twisted and false that many of the races on Earth have gone into hiding while their very existence was erased from human memory."

"So, what happened here?" Max asks, sounding impatient.

Avery glances at him. "Creator stopped the war before the races destroyed Terra. He banished the Dracans to the underworld and the Allarans to the sky, with a strong warning to remain hidden. As you know, they haven't exactly obeyed their directives. Now, let me finish, then we'll sleep."

I stifle a yawn. It has been a long, emotional day, and my eyes are tired. Still, I need to hear the end of the story.

"Satellite pictures of this region show another isolated rock similar to Uluru, along with other singular clusters of rocky outcroppings. Each one is the only geological anomaly in that immediate area of desert. In fact, there's a hint of an impact crater around the one slightly to the southeast. Uluru is shaped like a giant melted triangle. Does the shape remind you of anything?"

"Sure," Max says. "A Dracan ship."

"Exactly," Avery affirms. "A starship, to be exact. Two remained somewhat intact when they crash landed, but the rest of the fleet broke into pieces."

I close my gaping mouth and stammer, "B-but isn't Uluru made of sandstone?"

"Creator did not leave the Dracans any raw materials to rebuild their starships after the war. He turned them to stone. Uluru is one of the five starships that brought the Dracans here from their home world."

"How big is it?" Max's eyes snap with interest.

"All that's left is the core, which is three miles deep and nearly six miles in circumference. Aboriginals today rightly say the ancestors still inhabit the rock. We are a mile underground in Uluru."

She stands then and says, "Now get some rest, but wear your clothes to bed. We may have to leave quickly."

The fear her story had kept at bay rushes back with a vengeance. The food I ate sits in my stomach like a huge stone, and my heart races. For the millionth time, I miss Sky and her soothing gift. Are the kings still arguing about my fate? Will I survive this night?

Max and I ignore our own bedrooms and use some of the pillows scattered throughout Marla's room for bedding. No one wants to be alone.

"Jewel," Marla says, her voice heavy with sleep. "Don't worry, okay? Thuban won't let anyone harm you."

"How do you know?"

"He's my father. And you're my friend."

33
JEWEL

"Go away," I mumble when the hand on my shoulder shakes me again. Again? I thought I was dreaming, but the urgent voice in my ear sets off an alarm in my head, and my eyes fly open. The room is dimly lit with a holographic moon in the window and I wonder how late it is.

"Hurry, Jewel! Get up!" Marla keeps her voice to a loud whisper as she grabs my hand and tugs until I give in and sit up. When I notice Max with his ear pressed against the door, I jump to my feet.

"What is it?" I whisper back.

"I think Thuban has returned, but he isn't alone, and Max woke up to the sound of fighting."

The blood drains from my face and pools in the pit of my stomach. Fighting? That can't be good. Did Thuban lose? Are they coming to get me? What if he can't protect me? My throat closes and I can't speak. I make a choking sound and Marla puts her arm protectively around my shoulders.

There's no place to hide in the room, and no other exit. "Someone's coming," Max says, backing away from the door. The knob turns and the door is shoved so hard it crashes open against the wall. I'm glad

Max wasn't behind it. Marla hugs me tighter, probably to stop my violent trembling.

The outline of a huge Dracan fills the doorway, backlit by lights in the hall. As soon as he speaks, Marla tightens her hold to keep me from melting to the floor.

"Jewel Adams, the Council requires your attendance. Immediately." Shaula strides in, followed by two armed guards.

"Where is my father?" Marla demands. "She goes nowhere without his orders."

An evil grin spreads across Shaula's face. But then, every grin appears evil on him.

"I am afraid the good king is temporarily indisposed. Do not speak again. Guards!" One soldier grabs Max by the arm and pulls him out of the room. Marla and I hurry after him before the other has a chance to lay a hand on either of us. Shaula leads us out of the apartment. As always, the winding hallways quickly confuse me. A quick glance at Marla reveals her confusion, too. Are they leading us in the wrong direction? I don't dare ask her.

When we get to the cavernous room we entered yesterday, realization hits. We're not going to the council chamber. The transport vehicle bays are just ahead.

The dome echoes with our footsteps, empty of other traffic, Dracan or otherwise. I imagine everyone is still asleep and wish I were sleeping too, anywhere but here. Shaula opens a door and we enter one of the bays. Two Dracans sit back-to-back on the floor, bound and blindfolded. Shaula glares at us and the warning is clear. Do not speak.

We silently enter the transport. Max's guard shoves him into an empty room with seats bolted to the wall. Marla and I follow and take our seats.

As soon as the guard leaves, slamming the door shut behind him, Max says, "Thuban shouted something in the hall when the fight broke out. I'm pretty sure they subdued him, and that's why he's indisposed."

Marla hunches over, arms folded across her middle, and it's my turn to comfort her. "He's a king, Marla. Even Shaula isn't stupid enough to damage him. They probably tied him up, like the two in the bay. I'll bet he doesn't know it was Shaula who ordered the attack."

"You're right," Max agrees, throwing his arm around her. "I know a bully when I see one, and bullies are cowards at heart."

If the situation weren't so terrible, I'd laugh at the irony. Max should recognize another bully, since he was so good at it in Blue Mountain. This Max is a much different boy.

"Let's look at the bright side," I say for her benefit, with little hope there is a bright side. "We're still alive, which means Shaula still needs us. Marla, you know the Dracan hierarchy. Which of the kings do you think Shaula is working for? It might help to know where he's taking us."

"How would that possibly help us?" Marla says. "We'll never escape from any of their cities without transport, and I certainly don't know how to fly one, even if we could get our hands on one. Do you? Max?"

I agree it sounds hopeless, but I have an idea. "When Storm's aunt and uncle were abducted and taken to Superstition Mountain in Arizona, some of the Dracans worked with the Allarans to free them. They met us in the desert during the rescue. Vega said there's a faction that wants peace and knows the four of us are the only ones who can fix the artifacts."

"Even if that's so," Marla says, "how would we find them and enlist their help? We're captives, and I have no idea where Shaula is taking us."

"That's just it," I say, fingering the wristband my dad made sure would never come off my wrist. "If there's even a tiny window where my gifts aren't blocked, I can focus and send a picture of our location to the Allarans. They might stage another rescue with the help of their allies."

"Yeah," Max says, sounding as hopeless as Marla. "That's if we know where we are when we get there."

Lost in thought, we don't speak again. Since there's no sensation of moving during the trip, we don't know we've come to a stop until the door opens, and Shaula stands with hands on hips and a scowl on his face. "Follow me," he orders. "And remain silent."

His robe flares as he whirls around, and we practically run to keep up with his long strides. The two guards march behind us. When we pause at an intersection, I note which direction we take. We turn left down a tunnel like the ones under Clingman's Dome in North Carolina, where we followed the Watchers to the artifact. Smooth, unadorned walls curve seamlessly over our heads in a tube. Only the floor is flat, which is a good thing considering our rapid pace. There are no directional symbols and I wonder how Shaula knows where to turn.

We finally reach a plain metal door, which slides open to let us through to a square room. A female Dracan, flanked by four reptilian giants, stands placidly by a second door. She's wearing a doeskin dress that falls to her ankles and ends in a beaded fringe. Intricate beadwork adorns the bodice and three-quarter fringed sleeves expose wide silver bracelets on each of her wrists. If not for her scaled skin, she could be a Native American princess. Is it possible we're back at Superstition Mountain? Hope spikes in my chest. It crashes as soon as she speaks.

"Leave the prisoners with me, Shaula. Your work is done, and you will be rewarded."

"Please indulge me, Meissa. The humans are fragile, and I would see to their comfort before I leave them in your tender care." The way he says "tender care" sets my teeth on edge and raises the hairs on my arms.

Meissa narrows her eyes and bares her teeth, more than I thought could fit in one mouth, even one as large as hers. I didn't think it was possible to be more frightening than Shaula, but I was wrong. She is the first female Dracan I've seen up close, and her resemblance to a crocodile crossed with a shark makes my skin crawl. Apparently, she has the same effect on Shaula, because he quickly bows and backs away.

"As you wish," he says. "Your king should arrive shortly. Please inform him that I request an audience." He turns and leaves the room with his two guards hurrying behind him.

This is it. We're on our own against a she-demon, and she might eat us alive.

"Marla, dear," she purrs, suddenly all sweetness. "It's so good to see you again, and you've brought guests." Her sudden switch from evil queen to Snow White does not give me confidence.

34
STORM

The ride home yesterday was uneventful. We quickly unpacked and turned in early, letting exhaustion take over. I barely registered the alarm this morning, which is why I'm running late now.

The blood-red sky fades to orange as the sun rises over the ocean. By the time I get to the beach, Tony and Meg are already unloading scuba gear from the back of their jeep. Without thinking, I empty the rest of it, using telekinesis. I realize my mistake when Meg goes white and her mouth hangs open. Tony stands frozen, staring at the floating tanks, masks, fins, and other gear. It seems no one has told them about our gifts.

"Sorry about that," I say. "I guess I have some explaining to do."

"I'll say," Tony retorts. He wraps an arm around his wife. "Are you all right, honey?"

She nods and tilts her head in a silent question. Will they even believe me?

"Hi, guys!" Sky calls out cheerfully as she and Pax shuffle through the sand toward us. "Is something wrong?" I know she's sensing the tension in the couple, and maybe my contrition.

Tony speaks up, "It seems your buddy here can make things float in midair. Care to tell us what's going on?"

Pax, ever the peacemaker, chimes in. "Sure. It's time you two knew, in any case. We might need your help." Tony leans his back against the jeep and Meg shares the towel Sky has spread on the sand. I let him do most of the talking while he tells them about the Allarans and Dracans.

"Wait a minute," she interrupts. "Are you saying the lights we've been seeing in the ocean since we moved here ten years ago are alien spacecraft? We've seen them in the skies, too, especially at night. I'm not surprised. Why isn't this all over the news?"

"Both races intend to stay hidden," Sky says. "The Allarans altered our DNA, giving us our abilities, and they did it for a specific purpose."

"Keep talking," Tony says. His arms are crossed and the expression on his face makes it clear he's skeptical about all of it. Sky sends a burst of comfort, and his arms relax to his sides. I know she senses his unease at our admittedly far-fetched revelations.

"Did you do that, Sky?" Tony asks. "A minute ago, I thought you kids were crazy, but right now I'm ready to believe anything you say. You manipulated my emotions."

"It's how her gift works," Pax says, smiling at his sister. "She's a strong empath. I'm a tracker. I can smell the way dogs can."

Meg wrinkles her nose. "How awful," she says. "I can't imagine how overwhelming it would be."

"He can turn it on or off," Sky explains. "You know what Storm can do. As far as I can tell, his is the most practical gift."

"How can we help?" Meg asks. "Why would you even need our help? The three of you seem to have things covered."

"That's the problem," I say. "There are four of us, and we're going to find and rescue Jewel. With her gift, she's able to see millions of colors. She also sees the auras around people, and through disguises."

Tony asks, puzzled, "Sky, you said you've been given the gifts for a specific purpose. What is it? Why did the aliens change your DNA?"

Pax answers, "So we can save the world."

Megs face goes white again, and Tony laughs. "You're not serious. You kids? Save the world? How, exactly?"

He explains to them about the artifacts. By the time he's finished telling them about our finding and fixing the one in North Carolina, and how the Dracans took it and abducted Jewel, the sun is high in the sky and we haven't entered the water yet. I'm worried our instruction will have to be delayed until tomorrow, since morning is the time when the water is typically the calmest.

I shrug it off and address Tony, "Wolf says you've seen ancient rock paintings on the walls of some of the dry caves under the island. Would you be willing to lead us there so we can see for ourselves? We're searching for any clues that might help us find our friend."

"What makes you think you'll find clues in a cave? Those paintings have been there for centuries, if not longer." It's a reasonable request, and I'm glad Pax answers.

"The Dracans are holding Jewel in Atlantis, which we've traced to the bottom of the Tongue of the Ocean. We know she's there because she was able to get a short message out to us before we came here. The Dracans have been here for millennia, so the paintings might very well have clues."

"Do any resemble mermen, or a dragon?" Sky asks.

"Why?" Meg asks, both befuddled and suspicious. I wonder if my explanation will convince them to help us or confirm we've completely lost our minds.

"Because we've seen both, and we believe they might help us rescue Jewel."

35

JEWEL

Meissa leads us to a room resembling a cave, with smooth rock walls broken by pillars of stalactites and stalagmites fused together. The four guardsmen follow us in and stand at attention on either side of the door. She invites us to sit at a table between two of the pillars, where a pot of coffee stands next to a casserole dish with some heavenly smelling cheesy mixture. My stomach growls in anticipation, and I realize I'm starving.

"Please, eat," she says, still in a gentle voice. I'm beginning to hope this is her true nature and the monster that faced down Shaula was her way of rescuing us. I throw Marla a questioning glance, still too afraid to speak. She glances at Meissa and at me and gives her head a tiny shake. I gather I'm not to ask any questions. Max remains mute and stares at the plate in front of him, his face pale.

We eat in silence, and when we're finished, Meissa speaks. "Jewel Adams, I have heard so much about you. Allow me to introduce myself properly. I am Meissa, mate of Algol, King of North America. I am one of the few remaining full-blooded Dracan females."

Now that I think of it, she's different from the other Dracan females I've seen in my explorations of the palace with Marla. She's taller, stronger and has a more reptilian face. In fact, she's downright frightening. Are the others human hybrids, like Marla?

My curiosity is aroused. I swallow and find my voice. "Why? What happened to the others?"

"Ah," she says and smiles, showing her many sharp teeth. "I'm happy to see you've found your courage. Perhaps there is hope we may someday integrate. It may become necessary as time removes the purity of the Dracan race from us.

"Soon after your second world war ended with the atomic bomb explosions at Hiroshima and Nagasaki, the depths of Terra became toxic to the females of our kind. For some reason known only to Creator, our males were not affected by the radiation seeping into our cities, but the females of our race began to die off. A few of us survived the radiation poisoning, but we survivors are no longer able to produce young."

Her revelation startles me, and I'm surprised at my sadness for her. Sudden understanding hits me. Thuban took a human mate because there was no Dracan female for him. If Meissa survived the radiation after the war, how old is she? How long do Dracans live?

I'm about to ask when a commotion at the door draws Meissa's attention. The guards step aside, and I recognize the large Dracan entering the room as one of the two kings I suspect had something to do with the attacks on Storm's family and on our house.

As soon as Max and Marla jump to their feet, I stand up, too. From the moment he enters, Algol glares at me. This is not good.

Meissa calmly walks toward him and gets between us before he has a chance to come too close. "My dear Algol," she says in a soothing voice. "I have made your guests comfortable. Won't you refresh yourself now, and meet with them later?"

He turns his attention to her, thank God. "Of course, Meissa. We will meet in the conference room in an hour." He whirls and turns toward the door, but not without shooting one last glare at me. My stomach clenches and I dread that meeting with every fiber of my being.

As soon as he leaves, Marla asks, "What about Shaula, Meissa? Why did he kidnap us, and what does Algol intend to do with us?"

"I cannot answer that, my dear, although I am afraid the king is convinced humans are dispensable. He believes we Dracans can fix the artifacts, and when we do, we will no longer suffer the effects of the radiation. I fear his advisors, including Shaula, have lost touch with reality. Come now. You need to refresh and rest before the meeting."

We follow her to a room filled with comfortable couches grouped around tables, with bookcases lining the walls. She shows us the doors leading to the restrooms then excuses herself. "I must also prepare. I will not leave you alone with the king."

When she's gone, Max blows out air, as if he's been holding his breath all this time. "She is one scary female," he says, and Marla smacks him on the arm.

"If you think she's scary, just keep it up, Max. When you insult her, you insult me, too."

"Hey, you know I didn't mean it as an insult, babe," he says, more like the Max I'm familiar with. "You have to admit, she has more teeth than you do." She smacks him again.

"Hey!" he yells and rubs his arm. I imagine she packs a powerful punch.

"Max," I say, concern about our situation making me more exasperated with him. "When we get back to Atlantis, if we do, is there a way I can send a message to my friends without being blocked by the barrier?"

He and Marla don't know about my wristband, but they do know the Dracans have blocked my abilities. He must be wondering how my sight would translate into a message. I decide to keep my secret a while longer. When he doesn't answer, I continue.

"I think Cruiser and his people communicate telepathically. It's how he knew when to make us believe Triton was attacking Atlantis so Dr. Jenkins would sound the alarm."

"Even if he can, Jewel," Marla points out, "how would you contact him, and talk to him? You can't communicate the same way."

"If he can see me somehow, I can mime, like he did. I can see the life forces of sea creatures through the screens in your media center. Do you remember the first time we saw a merman, what he was doing? I think he could see us, too. Whatever is blocking my sight doesn't work through the cameras."

The door opens and four Dracan guards gather around us. The tallest says something in his language and Marla translates, "They're ready for us."

My legs barely hold me up until she links arms with me. I borrow her strength and the Dracans march us to a meeting that may or may not end with death for Max and me.

The conference room is more like a small throne room, with seats for the king, his wife, and the advisors. We're forced to stand in front of all of them. Butterflies take over my gut, and once again I wish I hadn't eaten earlier.

Algol is seated on the largest throne, next to a smaller one to his right, and Shaula sits on his other side, flanked by two other advisors. A door to the right opens and two guards escort Meissa to the second throne. I don't know why it hadn't occur to me until now, but Meissa is Queen of the North American continent, proud and royal in a glittering golden gown. I'm decidedly under-dressed in my slept-in outfit from the Council yesterday.

When Shaula stands to speak, Meissa rises to her feet and stares him down. He stammers something and sheepishly sits back down.

"My husband..." She turns to the king. "May I question our guests? I know you've brought them here for a purpose, and I am both curious and concerned."

Algol seems to be somewhat in awe of his wife and nods. I can see his reluctance, and I'm surprised to see his hands tremble before they grip the armrests.

When Meissa turns her face to us, I understand Shaula's terror, and why the king is afraid of her. She is no longer the gracious hostess from before. Her demeanor has transformed her into a fierce warrior. She wears the face she presented to Shaula when we first arrived, with narrowed eyes and bared teeth. Marla tightens her grip on my arm. Max's teeth chatter behind me.

"Now, Jewel Adams." She follows my name with a hiss. "Why should we not send you back to Thuban in pieces?"

36
SKY

The lagoon remains calm, and after a break for lunch, Meg and Tony agree to start Storm's training. Pax and I put on the equipment and join in. Although we've both been certified for several years, a refresher certainly can't hurt, and learning to use rebreathers instead of the tanks we're used to is a whole new experience. The adults don't know we've opened our link.

Watch what we do, Ryder, and you'll get it in no time, Pax says.

I'll get the hang of it with or without you, he retorts. He's teasing my brother, and I send a flash of approval. They're getting to be more like brothers.

At the end of the first session, when we're packing up the scuba gear and Storm floats it into the jeep, Tony remarks, "You're progressing quicker than most. Just be careful with details. If anything goes wrong in the cave system, you'd be in grave danger."

Meg adds, "Be here at first light tomorrow morning."

Dad, Wolf, and Charles are sitting on the veranda watching the beach when we return to the house. I smell fish cooking on the grill and can't help salivating. I hope we can stay on Andros for a while, even after we've rescued Jewel.

"How did it go?" Wolf asks.

"I did all right," he answers. "I learned all the safety procedures today. Meg and Tony say I need to complete at least four open water dives. If we do two a day, I can get my scuba certification by the end of the day after tomorrow. That is, if I continue to learn at this rate and they're up to two training dives a day. The rebreather certification will take longer, but since we're short on time, they've agreed to train me for the cave diving. They know the urgency."

"The sooner the better," Charles says, and I send him as much peace as I can. I'm hurting, too, as we all are, but Jewel is his daughter, and his pain is still acute.

Being in the water gives me a raging appetite, and I devour my fish and rice. Storm clears the table and Pax and I wash and dry the dishes by hand. We don't have a dishwasher on the island, and I find the chore comforting. After supper, we gather on the veranda. I sit apart, next to Sequoia.

"I love the stars here," she says, gently running her fingers over her belly.

The baby is content as she snuggles up to the caress through the wall of her temporary home. It dawns on me. Sequoia's baby is a girl. I send her my joy and she kicks happily.

"You sense her, don't you?" Sequoia asks and I nod. "I do too. She's an empath, like you, Sky. I've always known I am one, but her gift is much more powerful." She grows pensive.

"Your gift comes from Allaran DNA. Where does my baby's gift originate? Does she inherit it from me, or could she be part Dracan?" She says the name of the aliens in a whisper only I can hear.

I share her concern but send peace anyway. It doesn't matter, I tell myself. Wolf won't care, I hope. "Do you have a name picked out for her?"

"Not until she's born. Normally, my mother would have named her, but Mother passed on when Salali was fifteen and I was five. Her passing filled us with grief, of course, but my father was inconsolable. He deeply loved her and within a year, he also died. My grandparents died when Storm was only three. I know my sister is with them in a wonderful place, but my heart misses them." She's grieving, and I send comfort.

"Wolf and I will decide on our daughter's Cherokee name, and I'll pick an English name for her."

"Why would she have two names?"

"The practice has died down over the years, but we believe our Cherokee name holds much power, and only our family and most trusted friends are allowed to know it."

"Is Sequoia your English name, then?"

"Yes. My grandfather named me after one of our great leaders, Sequoyah, a silversmith and warrior, and the one who gave us our written language. When I was born, my grandmother had a premonition I would bring much good to my people. She gave me a name of power. After our baby is born, and when the four of you are together again, I will share my name with you. It's a measure of my trust in you."

Tears spring to my eyes. I'm deeply touched she would share such a precious gift with us. The baby stretches and Sequoia smiles at her little one's movements. We share the beauty of the night sky and allow the repeated whoosh of small waves hitting the sand to lull us.

"Speaking of the Allarans," Pax says, as he and Storm shatter the peace by pulling up lounge chairs next to me. "I wonder why they've left us alone all this time. Shouldn't they be helping us find Jewel?"

I know I'm projecting my frustration with the boys, but it escalates when I think of Jewel's so-called sentinels. I'm angry enough not to pull it back, until the baby's agitation stops me. My brother grabs my hand and the anger recedes, but only to bubble under the surface. I suddenly understand Storm's rage and fully empathize.

"We'll find her, Sky," Sequoia says, her voice calm and comforting. "We have to. The Allarans will show up when and if we need them to."

Storm speaks up. "When we do, and she's safely away from the lizards, I'll find a way to make the Dracans pay." His words deeply disturb Sequoia, and she gets up, kisses him on top of his head, and disappears inside.

"You know your aunt doesn't share your desire for revenge, don't you?" I point out. "Your mom was her sister, the only one left in her immediate family after her parents and grandparents died. Why is it you have all the anger while she has none?"

"She's unique, isn't she?" Storm replies, lying back in the lounge chair and crossing his arms behind his head. The dim light of the night sky turns his skin dark and caps his head with midnight hair. He's mysterious and wonderful. A few wavy strands escape the braid down his back and curl around his ear. I long to brush them off his face and kiss that finely sculpted mouth. I'd have to crawl over Pax first, and my brother shoots me a glare as if he knows exactly what I'm thinking.

"Humph," I say and lean back to watch the sky. Where are the Allarans? How will we ever find Jewel?

37

STORM

Today we dive near the lagoon before heading out to the reef. I'm impatient to finish the training and get to one of the blue holes. I want to see the cave drawings for myself. Scanning the horizon, I'm glad to see a tranquil sea and no humps silhouetted in the spectacular sunrise. I envy the years Pax and Sky lived in California, when they visited the beach all summer and enjoyed the sounds of the ocean and sunsets as glorious as this sunrise. When all this is over, I'll live in a place like this. I only wish I didn't see Sky in every fantasy of the future. What if she doesn't want to share it with me? I push the thought down and concentrate on my equipment.

Meg and Tony say rebreathers are easier to use in cave diving than scuba tanks, and I like how compact they are. They've checked out all the equipment themselves but won't allow us to dive until we've gone through the checklist, too. I appreciate the extra safety measures. I'd hate to run out of oxygen or have something else go wrong because of faulty equipment. Intellectually, I know what every piece of equipment is for, but I need practice using it and caring for it.

Pax yawns and stretches on his way to the beach, and Sky skips and hops with her usual enthusiasm. Tony plans for us to do the first dive in calm waters near the lagoon, and the second closer to the barrier reef wall. That's the one I'm eager to dive.

I move the equipment from his jeep into the Sea Runner, a twenty-six-foot Mastercraft speedboat included with our cabins. Dylan launched it earlier from the boat trailer, which is now attached to his jeep and parked under the house. He whistles as he comes down to the beach lugging a cooler full of beer and water. Fishing rods in the boat indicate what he'll be doing while we dive.

"We'll use the smaller boat in the lagoon. Then Dylan will ferry us out to deeper water to meet up with Michaels' Dream," Tony explains. The Dream is Meg and Tony's thirty-eight-foot cabin cruiser and dive boat.

"Meg will meet us around lunch time in deeper water. Dylan, you'll take us out there and I'll get the kids home this evening."

"Aye-aye, Captain," Dylan says, saluting smartly. He acts as if he doesn't have a care in the world. I suppose he needs a break as badly as the rest of us. With Tony's guidance, he pilots us to a location near the southern edge of the lagoon, where a mangrove stand, with its tangled prop roots, extends around a bend leading into an estuary.

"We'll dive here," Tony says, "but be very careful not to damage the mangrove roots. These trees sustain the ecosystem and are vital to the environmental health of the islands. Before you enter the water, there are a few things you need to know about mangroves." Sky's eyes light up and she sits back to listen.

"Mangroves clean the air by trapping and cycling pollutants, chemicals and inorganic nutrients. Barnacles and oysters attach themselves to the roots, and some of the algae and bacteria that live on the roots filter water and trap nutrients for the fish, crustaceans, and shellfish using the mangroves as their nursery. Without the mangroves, we wouldn't have sports fishing, or even fish for good eating, like snapper. Some of our birds use the trees for nesting, and animals find shelter there, too."

"Are you sure you trust us to dive here?" I ask. To be honest, he's making me nervous. What if I accidentally pull up some roots?

"I brought you here because you'll see fish in their early, most beautiful stage of development. Keep your eyes open and watch me for signals. Storm, if you see me or the others hightailing it out of there, it means get out now." I nod, more nervous than before, until he laughs.

"I'm pulling your leg, kid. We'll be down for forty minutes. Not much can happen in that amount of time."

One by one, we sit on the side of the boat, hold on to our masks and flip backward into the water. It's no different than the dive yesterday, except for the scenery. He wasn't kidding about the number of fish and shrimp swimming around among the roots. I recognize neon-striped angelfish and yellowfin snapper moving in and out of the tangle. Fish dart everywhere, in every color imaginable, some spotted, some with stripes, some with trailing pointed fins I'd never seen before. The mangroves are a city full of amazing sea life.

Sky taps on my arm and points upward. It's time to go, and I don't want to leave. I follow her to the sun and pull my mask off in the air. I hadn't noticed it at all underwater. I can get used to this life.

"That's incredible." Pax echoes my sentiments. "We never came across mangroves in California. Don't they grow there?"

"You can find some scrub mangroves in Baja," Dylan answers, as he reaches for Sky's outstretched hand to help her into the boat. "Florida has mangrove forests, and so do the Bahamas and the Caribbean islands."

By the time we stow our rebreathers and other gear in the boat, Dylan heads out to sea, to the coordinates where we hope Meg is waiting with Michaels' Dream. I'm starving and can hardly wait to chow down on some lunch. Pax sniffs the air and his face breaks into a huge grin.

"She's grilling burgers," he says. Sadness washes over me, and I turn to see a tear rolling down Sky's cheek. I fight the impulse to kiss it away. She avoids my eyes and stares at the horizon. I tap her private number on my wristband.

Is it Jewel? Is her absence making you sad? I ask her.

Partly, she answers. *Why hasn't the dragon returned? I really thought we made a connection the last time.*

The dragon? I don't know. Can you handle another emotional encounter with him?

I can handle anything if it helps us find Jewel, she says, and breaks the link.

We approach the bigger boat and Meg throws a couple of bumpers attached to ropes between our boats. Tony hops out and ties us to the side, and I float the heavy gear up to the deck.

"Thanks, Storm," Tony says, grinning. He's enjoying my ability. I want to warn him to stay on my good side, but I don't ruin the moment.

My stomach growls and I follow the delicious aroma of the grill to an open deck in the stern. Meg lays a platter of burgers on a small table and we dig in. I don't remember anything tasting this good.

3 8

STORM

"It appears the weather will hold for our next dive," Meg says, after we've eaten our fill. "Dylan, you have a radio and the coordinates for the lagoon. Let me know when you've made it back. If there's any trouble at all, please don't hesitate to call for help."

Sky hugs her dad and Pax helps him over the side to the Sea Runner. We wave as he heads back to shore. Tony fires up the Dream's powerful engines, and we move toward the line where aquamarine turns to midnight, where the wall of the Tongue of the Ocean meets the barrier reef.

We stop a good fifty yards from the edge of the reef, where Meg drops five dive flags into the water and goes to run up a larger flag on top of the bridge. We check our gear before putting it on for the second time today and double-check each other's equipment. It seems tedious, but I know how important every detail is.

Meg is the first to step off the platform in the stern, and the rest of us follow into water a few degrees cooler than the shallows.

I find Sky watching me through bubbles as I enter. She taps on her wristband. I'm glad Charles made them waterproof and able to withstand tons of pressure.

Are you enjoying this? Her voice is like soft music in my head.

What's not to enjoy? I love the water, the colors, and all those fish. And you, I add silently, hoping she didn't hear that. I squelch the thought as soon as it surfaces. I can't let myself care so much.

Pax breaks in. *It's beautiful in here. Jewel would love this.* He breaks off and presses his wristband. He's hurting. Sky swims over to him and touches his arm. He shakes her off. When we get this training over with, we can get on with the business of finding Jewel.

For now, I lose myself in the vibrant life of the reef. Sky points to a rock that seems to be breathing. She gently waves her hand over it, and it becomes a small octopus that scurries away, its skin texture and color changing as it moves. Man, I could use its camouflage ability. I let my mind drift into scenarios where I've turned into a Dracan, marching into their lair to rescue my friend. Then Pax and I mimic the skin of a triangular ship and slip inside and make ourselves identical to the equipment.

A sharp jolt pulls me back to the present. Pax's worried face melts behind his mask, while his arms go all soft and wavy like an octopus. Someone grabs me by the arms and pulls me toward liquid light. Am I going to heaven? My mask rips away from my face, and I gasp in a breath of sweet air.

Tony helps me up to the platform while I draw in deep breaths. My head clears and Pax is himself again. Tony unhooks the rebreather and Meg checks the sensors and warning system. They argue as they walk away toward the wheelhouse. Why is Sky crying?

We thought you were a goner, Pax says in my head. The link is still active, and he's obviously rejoined it.

What happened? I ask. A headache suddenly flares behind my eyes, and I bend over to hold my face in my hands. Sky's touch soothes me as she massages my neck and shoulders. I can get used to this.

Hypoxia, Sky says. *Your brain wasn't getting oxygen. When I was somehow able to see your hallucinations, I alerted the others.*

How did that happen? We checked the equipment.

It must have given faulty readings, Pax says, suspicion evident in his thoughts.

Deliberate? I ask, but I don't believe for a minute Meg or Tony would do anything to harm us or anyone else.

Of course not, Sky assures me. *I'm sure they'll investigate it and find a manufacturing glitch, or something.*

Meg brings me a bottle of water. "Lie down for a while. We'll get to the bottom of this." She reaches over the side to collect a flag and points to a cushioned bench in the stern. Pax helps me up and Sky holds my hand while I gingerly climb the small ladder and flop down on the bench.

"Are we still diving tomorrow?" I'm not going to let a little hypoxia slow me down. There's no time to waste. We've got to find Jewel.

"Are you up to it?" Meg asks.

"Heck, yeah. I wouldn't miss it for anything."

"Then we'll go. Tony and I will double-check the rest of the equipment tonight. You can bet we'll investigate how we ended up with a faulty rebreather."

Our first dive will be in the reef again, and the second down the wall. After the wall, I'll be certified, and we can hit the blue holes and get to the caves.

39
JEWEL

My mouth is so dry I can literally not speak, so Marla answers
for me.

"Honored King Algol and Queen Meissa," she begins. "Jewel
Adams is a guest of my father's and under his protection. If harm
comes to her at your hands, you will be at war with Thuban and all of
Atlantis."

"Good answer, daughter of Thuban," Meissa says, and her grimace
begins to resemble a grin. I wonder if she's enjoying this. "However,
we must hear from Jewel Adams. Now, my dear, what makes you so
very special?"

I glance at the king and catch Shaula's eye. His sneer turns my
stomach in knots. "King Algol heard my story at the royal council," I
squeak out. "If it pleases you, I'll tell you, too, but the king may not
want to hear it again."

I glance at him hopefully, but his glare makes me want to melt into
the ground.

"Please," he says with a sneer. "Repeat your entertaining account to
my wife. When she has heard enough, we will decide what to do with
you."

It's obvious he didn't intend his comment to reassure me, but to my surprise, it accomplishes the opposite of intimidation. Righteous anger rises inside. I straighten my back and this time when I speak, it's with power and confidence.

"I am Jewel Adams," I say unnecessarily, "one of the four who were chosen to save this planet for the likes of you."

Marla quickly steps back from me and stands beside Max, shock on both their faces. I glance at Shaula, and my confidence grows as his sneer disappears. His scowl emboldens me.

"Terra is in danger because your cities have depleted the earth of nutrients vital to the well-being of the tetrahedra, the organs keeping the planet alive and balanced. They, the ones we call artifacts, chose us from the time of our birth, and we alone can repair them."

Shaula jumps to his feet and roars. "You lie! Our scientists are on the verge of a breakthrough. We will soon know the secrets of the one we captured from you, and we will repair the rest. We do not need you humans."

"Yes, you do," I answer with confidence. "The tetrahedra are made for Terra, and only Terrans can approach them. In fact, the only Terrans they allow near them are my friends and me. Tell the king, Shaula, exactly how close your scientists have been able to get to the artifact."

I don't know the answer, but I cross my fingers and hope and pray I'm right in assuming they've gotten nowhere.

"We have cracked the outer shell and stopped it from spinning."

"If that's so, then what is depicted on each of its sides?"

"Nothing, human. There is nothing there."

"Now I know you lie, Shaula. Meissa, if you don't believe me, please ask to see it for yourself."

The giant Dracan female turns her dirtiest look on Shaula, and I'm almost sorry for him. The moment of sympathy is shattered when Algol jumps to his feet and shouts, "Guards! Take them to the prison."

Meissa whirls and grabs him by the upper arms. "What are you doing, Algol? Do you mean to declare war on Atlantis?"

The guards surround us and force us to keep up with them as they march us out of the room and down a winding hallway. We enter a doorway to a steep stairway dropping into the dark. The lead guard shines a flashlight on the stairs and stomps down, followed by Max, Marla, and me. Another guard brings up the rear. I imagine the light is for my benefit and Max's, since they, like Marla, can probably see in the dark.

We go down several flights when the guard opens a thick door into another patch of blackness. "If you allow us to stay together," Marla says, "I will ask my father's mercy on you men when he and his armies destroy your city."

The guardsman laughs, opens a cell and says, "Princess, it is my pleasure to welcome the three of you to your new home." As soon as I clear the cell door, he slams it shut and roars in laughter.

"My orders are to keep you together, but by all means, ask your father for mercy for me and my companions." Still laughing, he and the second guardsman march up the stairs, leaving us in the pitch dark.

Marla gently takes my trembling hand and leads me to a bench along the far wall. Max sits down next to me and scoots close. My eyes follow the sound of Marla pacing, but I see nothing.

"What now?" he asks. No one answers. Marla hisses and I imagine she's seething with rage. This king will certainly pay.

"Marla, would you explain something to me? Why did Meissa turn from a kind hostess into the chief inquisitor? What's her story?"

"My mother warned me about her," she answers from somewhere to our left. "Imagine if you were one of the last of your kind, knowing you'll never have children. Human women are the Dracans' only hope of procreating, and she has had to watch the kings take humans as mates. Do you remember how she explained it all happened after the atomic bomb blasts that ended World War II? Humans did this to her and her people. Meissa was a warrior before she became Algol's queen, and she is the one who turned her husband against humans."

"Wow," Max says. "Then there's no hope we'll get out of here alive, is there?"

"Of course, there is," she answers impatiently. "By now my father knows who has abducted us, and he'll send help. Dracans cannot afford to war with each other. Their existence is as tied to the artifacts as everyone else's.

"Meissa is not stupid. You said the right things in there, Jewel. You made sure she understood you and your friends are the only ones who can fix the remaining artifacts."

"What do we do now?" Max asks.

"We wait," she answers.

"We sleep," I add, yawning loudly.

40

JEWEL

"Marla!" A woman's voice calls from the top of the stairs. There's a commotion, a fight, and a beam of light jerkily moves down the stairs. I can't see who's carrying the flashlight, but I can guess.

"Mom!" my friend answers. "I knew you'd come. Do you have the keys to let us out?"

Avery fumbles with something in her hands, and the door springs open. Marla falls into her arms and her mother drops the flashlight, which Max is quick to pick up.

"Hurry." Avery's voice is tight with urgency. A large body tumbles down the dark stairwell. Max shines the light on the dead face of the laughing guard. He won't need mercy, after all.

I stumble up the steep stairs toward the light at the top. A soldier dressed in green holds the second guard, hands tied behind his back. Thuban's man. I never thought I'd be so happy to see Dracans.

I notice Avery's clothes for the first time. She's dressed like a warrior, with dark green pants tied tightly at the ankles, a matching vest over a long-sleeved green shirt, steel-toed boots, and belts loaded with knives and ammunition crisscrossed over the vest. The giant soldier hands her a rifle and she heads down the hallway, the three of us right behind her.

We come to the room where Meissa interrogated me. Algol clenches his hands, tied to the armrest of his throne, while Thuban paces back and forth in front of him. Two guards hold Meissa's arms, but her relaxed face makes me think she's allowing them to touch her for her own reasons. Being one of the last Dracan females would certainly give her immunity, and I can see her as a formidable warrior. There is no sign of Shaula.

"My daughter," he roars when we enter. "What have they done to you?"

"Nothing, Father," Marla answers, surprising Meissa.

"Meissa welcomed us with a warm meal and good company. She is a gracious hostess." She bows slightly at the queen. Thuban waves at the guards and they let her go.

"Then it was Algol who ordered your imprisonment?" her father asks.

"Yes," she answers. "But it was your advisor Shaula who ordered the attack on you and who abducted us and brought us here."

I would not want to be Shaula at this moment. The expression on Thuban's face promises a long and painful punishment. Marla steps back and respectfully lowers her eyes, and I do the same.

"Max Green," Thuban's voice grows deceptively quiet. "Were you not complicit in my daughter's abduction?" I find it ironic he's concerned with placing blame for Marla's abduction when he's the one who ordered my own kidnapping.

"No, sir," Max says. Given his penchant for running from trouble, I'm surprised he's able to answer at all. "I love your daughter and would never do anything to hurt her."

Oh, wow. That's not what I expected to hear from him. Excuses, blame shifting, maybe. A declaration of love to her father? Apparently, Thuban is just as astounded.

"What?" he roars. "You, a human?"

"Thuban," Avery places her hand on his bicep, and her touch seems to calm him down. "May we speak of this later? This situation with Algol requires your attention."

Marla's father turns to stare at the bound king. "Guards!" he roars. "Take him to my ship. Meissa, my dear, are you able to handle his duties until the Council decides his fate?"

The queen grins, and I have the impression she's been handling his duties all along. She's the true power behind the throne of the North American kingdom.

This time, we board Thuban's craft, and follow the king and Avery to the bridge, where we're given seats next to viewports. It's the first time I've seen the real outdoors since before my friends and I followed the Watchers into the caves. When we lift off, I allow the tears to flow. The craft is so fast, I only get a glimpse of the Arizona desert as it recedes from view. Then we're above the clouds and I close my eyes and let my face absorb the sun through windows coated with the substance blocking my ability to see the sky in all its colors.

We slow down as we approach a long island, raggedly torn into three sections. Aquamarine waters surround it and band through the separations in the land. A patch of dark blue grows second by second until it fills the viewport and we're in it, without a single splash. The water becomes black so quickly I want to reach up and grab the sun. We dock in moments, not sensing the deceleration any more than the craft's acceleration. I wonder when humans will get around to inventing technology like this. I wonder if I'll live to see it.

Oh, my friends, I miss you all so much.

4 1

SKY

I'm nervous about diving today, for the first time ever. I know what happened to Storm is a rare and isolated incident, but the timing is suspicious. Jewel's last warning comes to mind, and I shudder. "Stay away," she'd said. Is someone actively trying to stop us?

The morning light bathes my friends in a rosy glow as we head to Storm's jeep. I turn toward the sea, where water birds in silhouette scurry along the sand in search of small crabs. In the distance, two dolphins leap out of the still water side-by-side. I wonder if they're the same ones we met snorkeling.

We'll meet Tony and Meg at their dock today, and Storm seems as eager as we are to get going. In twenty minutes, we're aboard Michaels' Dream and Tony sits us down before we leave the dock.

"At first we thought the rebreather itself was faulty," he says. "I took it to the dive shop as soon as we docked yesterday, while Meg drove you home. The owner, Mark, tested the canister, and found it contained a mixture that was meant for a much deeper dive. The gas mixture didn't deliver enough oxygen to your brain.

"He recently hired a new guy who worked a few days and disappeared. He could have tampered with the labeling. Do you have enemies here?"

Storm's eyes narrow and he turns away from Tony. If he only knew.

Tony shrugs and continues, "Unless they find the guy, they can't be sure, so today we each take a spare tank down with us."

While Meg fires up the engines and skillfully steers the Dream to open water, Tony shows us how to switch the tanks out, both on our own and for each other. "If we're in a deep dive, or exploring the blue hole cave system, we can't surface quickly. You must get very familiar with emergency procedures before Meg and I take you into the hole. Hit the books tonight and review all the procedures. Storm, we'll certify you as soon as we're satisfied the three of you can handle any emergency."

Storm is frustrated, and his rage beats against its cage. He takes a couple of deep breaths and nods. He, of all people, knows how vital this is. I send him peace and my approval, and he relaxes.

Meg takes us to a spot where several other dive boats are floating, with flags marking the spots where the divers went down. We check and re-check our equipment as we put it on, until we're finally ready to hit the water.

I hold my mask and step off the platform into a magical world of weightless wonder. I'll never tire of the ocean. I decide I want to be an oceanographic scientist of some sort. The possibilities are endless.

Storm is delighted as soon as he's in the water. I tap my wristband.

It pays for us to stay in mental contact, I say.

I agree. Pax points to him and nods.

We should probably stay close, Storm adds, without anxiety.

Life in the reef delights me no end. Tony leads us into a shallow coral canyon, where moray eels poke curious heads out of holes and cuttlefish blend with the sand and coral when they sense us coming. My heart fills with gratitude and wonder at the living display of astounding creativity. How I wish Jewel was here with us.

Meg signals for us to surface much too soon. I'm surprised to find we've been down an hour already.

I didn't sense any time passing, Storm says. *Did you?*

Pax answers, *it's always that way down here. It's why we're so careful to check our gauges.*

Don't you wish we had gills in addition to lungs? We could choose to leave when we want to, I say wistfully. I've often fantasized about having the ability to live in the ocean as well as on land.

Tony pulls himself up on the platform and helps Meg out of the water. By the time the three of us are on board, Meg is in the galley preparing lunch. I shrug out of my gear, stow it and help her set the table.

After we eat our sandwiches, Tony heads the Dream out to the blue water of the Tongue. Land is still in sight and I marvel at how close to the island the sea drops into the depths. It's like living at the rim of the Grand Canyon. The waves are higher out here, rocking the boat from side to side. I hope Storm doesn't get seasick.

Meg stays on board while the rest of us drop into the sea. Just like the reef, the wall teems with life in motion. Sea fans wave with currents, corals of all types dot or cluster on the wall. I spot some banded butterfly fish darting among the fan corals and watch a reef shark glide toward a school of shiny bait fish forming a large fluid ball in a futile attempt to try to make predators think they're some huge sea creature. They aren't fooling the shark.

Down there, I say over the link, and point to a spotted eagle ray flying gracefully below us. Storm continues to watch the shark.

Do a lot of sharks swim out here? He sounds a bit nervous.

Oh, yeah, Pax replies. *Bigger ones. They've spotted some great whites in these waters recently.*

He spins around in the water but relaxes when he doesn't see any. I don't tell him a second reef shark just swam past behind him.

I suddenly sense a spike of anxiety in him. *What is it?* I ask, expecting another shark sighting.

The wall! It's moving!

A roar fills my head and a wall of water pushes me against spiky anemone that tear at my wetsuit. Chunks of rock and coral pull away and tumble into the depths as the wave recedes. An underwater wave? I wonder if it registered on the surface. Did Meg experience it?

Are you all right? Is Tony okay?

Pax answers, *Tony and I are fine, but we can't locate Storm.*

Panic stops my heart for a second and I'm sucking in air faster than I should. I search through the muck and silt the wave stirred up. I head down and notice Pax and Tony have the same idea. The canisters in our rebreathers contain a gas mixture meant for shallow dives, but we can't lose Storm.

Pax has stronger legs than I do, and he's moving deeper more quickly. He suddenly stops his descent and points downward. *Do you see it?*

A vague outline of a long tail and ridged back fin comes into view. Then I spot the arms. Human arms ending in webbed hands are wrapped around an unconscious diver.

The creature spies us, pushes the diver toward us and darts away, as fast as any of the small reef fish. A picture forms in my mind of a monster with great webbed feet and worm-like appendages where the mouth should be, and a cloud of bright red blood flowing from its head. Horrified, I spin around searching for the beast. Then it dawns on me the blood is my hair, and I'm seeing myself through the creature's eyes. Is it communicating the way the dragon did?

Pax and I quickly swim to Storm, and each grabs an arm. Tony gently nudges me aside, takes my place and points upward, then at the gauge on his wrist. He points to me and to his eyes. Watch me.

I follow the men and stop when they do. I know how dangerous it is to ascend too quickly after a deep dive. We didn't go down that far, but there's no telling how deep Storm went before the sea dweller rescued him. I wish I had gotten a closer look at it. Is Jewel aware of these undersea people? Apparently, they can live at extreme depths and here in the shallows, too. How have they remained hidden for so long, and why appear now?

Back on board the Dream, Meg calls in the emergency, gathers the flags, and turns us toward the main dock in town. Tony and Pax take his mask and gear off him. He's breathing, but a rock or something has knocked him unconscious and he'll need medical attention. Poor

Storm. It's the second time in two days. I sit with him, holding his hand and sending comfort to him.

"Water." I've never been so happy to hear his voice. Pax helps him sit up and hands him a bottle from the cooler. He takes a long drink and clamps his hands around his head.

"Hold on there, buddy," he says, pulling his hand away from the obvious cut behind his ear. "You've been injured. Let the medics check you out before you go messing with it."

Tony comes back to the stern with an ice pack. "Here. Hold this against it. It's stopped bleeding. We won't be diving again for a few days, kids, and it isn't just the injury." I know he added that because of Storm's angry glare. He'd go back in today if it would help us find Jewel faster.

"A weather system is heading our way from Florida, and we can't dive until it passes."

"When will that be?" I ask.

"The forecast is for thunderstorms, heavy rain, and four to six-foot seas for the next three days. The good news is the bad weather will give the three of you time to study for the rebreather certification, and Storm will be scuba certified at the same time. By the time it passes, you'll all be ready to dive the holes. The one we're going into is known only to the natives and a few of us dive masters. We don't take tourists there."

"Why not?" I ask.

"The small entrance is one reason, and once inside, the caves aren't easy to get into. Also, the Black Seminoles of Red Bays say they hear moaning sounds and sometimes see lights in it. They call it Skyhold. Some other Andros natives claim the ghosts of pirates haunt the caves in there. When Meg and I investigated for ourselves, we found the rock drawings."

Storm says what I'm thinking, "So, because of the weather, we can't get into an inland cave system? Why not?"

"All of the caves are connected to the ocean. When the sea is agitated or high, strong currents can pull you out to sea through openings small enough to shred a human. We're not taking any chances."

I agree. The prospect sounds terrible.

42
JEWEL

With Shaula gone, I have the freedom to roam with Marla again. I'm happy to see she's in my room when I wake up.

After breakfast, I ask, "Could we go back to the lab and see if Ashley is all right?"

"Sure," she replies. "I want to see those dragon scales you told me about. I also want to see the tank Cruiser escaped from."

Marla leads the way, and this time I pay attention to the turns and landmarks, like the statue of Athena where we turn right, and the bust of some Roman emperor in an alcove where we turn left. I'm tired of being lost like a mouse in a maze.

We soon arrive at the door with the Eye of Horus, and once inside, hurry down the hall to the science center. Marla pushes the door open and I follow her in.

"Hello?" she calls out.

"In here," a woman's voice answers from the second room, and I breathe a sigh of relief. Dr. Jenkins comes into the main lab, wiping her hands on a towel. Green goo decorates her lab coat, just like the first time. It looks beautiful to me.

"You're all right!" I exclaim and rush to her. She puts her hand up in warning when it becomes obvious I intend to hug her.

"I'm a mess, Jewel. I'm happy to see you, too."

"I was so afraid Shaula had done something to hurt you after you set off the alarm and Cruiser escaped." I'm surprised to be fighting tears again. What is it with me, lately?

Marla glances from Ashley to me and back again as she leans against a table with her arms crossed. Her smug face is the same one she often wore in North Carolina. Is it a defense mechanism? I draw her in and introduce her to Ashley.

"You're the princess," Ashley remarks. Her statement confirming Marla, the daughter of a king, is truly a princess, suddenly strikes me as funny, and I begin to laugh.

Marla's astonishment makes me laugh harder. In moments, she's laughing, too. So is Ashley, and they don't have a clue why.

As soon as I can catch my breath, I blurt out, "A princess! A princess and a dragon! We're living in a fairy tale!" Fresh laughter bubbles up, and I double over with it and sink to the floor.

"Don't forget the mermaids," Marla croaks between laughs, while she drops to the floor and curls up holding her sides.

Ashley, leaning against the wall, pauses to breathe and adds, "and the evil advisor."

It takes some time to regain our equilibrium because the minute one of us starts, all of us laugh all over again.

I'm still gasping for air when Ashley leaves the room and comes back with three mugs of steaming coffee. The aroma reminds me of home, and once again, my laughter turns to tears. Marla scoots over and pulls me close in a hug. When I get out of this mess, I'm taking her with me. I'm irrational.

"Jewel, I should tell you what I've learned about Cruiser and his people," Ashley says as she hands me a mug.

"What you've learned?" My tears instantly dry up. "How?"

"You won't believe me, so I'll show you." She walks over to the empty tank where Cruiser had been held prisoner.

She taps a pattern of sounds on the glass reminding me of the Morse Code that connected me to my parents through the wristband. In a few minutes, the water in the tank swirls violently, and suddenly, there he is. Cruiser sees me, grins and takes a bow. Are you kidding me?

"Why? How? What is he doing here? Does he want to be caught again?" The questions pour out of me in a torrent. Marla is stunned to silence. She simply stares at the merman on the other side of the glass.

He turns to her and bows again. He makes a series of clicking sounds and, to my astonishment, Ashley says, "He's greeting the Princess of Atlantis."

"How do you know what he's saying? Wait a minute…" I pause, thoughts jumbling my brain. "When Shaula brought me here, you seemed surprised when Cruiser mimed Triton attacking, but you knew what he meant right away. How long have you been able to communicate with him?"

Instead of answering me, she turns to Marla. "Princess, before I reveal anything, I must have your solemn word you'll say nothing of this to anyone else. Not even your mother."

"What will happen if I tell her?" Marla asks.

I know I couldn't keep this a secret from my own mother.

Ashley frowns. "If she tells Thuban, at the very least I won't be allowed access to these labs again. It's imperative I continue to study the sea people. The fate of the world might depend on it."

That phrase sounds too familiar, and my stomach drops like the first time Wolf told my father the fate of the world depends on me and my friends. Is this something new to worry about?

"In what way?" I ask. Do the sea folk know about the artifacts? Do they know where they are? I glance at Cruiser, who is studying us with a great deal of interest, as if he understands every word we're saying. He doesn't, does he? He sees me watching him and his fishy face breaks into a wide grin.

Before she has a chance to answer, my friend gets to her feet and fixes Dr. Jenkins with a cold stare. "Would you put us all in danger by withholding vital information? Do you think my father so volatile he would not allow you to continue this line of study, especially if, as you say, our fate depends on it?"

Ashley's face goes a shade paler. "Since you put it that way, then

I'll be happy to share what I've learned. You decide how much to tell your parents and when. Forgive my presumption."

Marla relaxes and says, "Then spill it. I'm dying to know how this communication happened, and what Cruiser is saying."

"Okay," Ashley takes a deep breath, sits on a high stool and leans her elbows on a lab table, while Marla and I sit across from her.

"Dracans captured Cruiser during one of their sweeps for saltwater fish in an upper layer of the midnight level of the ocean. He told me later he'd been hunting with his people, and when the craft approached, he slowed down so the others could escape. He's a hero."

I make eye contact with him and he takes another bow. "He understands your speech, doesn't he?" I ask.

"It's more like he sees the pictures in my mind as I form the words."

"Is that how he communicates with you?" Marla asks. "Do you see pictures?"

"It's part of it. My mind isn't naturally attuned to telepathic communication. He's patiently taught me the patterns of his clicks, using pictures and hand gestures until I understand. The telepathy is getting a little easier, but I rely on his verbal and visual cues much more."

I visualize the tetrahedron spinning in its force field, and Cruiser nods. He reads me! I should receive whatever he sends me, given my practice with the wristbands, but I get nothing.

"How does he get in and out of the tank?" The question has bugged me since he first showed up in there.

"His people rigged the tube so it won't close. They've somehow jammed the signal that alerts the technicians. The Dracans don't know anything is wrong with it."

"If they can do that, can they rig something else so I can get back to my friends? You know the fate of the world depends on the four of us, don't you?" Cruiser nods again. I wonder what he's shown Ashley, and whether his version of saving the world is different from ours.

43

PAX

Internet access is slow at best on Andros, and the thirty-mile-per-hour wind isn't helping. I slam the laptop shut in exasperation. Rain pounds a steady rhythm on the metal roof, and I'm stir-crazy. If it weren't for the frequent crashes of thunder that follow nearby lightning strikes, I'd take a run in the warm tropical rain.

I find Sky in her room, reading a novel left by one of the previous vacationers. "Did you get much studying done?" I ask.

"Not since the storm knocked out the internet," she says with a smile. "This would be a good time for a nap. The sound of the wind and rain is making me sleepy."

"Not me." I do a few jumping jacks. "I'm ready to practice some katas and do a little sparring. This inactivity is driving me crazy."

"It's only been a couple of hours since it started. I think I spotted some board games in a cabinet in the great room. Want to play one?"

I know she's trying to be helpful, but I can't shake the sense of urgency I've had since we got here. It's taking too long, and we still don't know how to find Jewel. What good will cave diving do when we can't get to where she is?

I barely hear the knock on the front door over the noise, when Mom welcomes Storm inside. He's dripping all over the floor, but even as soaked as he is, I envy his walk outside. Lightning crackles and booms, hitting too close to the house.

"Hey, Fletcher," he says, shaking droplets of water off his hair. Mom hands him a towel, and he pulls her into a damp hug. She laughs and pushes him away.

"How's Sequoia?" she asks.

"She and the baby are napping," he answers. "At least she is. Baby can get pretty active when she lies down."

"I remember those days fondly," Mom answers, giving me a warm hug. She heads back to her room and Storm follows me into Sky's.

"Do either of you have any thoughts about how we're going to get to Atlantis, much less rescue Jewel?" I let my impatience sharpen the tone of my voice and reject the comfort Sky is trying to send. We've had too many delays. First the Navy sent the Proteus away, along with our chance of using Theseus to dive to Atlantis, and now we all need to be certified for rebreathers in order to dive the caves to search for clues. Where will clues lead us when we can't dive deeper?

"If only the dragon would surface again," Sky says. "He sent me pictures of the artifact, which he thinks is his egg. If I can send pictures back, he might understand what we need to do to help his egg."

"His grief nearly killed you," I remind her. "If you hadn't been able to diffuse it by sending it to the rest of us, who knows how much you could have taken? How will you handle it when he resurfaces, if he does?"

"I wasn't there," Storm says.

"You were busy fighting whatever shook up the submersible," Sky excuses him.

He shakes his head. "If I had been, could I have helped? We shared a connection when we fixed the first artifact."

"We had Jewel with us then." I remember the flood of love we released and can't imagine how it will ever happen again without her.

"Do you think we can call him, like we did the Allarans?" Sky fingers her wristband.

"Wouldn't we need the adults to do that?" I ask.

"Maybe not," she says, and chews on her lower lip. "It won't hurt to try with just the three of us."

It could hurt a lot, I think, if he does surface. I can't forget how broken my sister was the last time. It took hours to come out of the dragon's dark despair.

"Maybe we should wait and let our folks know what we're planning to do," I suggest. "After all, if Triton hits them with his grief, they'll know what we're up to, and they'll hate that we didn't warn them."

"True," Sky says. She glances at Storm. "And we must consider your baby cousin. She'd be especially sensitive."

"Why?" I ask, surprised she would know that.

"She's a strong empath, like me. Sequoia is, too, but not as strong. It's why she collapsed and wailed when the dragon surfaced. His sorrow was amplified by the baby and me. We can't put her through that, especially now we know about the baby."

"We could take the boat a few miles down the coast and try it there," Storm suggests.

"Sure," I agree, "but not until the weather clears."

Tony said it's going to hang around for two or three days. There must be something we can do in the meantime.

"Why don't we call the Allarans?" I suggest. "The storm won't affect their craft, and they might have new information that can help us."

"Let's try it tonight, after supper. If the weather clears enough, we can gather at your house, Storm, so Sequoia doesn't have to go outside. I'm sure Charles and Analiese are chomping at the bit, and I know Mom and Dad will help us." Sky sounds more cheerful now we have a solid plan of action. Any action is good right now.

44
JEWEL

Marla tugs at my arm. "We have to get back, Jewel. My mother invited us for lunch, and we'd better leave now."

I hug Ashley and turn to wave at Cruiser, but he's gone, and only a mini whirlpool remains.

"Does he do that often?" I ask her. "Disappear like that?"

"He must sense someone coming."

A knock at the door proves her right, and a Dracan I hadn't seen before enters. He's smaller than Thuban, but larger than an average human, with light blue-ringed scales fading to yellow in the centers. It gives him a glow that reminds me of Pax's aura. He's wearing an unbuttoned lab coat over loose black pants, and like every other Dracan male, he's shirtless.

"This is my son and colleague Murphrid," Ashley introduces him.

Her son? He must be a hybrid, then, like Marla.

Murphrid bows to Marla and reaches out his clawed hand toward me. I automatically shake it, and he grins, showing his sharp teeth. I smile back. I have a good feeling about this one.

Marla tugs again, and I wave as we leave.

"What's the rush?"

"She didn't say, but when Mom talked to me this morning, she seemed anxious to meet with us. You can't get too comfortable here, Jewel. You need to get back with the others."

I silently agree and follow her, paying attention to landmarks.

Avery meets us at the door of Marla's sitting room and quickly masks her annoyance when she sees me. I wonder if she invited her daughter and wasn't expecting me.

"You two are late, and we have much to discuss." It sets me at ease. I'd rather be late than unwanted.

Marla's sitting room is the size of our great room back home, with wall-to-wall bookshelves along one wall and three groups of tables and chairs, as if she were planning to hold a game tournament in here. Two couches face a stone fireplace where a holographic fire blazes. Thankfully, it doesn't give off heat. The opulence is a striking contrast to the little cabin she and her mother shared in Blue Mountain. Before I could ask Avery about her time back there compared to living here, she spoke.

"While you two were in Arizona, Triton was more active than usual around the perimeter. We had two breaches, including one where he actually cracked a hole in the dome big enough to let quite a bit of seawater through before it could be repaired."

"Dr. Jenkins never said a word about it," Marla remarks. "I wonder why not."

"We were pretty busy discussing other things," I remind her. "Maybe she would have if we had stayed longer." Even though her mother helped plan the first failed escape attempt, for some reason I don't want her to know about Cruiser. I hope Marla doesn't mention him.

Instead she says, "Why would Triton suddenly get active? The first time he tried breaking the perimeter was before Shaula abducted Jewel. Do you think her presence has anything to do with it?"

"I wish I knew," she answers. "How would he know about our Jewel?"

Our Jewel? Coming from her, it sounds nice, like I belong to her family, but it gets me thinking of my mom and dad, and longing washes over me. Tears sting my eyes again and it scares me. I've never been this emotional. Am I getting sick? I determine to pay attention to what my emotions and body are telling me. I've never had to live without my gift before. Is it why I'm so unpredictable?

Avery says, "Thuban thinks it may have something to do with the artifact kept in a vault underneath Dr. Jenkins' laboratory, one which she and her son Murphrid have access to. Shaula wanted you to show them how to fix it, Jewel, but Thuban and I know you can't do anything without the others. Ashley knows it, too, but Murphrid believes he can figure it out."

"I can't imagine how. It took all four of us to fix it, and I don't know how anyone can break through the force field while it's healthy. It was hard enough when the poor thing was sick."

"Thuban is convinced there's another one nearby, one that isn't doing well. The ocean has become unstable. Abnormal weather, sudden rifts in the sea floor, erupting volcanos, unexplainable whirlpools, these things are intensifying. Underwater tsunamis and rogue waves pose a real danger to Atlantis, even in our semi-protected location in this trench. During the rift that occurred when you two were in the throne room, you heard the sound filling the palace. Do you remember?"

"Of course," I say. "It was like the sounds we heard at Blue Mountain, but much sadder. I thought my heart would break."

"Yes," Avery says. "Triton's call. We've heard it before, but never as close, and never as mournful. We believe he knows where the ailing artifact is and that he cares deeply about it. If he knows about you and that you can help, it could explain his increased activity."

"The sound we heard in Blue Mountain came from the artifact itself. If it's failing, then why isn't it calling, instead of Triton?"

"There's a difference. We've heard other sounds that may come from the artifact, just as loud but lacking the emotional tone of the one Triton makes. His carries intense grief."

Marla interjects, "If he's trying to get to Jewel, doesn't he know breaking the barrier will kill her?"

"He may know of a way to get her and her companions to the artifact safely."

"You're assuming he's intelligent and can reason," I say. "What brings you to that conclusion?"

"You cannot tell Dr. Jenkins or Murphrid what I'm about to reveal. I trust her, but he's determined to find a way Dracans can fix the artifact, and we don't know if scientific curiosity motivates him, or if he's sold out to the ones like Algol, who would wipe humanity off the face of Terra."

Marla winks at me and I stifle a laugh. Avery sounds like Ashley right now.

"I can understand not telling Murphrid because we don't know him at all, but you may be surprised to discover Ashley knows more than you think," she says.

Avery gazes into her daughter's eyes for several seconds, nods, and drops a bombshell on us. "Triton has mentally projected pictures of your friends to me. He knows them and knows where they are."

45
PAX

A flash of lightning reveals the Allaran ship hovering over the beach. Storm and I watch through the picture window, while Sky gathers umbrellas and hugs our parents. We're going out to meet it.

"Are you sure you don't want us to come with you?" Dad asks.

"We've been aboard their craft before," I reply. "I trust they won't hurt or abduct us, and they might know of a way we can rescue Jewel."

"I'm going," Charles says. He wipes his sleeve across the window, but it doesn't clear the curtain of rain away. We wait for a flash of lightning to get a glimpse of the ship. "She's my daughter, and I hate being helpless. I need to hear what they have to say."

Storm nods in agreement. I open the private link to him. *Do you think it's a good idea?*

He's her dad. Whatever they say, he needs to hear it first-hand.

We'll keep the link open to all the parents while we're there. Won't that be enough?

He shakes his head. *Remember how they cut off Jewel's link when she left it open the first time? They allowed the open line up to a point. He needs to be there with us. I don't trust them.*

I close the link and nod to Charles. "You're right. You do need to come with us."

Before we leave, all of us gather in the great room. We've gotten better at joining our minds to call the Allarans, and we open the links to each other once again. We won't close them until we've returned, even though we know the Allarans can block us if they want to.

Wolf stands by the door when we're ready to leave. Strong wind blows it open the minute we unlatch it, and he and dad wrestle it closed behind us. We struggle with the useless umbrellas, and by the time we reach the shelter of the ship, we're soaked to the skin. Thank God it's warm rain.

The hatch opens and we float up, one by one, to a room lined with space suits and gear. An unfamiliar female Allaran welcomes us with her honey-toned voice, "Please follow me." I drop my guard and breathe in her exotic perfume. I'm intoxicated.

Storm shoves me out of the way to be the first behind her. I'm next, and Charles is panting behind me. Strong pheromones filling the small space fuel a primal rage and a nearly irresistible desire to attack my rivals. I send my guard back up before I lose all my senses.

Pure disgust from my sister nearly knocks me down. Sky is not happy with us. I glance back at her and see her eyes flash fire, burning a hole in the back of Storm's head. I don't envy him.

We enter the observation room, where the female gestures for us to take a seat. As we bend our legs to sit in thin air, four bubbles rush to position themselves underneath us and mold themselves into comfortable chairs in time to catch our weight. Once again, I marvel at their advanced technology.

"I am Belena, the chief scientist of this vessel and DNA donor for Jewel. I am as concerned for her as you are and will tell you what we have discovered. We will not block your telepathic signals to your families."

"Is she all right? Are they hurting her? Is she being kept in prison?" Charles erupts with questions.

"I assure you," Belena says in a voice full of concern and kindness,

"Jewel is being well cared-for. She is with King Thuban's family. He believes an alliance with humans would benefit both races."

"Do you believe it? If it's true, then why haven't they returned her to us?" Storm forces out the words, wrinkling his nose like something stinks. His hatred for the Dracans overrides his attraction to the Allaran. Sky would normally try to calm him down, but she's struggling to control her revulsion of Belena.

"We have tracked their movements with Jewel. Thuban took her to attend the Royal Counsel in Uluru. From there, she was taken to Algol's domain in Superstition Mountain and is now back in Atlantis."

I break in, "Your people told us you couldn't rescue her from Atlantis, but what about those other places? Didn't you get Wolf and Sequoia out of Superstition Mountain? Why not Jewel? And what is Uluru? What's keeping you from returning her to us? Aren't you interested in saving the planet anymore?"

She laughs, the sound like water running over stones in a brook. "Paxton, we are monitoring Jewel's situation. You know from Wolf and Sequoia's rescue, we have Dracan allies. The truth is, Creator has forbidden us to do more than observe. We do not yet understand his purpose, but it must be vital, or he would allow us to intervene as we did before."

"If you won't help, then is there anything you can tell us that might help us rescue her ourselves?" Charles asks. Deep furrows line his forehead, and his eyes fill with unshed tears. My own grief and anger are rising. It must be worse for him. He's loved her a lot longer than I have.

"Just as the Watchers led you to the first artifact, the sea dwellers hold the key to the chamber where this one dwells. The dragon, whom the people on the islands call Lusca and the Dracans call Triton, guards the artifact, believing it to be his egg. Perhaps if the sea dwellers and the dragon are made to understand the importance of freeing Jewel and getting the four of you to the artifact, everything will fall into place. We will interfere only if her life is threatened and we know about it. I am deeply sorry, but we cannot make this easier for you."

"Is there any way we can see where she is? Can you show us where Atlantis is?" Sky asks, choking back the rage pouring from her.

"According to the coordinates our allies have sent us, we are directly over the city now. It's more than a mile below the surface of the ocean. Observe."

The screen lining the room lights up with a view of towering black clouds all around us. We watch as the ship descends below the clouds and a slate gray ocean spotted with whitecaps comes into view. The scene expands and suddenly we're below the churning waves.

"There's no way we can tell where this is, Belena." Storm sounds angry and frustrated.

"Yes," she replies. "The weather is uncooperative, but I am sending the coordinates to Dylan through your link. Perhaps you can enlist help to reach the city, but it will be up to you. We will remain on standby, of course, and render aid as we can. I am sorry we are otherwise limited."

The view screen becomes blank and Belena leads us back to the room with the hatch. This time, the ship drops us on our veranda. I'm glad the link was open. I would hate to have to report the bad news. The Allarans will be no help.

4 6

STORM

Sequoia's song reaches me through a thick fog of sleep. She opens the shades and windows, letting in fresh sea air and sunshine. Judging from the quality of light, it's way past daybreak. How late is it?

I jump up, run to the window and spot Sky and Pax already on the beach with Dylan, running through their katas. I'm ready to go in ten minutes, a record, even for me, but Sequoia won't let me leave without breakfast.

"You're going to have a full day, son. Aren't you getting your scuba and rebreather certifications today?"

"Yeah," I answer through a mouthful of toast. "Gotta run, Auntie." She gives me a quick hug and a little shove through the door. I don't know why I'm so happy, unless it's coming from her baby. Too many empaths around.

I'm happy all the way into town, where Tony and Meg are getting Michaels' Dream ready at the dock. Dylan, Wolf and Charles join us for our trip, where we'll pass the final dive test and receive our certifications. Dylan is also getting the rebreather certification. He plans to dive the caves with us.

We head out to one of the offshore blue holes Andros is famous for. Boats are already floating around the perimeter of a perfect circle of midnight blue surrounded by the aquamarine shades common to the shallows around the islands. I count five boats and at least fifteen dive flags.

Scared? Pax's voice in my head is serious, and I don't blame him for asking after my last experience on the wall.

Nah, I answer, but I'm pretty sure Sky reads my nervousness. Truth is, I'm scared, but I won't let it stop me. The curl of her lip and raised eyebrows confirm my suspicion. I can't hide anything from her.

As soon as we've checked out each other's gear, and Meg finishes securing the boat and dropping in the dive flags and six tanks secured to a long line, we splash over the side, one by one. Wolf and Charles will be testing some new sonar and communications equipment while the six of us dive. I suspect their fishing poles won't go to waste, either.

As soon as the silent water closes over me, I relax. Smooth walls extend down beyond the light. We each have three dive lights and two extra tanks, which we can switch out if we have problems with the rebreathers. Dylan is recording everything he sees with a sophisticated underwater camera. I wonder if he'll get a shot of the sea dwellers, or maybe even the dragon.

Sky is delighted as two bottlenose dolphins swim around her, clicking madly. She reaches out, and one of them touches her hand with its nose.

Are you seeing this? They like me! I can hear her squeal in her thoughts. A sudden rush of sadness replaces her joy. *Jewel would love this so much. I can't stand that she's missing it all.*

Pax kicks hard and shoots down past us. We've got to find her soon. My rage rattles its cage, and I concentrate harder on the life teeming on the wall.

As soon as we meet up with Tony hovering in place, he points to a dark opening. He takes the end of a line from a reel attached to his belt and ties it to a pylon someone had left embedded in the rock between two corals. I spot a few other pylons around the opening, some with lines attached and some without. I assume the lines belong to other divers already in the cave. If any of us should be separated from the others, any of the lines would lead us back out. It's a comforting thought.

Dylan follows him into the cave, while Meg takes up the rear, after tying her own line to another pylon. Tony had emphasized how vital redundancy is in cave diving, which is why we're carrying extra equipment. It makes sense. If anything should go wrong, our extra gear could save our lives.

We swim along a winding tunnel, pocked with smaller openings and lined with irregular sandy shelves. Oddly transparent shrimp and worm-like creatures swim through the beams of our lights. The cave dwellers are blind and don't need pigmentation in their skin. Amazing.

Did you notice there aren't any stalagmites or stalactites in here? Pax points out.

Remind me to ask Tony and Meg, Sky replies. *Instead, there seem to be a lot of slabs around, like the remnants of a wall, or road.*

The Bimini Road is northwest of here, I remind them. *Maybe they're related.* Dylan nods and I know the twins have opened their link with him. He can't hear me directly, but they can open their thoughts to him and relay anything I send to them.

We reach a large chamber lined with more shelf-like structures along the walls. Tony leads us to one of the shelves, where we stop to rest. Lights of other divers in the cavern illuminate odd carvings in the walls. I wonder if they're original to the cave, or if tourists left their brand of graffiti. I'll have to wait to ask any questions.

Meg points to her watch and turns to lead the way out of the cavern and back to the surface. I hate leaving, but this place won't take us closer to Jewel or the artifact.

This is just for the certification. Sky gentles my mind, and Pax chimes in.

The real test will be when we explore Skyhold on Andros. It's where Meg and Tony found the dry cave, and where we might find a way to get to the artifact.

What good would it do without Jewel? she asks, discouraged.

One thing at a time, Pax assures us. *When we find her, at least we'll know where to go from there.*

We ascend slowly, stopping at the tanks hanging from the line Meg threw in. We each grab one and switch from our rebreathers to the new tanks, which have pure oxygen to push out the nitrogen in our blood from the dive. This will be standard procedure for our cave diving expeditions, no matter how deep we dive. The bends can kill you, as if we didn't have enough to worry about.

Back on the Dream, Charles and Wolf have lunch prepared and we dig in like starving animals. I'm amazed at how hungry diving makes me. I take a bite of the best sandwich I've ever tasted.

The sound starts low over the horizon and quickly builds to fill the atmosphere.

"Hurry," Meg shouts. "Get below deck! Cover your ears!" She's heard this before.

It isn't the dragon, Sky says. *This must be the artifact.*

It's in my gut, in my bones, reverberating off the cabin walls and vibrating the boat so much I'm afraid it'll shake itself apart and we'll sink. A tsunami of sound washes over me, endlessly tossing me in a violent gale of agony. The ocean carries the wave and amplifies it until I'm afraid my eardrums will burst, or my brain will. Then it ends, suddenly, as if someone simply turned it off, leaving me completely deaf. This is familiar.

Are you two all right? I ask, not expecting an answer just yet. This was a bad one. The artifact must be in imminent danger.

I crawl over to Meg, who had jumped into the cabin right behind me. She's unconscious but breathing. My movements are sluggish, and I can't quite get to my feet yet, so I crawl out on deck and find Wolf, also alive. Dylan, Charles, and Tony are stirring near the stern. Good.

Sky? I call out mentally, knowing no one can hear yet.

I'm okay. I breathe easier at her answer. She calls out to her brother, *Pax?*

When he doesn't answer, I regain my feet and scramble around the cabin. There's no sign of him. Was he on deck?

By now, Dylan is also up and searching. Sky must have alerted him something is wrong. Then I spot him, floating face down about twenty feet from the boat. Without thinking, I lift him out of the water and float him to the deck.

Dylan quickly checks for a pulse, nods and starts rescue breathing.

His pulse is strong, Dad says, but his lungs are full of water. Sky turns to me and buries her face in my chest. I hold her tightly while she sobs, still in silence. My gift seems useless now. I can't empty his lungs or get him to breathe.

Some of the other boats have pulled in their dive flags and are heading toward shore. About a hundred yards from us, someone is struggling to pull in a line. I reach down with my mind and find a diver stuck on one of the slabs along the wall. I move the slab and free him, and sense Sky's approval as we watch the diver surface and his friend pull him in.

Suddenly, Sky pulls away from me and runs to her brother's side. He's up, coughing violently and breathing. Tears spring to my eyes, but I turn away before anyone can see. It wouldn't pay for him to know how relieved I am that he's still with us. The engines come to life under my feet, and Tony steers us toward shore.

The lights of an ambulance reflect off the boats tied up to the dock as we pull in, and I can hear Tony shouting to the medics. Hearing has returned, as I expected, or at least hoped. Pax insists he's fine.

"Let them check you out here," his father insists. "If they think you're okay, then we'll go home. Deal?"

"Sure, Dad." What else is he going to say? I know how he feels. Sequoia is a much better bet when someone needs help than any doctor or hospital. Dylan knows it, too, after the way Sky healed from her accident back home. We wait while the medical guys examine him.

"Are they called EMTs in the Bahamas?" I ask. Sky knows full well I don't care what they call them.

"He's fine," she says, answering the question I didn't ask. "I don't sense any anxiety from him."

She sends me love, which reminds me I haven't paid attention to keeping my wall up. Maybe I don't need it after all. I send some back, and watch her beautiful mouth widen in a happy smile, and tears well up in her incredibly blue eyes. I pull her close and lean in for a kiss, and just like in the movies, her dad picks that moment to yell, "Let's go! Pax is fine."

4 7
STORM

I'm up before daybreak and watch the sunrise from our deck. Water birds skitter along the shore, and long-legged birds stand patiently in the surf, silhouettes against the reddish-orange sky. Dolphins leap in the distance, and I wish life could always be like this.

I'm too excited to sleep any longer. We're going to Red Cays this morning, and Lucaya promised to give us access to Skyhold. After hearing her description of the sounds coming from it, coupled with the lights her people often see, I think they named it well. It may very well be a link between worlds.

We're on the road at full light, Dylan riding with Tony in the jeep with most of the equipment, while I drive the second jeep with Meg, Sky, and Pax. Meg tells us more about what to expect.

"The inland blue holes are very different from the ones at sea," she says. "Unlike the ocean blue holes, they have sharp layers of water chemistry, starting with a lens of fresh water from rainfall that lies atop a denser layer of saltwater. Bacteria between the layers survive by using sulfate, generating hydrogen sulfide as a by-product. That stuff can kill you. When we hit that layer, you'll know it, and we'll sink below it as quickly as we can. You might experience a headache, slight nausea or itchy skin where the water touches you. It'll pass once we're below it."

We turn onto the road leading to the village. Fresh green growth is already showing among blackened tree trunks and brown vegetation. Sometimes I think forest fires are nature's vacuum cleaner, clearing underbrush for healthier growth.

Meg speaks up again. "Most of the caves under Andros were once dry, and you'll see stalactites and stalagmites that grew into columns over millennia before they were flooded after the end of the last ice age. The caves will seem more familiar to you than the ocean hole we visited yesterday."

"You and your husband found dry caves in there," Sky says. "Are they only accessible from the water? If they're dry, then aren't they close enough to the surface to have an opening on land?"

"I'm afraid the only way in is through the water. Since we have coordinates for where the dry caves are located, it's feasible a way could be blasted in, but no one is going to do that here. In fact, only the natives and very few others know about them at all. They're sacred to the natives. The Black Seminoles are giving you kids a very special privilege."

She continues, "Once we're in the dry cavern, you can remove your masks and mouthpieces. We don't know where it comes from, but there's ample air in there. I hope the cave drawings will be helpful in your search for Jewel."

We pull into the village and park in front of the church, where Donny is jumping up and down with a huge grin on his face. Lucaya's perfect white teeth make a pleasant contrast against her dark skin as she moves forward to greet us with a smile of her own. It fades when she sees Sequoia isn't with us.

"Where is my friend? I thought she'd come with you," she says, obviously disappointed.

Sky gives her a hug and explains the pregnancy is making her tired lately. Lucaya nods.

"I will come back with you when you leave. Donny and I will pack a few things. You do have room for us, don't you?"

Meg assures her we can fit them both in one of the jeeps. I help Dylan and Tony unload the gear and float it along as Lucaya leads us into the burned-out forest, Donny skipping ahead.

"I might want to take you along on all our interior dives," Tony says with a grin. "These places are not easy to get to, and it's no fun lugging the heavy tanks and gear along."

"Yeah but think of the exercise you'd be missing, and I'll bet the water feels awfully good after you've hiked in with the equipment."

When we arrive, the hole is nothing more than a small pond twenty feet across, surrounded with scrubby vegetation. Some shows signs the fire licked a few lines this far, but didn't burn as much as it did closer to the village. A flat rock full of scratches and scrapes juts out over the water, and I set the gear down on top of it right after Donny cannon-balls into the pond. The cool splash tempts me to jump in after him. We'll be in the water soon enough.

I squeeze into the full wet suit like a sausage, and I understand why Sequoia refuses to wear panty hose. We all grunt and groan from the effort of pulling them on in this heat. Meg and Sky wear their hair in braids tucked into the neck of the suit.

"The last thing we want is to get our hair tangled or caught some-where," Meg explains. "Storm, I suggest you braid yours, too."

Pax grins while Sky braids my hair. He keeps his short, like Dylan and Tony. I'm rethinking letting mine grow long.

We tap our wristbands while the adults go through checklists. Donny's bright eyes peek out from the middle of the pond. Did he see that? Meg dives in without her tanks, and Tony tosses her the oxygen canisters we'll use before we come up. She ties them to a seventy-five-foot line, drops them, and once she's sure they haven't caught on anything, she comes back out and puts on her gear.

We check each other's equipment, including the extra lights and tanks attached to our belts, and drop into Skyhold. Tony leads the way, with Dylan and his camera right behind him. Meg takes up the rear, and we sink into the path of our dive lights. The layer of poisonous bacteria shows up about fifty feet down, like a fibrous peach-colored river. Jewel would love the color. I dread going through it.

Does anyone else fear that thing? I ask through the link.

If we swim fast, we should break through in a few seconds. We'll be okay once we're below it. Sky's words are reassuring, but she's concerned. I wish I could send her peace like her brother does.

Tony waves for us to follow and his flippers churn up the murk as he turns up the speed. It's disconcerting to see him disappear in it, followed by Dylan.

Here goes nothing, Pax says, and he disappears.

If he can do it, I can do it, Sky says, following her brother. I love her spirit and echo the thought in my mind. If she's willing, then I'm game.

48
STORM

The layer isn't thick, but the effect is immediate. I'm nauseated and the skin on my face burns by the time I'm floating in the saltwater below it. I take deep breaths and pray I can keep my breakfast down.

Sky, are you all right? When she doesn't answer I swim over to her and turn her toward me. Her complexion is a little green, but it could be a trick of the dive lights.

Better, she finally says, and shakes me off. I'm more stable, too, and remember Meg telling us it would pass quickly. I locate the tanks we'll use when we're ready to ascend. The sight is reassuring.

This way, Pax says, pointing to Tony's bright orange fins disappearing into a large opening. We each attach the lines from our spools to pylons other divers had driven into the wall, and we follow Tony's line inside. I'm struck by how eerily beautiful it is in the passage. Our lights turn everything shades of blue. Stone formations fall in drapes from the ceiling, and we swim around columns like the ones in the artifact cavern back home. Transparent centipedes and shrimp swim past, and I'm surprised to find a variety of other fish here, as well. They must come in through openings along the sea wall. I lightly brush against what I thought were a group of reeds and the one I touch crumbles.

Those are straws, Sky explains. *They're calcite formations like the columns, but more fragile, as you just discovered.*

These formations are called speleothems, Pax says. *Scientists study them for clues about past climate changes. Dad says he'd love to study these. I have no objection. Sun, surf, reef, caves, I could spend a lot of time here. The only thing missing is Jewel.*

We swim in silence until Tony stops and we gather around him. He points to a ledge near the ceiling and mimes a tight squeeze. He leads us to an opening just large enough for one diver. Everything in me wants to stay on this side of that hole. A rising sense of anxiety tells me Sky doesn't want to go through it, either.

I'll go after Dad, Pax says. *Sky, you follow me in. Then you, Ryder. Meg and Tony have already done this, and they didn't say anything about it being dangerous. We can do this.*

Sky relaxes. Pax is magic balm to his sister. Tony and Dylan disappear into the small opening, and Pax gives us a thumbs-up and slides in after them.

I'm in, he says. *Your turn, Sky.*

I wait for her go-ahead, then push my way into the opening. There's about an inch of room around me, enough to move my flippers to propel me the ten feet to the other side. We're in a chamber half-full of water. I swim to the surface and, like Tony and Dylan, take off my mask. Meg bobs up next to me, and we pull ourselves up on a stone ledge in the interior of the cave.

Our combined dive lights bounce off the walls, too bright for this small space. The two men keep theirs on, while the rest of us douse ours. The walls are gray, shot through with red streaks flowing down from the ceiling and small ledges, like the blood of ancient sacrifices. The paintings are black and amber in color, some faded but most as sharp as if they'd been done yesterday.

Pax stands near one painting and Sky gasps as she joins him.

What is it? I ask, and he points to a vertical half-moon drawn over an arrow pointing to the right, with a winged serpent, or dragon, under the arrow, exactly as the group of symbols appeared on one side of our artifact.

It's one of the symbols on Sequoia's blanket, the one she copied from the design in the crop circle your parents photographed in Oklahoma. Sky's face is pale, and Dylan comes to see what we're staring at. I can't hear his thoughts directly because he can only link with his children and the other parents. Charles had to limit the number of connections when he made the wristbands.

Dad thinks the dragon might be the one the Dracans call Triton. Ryder, you said the symbol is ambivalent and can mean either good or bad. We still don't know if it will help or hinder us. He shrugs. *We should probably speak out loud, so Tony and Meg know what's going on.*

Dylan explains the significance of the symbol to the dive masters while he photographs every painting on the walls.

"That one could be an Allaran in a beam of light," I point out. The figure is an oblong with a round head, long hair, and no facial features. The streak like a light beam might be bleached stone and not have anything to do with the drawing.

"These could be watchers with big bald heads, huge eyes, and vertical slits for noses." Sky points to another drawing. "Didn't the Allarans say the sea dwellers are the artifact's keepers here? I wonder why the artist drew watchers."

"Over here, kids," Dylan calls out. "Apparently, the sea dwellers and Triton joined forces against men in ships. I'd love to know the history behind these drawings."

We quickly scan every picture in the chamber, hoping for a map or some indication of how we can get to Atlantis. One drawing makes the hair on the back of my neck stand up. A perfect triangle, with circles at each corner, is drawn over a lizard standing on its hind legs, with sharp teeth and triangular scales. The artist had seen the Dracans.

"It's time to go," Meg announces, glancing at her watch. "Getting through the slime layer will be just as bad going back, but you've been through it and know what to expect."

"I can help," I say. "After we've breathed from the oxygen tanks, let's all gather closely together. I'll take us up in a ball of saltwater. We won't experience the effects of the bacteria at all."

Tony laughs and says, "I really need you along on these dives, Storm. When this is over, you'll have a job with us anytime."

The trip back through the passage is uneventful, and we're soon gathered beneath the pinkish curtain. I pull a ball of water around us and hold it there like a bubble, which I float to the surface with us inside. Donny's astonished face stares as I lift us, water ball and all, to the flat rock. He scrambles out of the way and squeals when I let it go and the water cascades over him. His laughter is contagious, and we quickly pull out our mouthpieces and join him.

I glance over at Sky, who's holding her belly, doubled over, and suddenly realize she isn't laughing. She's crying, and her grief hits me in the gut, only this grief is too big to be hers. The dragon is calling to her. Donny stares at her, the whites of his eyes like two full moons in his brown face. Lucaya runs to her and wraps her in a tight hug, the two of them rocking back and forth and keening.

Dylan huddles with his daughter and Lucaya while Pax abruptly sits and hides his face in his arms. The sound is not like yesterday's noise that hit us like a wall and nearly killed us. This is a deep cry, crushing us from the inside with an emotion I wouldn't wish on my worst enemy, except for the lizards.

Donny's wide-eyed gaze flits from one of us to the other and finally fixes on me. I bend down and open my arms, and he flies into them, clinging like a burr.

This is my first encounter with the dragon's emotions, but at least I know what it is. Tony and Meg are completely bewildered.

"What's wrong with everyone?" Meg asks. "Why are you all acting so strangely? Did the bacteria get to you?" She bursts into tears, and Tony has obviously had enough.

"Stop it, whatever this is. What the heck is going on here? Snap out of it!" He hugs his wife and glares at Dylan, who glares back over the top of Sky's head.

Pax stands up. "He's right. We've got to take control of this. Sky, can you form a picture of where we are and send it to him?"

"What are you talking about?" Tony's face is bright red, and he seems ready to hit someone.

"It's the dragon," I answer before I'm the one he punches. "The dragon and Sky have a link. She's communicated with it before."

Maybe if we link, I can do it, she says.

I'm game, I answer, *but someone will have to make up something for the ones who don't know about our link.*

Dad says he'll talk to Tony. Can we do it without him? Pax asks his sister.

We must try, she answers, and with a final squeeze, leaves Lucaya and comes over to Donny and me. I don't think I can peel him off, and I don't really want to.

Pax joins us and we sit in a circle. Donny's curiosity is palpable, and I explain to him we need silence to communicate with the dragon. He nods and settles down next to me.

Sky forms a picture in her head, of the three of us next to an artifact. A stillness follows, as if the dragon sees it and is waiting for more.

She forms a picture of Jewel held by a Dracan in a city under the sea. We've never seen Atlantis, so she pictures what she imagines it to be. I hope the dragon understands what she means. Then she pictures us all together, laying hands on the artifact.

Triton doesn't like that one, becoming agitated as he withdraws from us. Thankfully, the grief also leaves, but Sky breaks down crying.

"It didn't work," she says between sobs. "He doesn't understand his egg needs us. How will we get him to help us now?"

49
JEWEL

"Marla, wait up." I stop and bend over, holding my side and gasping. I hate training, but Marla insists we run around the edge of the palace circle twice a day. It's a beautiful track, winding through meadows and woods, with the clear water of the canal always in sight on one side, and the imposing palace on the other. The light appears to be from the sun and perfectly mimics early morning and late-afternoon, complete with a comfortable breeze. I wonder at the genius behind the holograms and air flow.

"What's wrong with you?" she asks, every bit as haughty as she was in Blue Mountain. "This should be getting easier. Don't forget the stakes, Jewel."

We've been training since we had the conversation with Avery four days ago. Not only is it not getting easier, but my emotions have continued to go haywire, and my muscles aren't getting stronger. I wonder, too, what's wrong with me.

We return to the palace and a shower helps restore some semblance of normalcy. Marla knocks and comes into my room, followed by Juliana with our lunch.

"Won't you join us, Juliana?" I ask. She shakes her head and turns to go, but Marla stops her.

"Please, sit and eat with us," she insists. The girl nods and gingerly takes a seat at the table, hands folded in her lap. I've barely heard her voice in the time I've known her, so I try to draw her out.

"How long have you been here?" I ask, wishing I'd asked a better question. Who is she? Why wasn't she jailed when we were caught trying to escape? Is she a hybrid? Who are her parents?

"All my life," she answers.

"How old are you?" The probing questions just keep popping out.

"I'm nearly seventeen. How old are you?" She looks up, then, and I'm startled by the twinkling humor in her eyes, as familiar as my own. Besides being brown instead of aqua, they're shaped exactly like mine. How is it possible? Could she be part Allaran? For once, I fumble for words.

"I'll be eighteen in a short time, but I can't be sure exactly when. Marla informs me time may operate differently here and I'm not sure how long I've been here." Now I'm rambling, and I can't tell if I want to laugh or cry. Her eyes soften, and she opens the lid over the main dish. She serves Marla first, then me. Marla points to a dessert plate and at Juliana, who takes it and serves herself.

We eat in silence until Marla says, "What have you learned about alternate ways out of Atlantis, Juliana?"

"Max has found a cache of deep-sea suits the Dracans sometimes wear for sport fishing near the city. He was able to hide three of them. A few problems will have to be worked out. They'll run out of air before someone is able to reach the surface, and the gas mixture is all wrong for a human. They'll need to be outfitted with specialized depressurization gas."

"Who can adjust them, and how long will it take?" Marla asks. Was Juliana part of the planning committee for our last attempt to break out of here? I thought she had just come along for the ride.

"Murphrid is already working on it. Cruiser has a plan, but we'll need the suits to carry it out."

It seems Murphrid is on our side after all. I hope he isn't planning to sell us out.

"Can we trust him?" I ask.

"Of course," she answers. "He would do anything for me." Her light brown eyes go soft and trigger a sudden sharp pain. It doesn't surprise me that she loves a Dracan hybrid. She's lived among them all her life, and I've come to care for them, too. No. Storm looked at Sky the same way in the cave. There go my emotions again, completely irrational.

We help Juliana pile the dishes on the cart, and she promises to meet us in the lab. It's time we see for ourselves what the others are planning for us.

Ashley welcomes us, and we go directly to Cruiser's tank, where he's conversing in sign language with Murphrid.

"Don't you speak mentally?" I interrupt the conversation and Cruiser bows his head briefly at me. Then he spots Marla and takes a full formal bow. How odd.

"I can't see the pictures my mother describes," the Dracan scientist answers. "I really wish I could. Maybe he can project to humans, but my Dracan genes might be interfering."

"May I try talking with him? I'll tell you what he says," I offer.

Cruiser nods and says something with his hands, and Murphrid says, "Of course. He's willing to try."

I close my eyes and a picture of the inside of his tank appears on my eyelid, like a tiny television screen. He shows me where the tube exits the barrier. Three bulky suits float up the tube, escorted by a group of sea people moving toward the surface. I relay the scenes as they come to me. It seems so simple. When I open my eyes, Murphrid is pacing, worry written on his face. Ashley glances up from the screen in front of her and frowns at Cruiser.

"How on earth do we get her into the tank, Cruiser?" she asks aloud. "It's completely sealed. So is the tube."

She glances back down and announces, "Someone's coming." In a flash, Cruiser is gone. The door opens and Max and Juliana come in, and she rushes to Murphrid and hugs him. The Dracan's scales glow brighter for a second. I really miss my sight.

Marla smiles at them and continues the conversation. "There must be a way for the divers to get into the ocean, Ashley. Why else would they need the suits at all?"

"They're beamed out of the ships," Max says.

"We tried stealing a ship before, Max," Marla reminds him. "It didn't work out so well."

"We wouldn't have to steal it," he says. "We hide in one going out to fish. When they beam up the catch, we drop out into the ocean."

"I can see two problems," I say. "Why would they take us on a fishing expedition, and how will the sea people know where we are when we drop out of the ship? And how do we get around the Dracans inside the ship?"

"Three," Juliana says.

"What are you talking about?" Max asks her.

"Those are three problems," she answers. "And there are bound to be more of them."

50
SKY

It's late afternoon by the time we head back home, and I can't seem to shake the sensation something is terribly wrong. I hope it's no more than the aftereffects of the dragon's rejection, but my gut tells me I'm missing something. Pax sends calmness, but it doesn't help. The closer we get to our houses, the more uneasy I become.

Donny is asleep with his head on Lucaya's lap and his feet on mine. His mom observes me gravely.

"You feel it, too, don't you?" she asks. "A big storm is brewing. Won't be long before we're at your place. By then we should know where it's coming from and how bad it'll be."

The sky has filled with clouds and I think of the cloaked Allaran ships. I'm not sure I believe they're still watching us and keeping tabs on Jewel. Can we trust them? Their inaction doesn't seem like something an ally would do. A dark gray curtain falls beneath a shelf cloud over the ocean to our left. A downpour. I spot something odd in it.

"Do you guys see that rain shower? What's inside it?" Storm, who's driving, turns to look as Pax leans over him. We swerve a little, until a sharp beep from the jeep behind us pulls his attention back to the road. He signals and we pull over, followed by Tony, who has Dad and Meg in his car.

Donny wakes up when Lucaya and I get out, and we all stand outside and watch four dark shapes, like the legs of a table, swirl slowly inside a dark gray curtain of rain.

"Waterspouts," Tony says. "We've seen them before, but never four of them at the same time, and never in one small downpour."

As we watch, sunlight glints off two triangles as they shoot up out of the ocean and disappear into one of the spouts.

"Are those what I think they are?" Meg asks.

"I believe we just witnessed two Dracan ships using a wormhole," Dad answers.

Storm's rage builds up and pain stabs my brother. Is Jewel on one of those ships? This day keeps getting worse, and it doesn't help that my sense of urgency is increasing.

"Let's go," I say, "something isn't right at home."

As we pull up to the houses, I spot Charles and Analiese rushing up the stairs to Storm's house. My mother opens the door for them, sees us and waves. I don't bother helping to unload anything, but run to her as quickly as I can, while she comes downstairs to meet us, followed by Charles and Wolf.

"Is Sequoia all right? The baby?" I ask, knowing they are. But what else would cause everyone to rush over?

"Everyone is fine, Sky," my mom says and gives me a hug. "Wolf just heard a hurricane is brewing south of us, a bad one."

Mom greets Lucaya and her son and hugs Pax and Storm. Dad hands her a bag of wet swimsuits, and Storm lifts some of the heavy gear out of the jeeps. The men stow the gear in the storeroom under Wolf's house, then follow Dad to our house to listen to his weather radio. Lucaya and I go with mom to see Sequoia and Analiese.

I help the women get supper ready while Lucaya tells them what we shared with her about our dive and the communication with the dragon. I don't want to speak. The sense of impending doom weighs heavily on me. Sequoia hugs me briefly and whispers, "I know. I'm sorry." Her baby is content, and I'm comforted.

After supper, when Tony and Meg head home, Dad fills us in.

"Hurricane season officially starts in June, but this is the second one this year already," he says, sounding worried. "Hurricane Beth is projected to take a northeasterly track, and the National Weather Service has issued a warning for all of the Bahamas. They've never seen one form or intensify this quickly, this early in the year. It's already a category two and could become a three before we're hit with the worst of it. Rain bands are already whipping across the southern Bahamas. They'll reach us tonight.

"We don't have much time to prepare. Tony showed me where he keeps the storm shutters, so you boys come help me get them out. We'll install most of them tonight.

"Charles and Wolf, you get the boats and outdoor equipment into the sheds under the houses. The rest of you, bring everything indoors off the verandas. Once the outdoor furniture is secured in the great rooms, let's get the two windowless safe rooms ready in our house. We'll want to stick together. Ladies, please pack our computers and belongings to store in one of them. Put pillows, blankets, water and some food in the other so we can huddle there until the worst is over. Don't forget lanterns, fans, batteries, and the weather radio. We'll be crowded, but it won't be for long. This is a fast-moving storm."

"Do we have to get it all done tonight?" Pax asks. His face is pale and drawn with exhaustion, his tiredness feeding my own. Between the dive and the dragon, our energy is nearly spent. And now this.

"We'll do as much as we can, but we should have time to put up any remaining shutters tomorrow, if we get an early start and work between rain bands. The worst of it will be here by early afternoon."

Dad, the climatologist, has lived through some horrific storms. I don't want to share that experience with him. Maybe, if we're lucky, this one will blow out to sea and miss us entirely. I send the request to God and rush after Mom to help batten down the hatches. The pylons holding our houses seem flimsy to me. I wonder if they'll be strong enough to weather a major hurricane. A category three storm has a sustained wind speed of between 111 and 129 miles per hour, with much stronger gusts. Wind like that could take the roof off, knock out power, and down a lot of trees. Any higher, and the houses could end up in the sea, and Dad says this one is still intensifying.

"Mom," I ask after I've brought the last deck chair into the great room. "How old are these houses? Do you think they'll hold up?"

"Don't worry, Sky," she says, even as she projects concern. "When we rented these houses, the owner said they're twenty years old and have weathered many bad storms. We'll be fine."

I'm not reassured, but since I can barely lift my feet to walk, I drop into bed fully clothed, and remember nothing until Mom shakes me awake at first light.

THE BOYS ARE ALREADY hard at work, wrestling shutters in place against the wind and rain. I watch Storm position two shutters at once, holding them against the house while a horizontal deluge of gust-driven water nearly knocks him off his feet. He has a firm hold on grinning Donny, who hugs a bucket of wing nuts to his narrow chest. The kid is enjoying the adventure.

When they have all three houses secured, Pax, Storm, and Dad each hop into one of the jeeps and take off, Donny riding with Storm. Dad is towing the boat on its trailer, and I open the link.

Where are you going? I ask.

To help Tony and Meg, Dad says. *We'll leave the cars inland to avoid the storm surge and get a ride back with Tony. He and Meg will stay at their house.*

The women chat while they chop veggies and make sandwiches for the large coolers we'll keep in the safe room. I listen to their talk of the baby and the pregnancy, happy for Sequoia. I send a beam of joy to the baby and she responds. Sequoia touches her belly where her baby kicked, and grins at me.

I leave them and go back to the empty deck. The rain has stopped for the moment, but the sea churns under clouds rushing ahead of the impending hurricane. I wonder if our Sentinels are up there watching it. Will they rescue us if we're swept away, or the house splinters around us? I wish I could see them like Jewel does. I hate that they're doing nothing to find and rescue my friend.

Mom joins me and hands me a sandwich. "Really, Mom? Peanut butter and jelly?"

She grins and says, "We both need some comfort food right now."

I savor the sweet nutty flavor and sticky peanut butter in my teeth. Mom is so right. We listen to the shouts of the men as they collect and store anything loose around the houses, which now resemble something out of a horror movie, all boarded up and dark. Most of ours is done, but they'll finish the last panels once we're all settled inside. I wonder how much time we have.

I miss the squadron of pelicans that normally dives for supper around this time every day. An occasional gull screeches as it sails with the wind, searching for cover. I can't imagine any of the small trees or palms dancing wildly in the wind would afford much protection for the birds. I wonder where they go for safety.

Mom points to the horizon. "Do you think that dark smudge might be our dragon?" I squint to get a better focus. The lagoon has grown more agitated in the last few minutes. Waves lick higher on the shore, with bigger ones coming in the distance.

"I don't think so, Mom. I believe it's our hurricane. And here come the men."

5 1
STORM

Donny and I are crammed tightly between two coolers filled with water and food. Battery-operated fans barely stir the humid air and scattered lanterns cast a dim light through the small safe room. The power went out a couple hours ago, and it's hot and tight in here, with each of us wearing life jackets and holding pillows over our heads to muffle the screech of the unrelenting wind. The men sit with their backs against the walls, forming a circle around the women huddled in a mass in the middle. I'm surprised at their relative calm while the world screams around us, but I suppose I wouldn't hear their cries anyway. Tiles or flying branches skitter across the roof. With the wind coming from the sea, I wouldn't be surprised if some of the debris hitting us is from fishing boats or passing ships.

I use my ability to hold the roof on the house. Pax shoots me a worried glance when something big crashes against the side, shaking us violently. Another crash and I realize we're hearing the storm surge Dylan warned us about. These waves can knock us off the pylons and sweep the house out to sea. None of us anticipated the surge to be high enough to reach us. I don't like the groans and creaks coming from underneath after each impact. I will the house to settle firmly on the pylons, and the creaking stops for a moment. God, how long will this keep up?

Dylan holds the weather radio to his ear and shouts, "The eye is approaching. We'll have a breather in a few minutes."

I need one. Telekinesis is as natural to me as walking but requires a lot of energy for something this massive. The wind tries to rip the roof off again, and I fight it with everything I've got. Then it suddenly dies, and the silence seems strange.

I'm glad to hear Wolf ask, "How big is the eye, Dylan?" He has Sequoia wrapped tightly in his arms and seems reluctant to let her go, even in the stillness.

"Not big. It's tightly wound, which makes it fast but dangerous. The smaller the eye, the faster the wind, usually. We stay inside, but we should use this opportunity to stretch and use the bathroom. He reaches into a cooler in the corner. "Water, anyone?"

Sky helps her mom and Analiese to their feet. Lucaya pulls Donny up, while Wolf helps Sequoia to hers and the five women take flash-lights and head to one of the bathrooms, leaving the second one for us. The shutters have kept out flying debris, and nothing on the inside seems damaged. I take a long swig of water and stretch my legs. We've been in here for three interminable hours, and we have at least as long when it comes again.

While the women are gone and Charles walks Donny to the bath-room, Dylan says, "The last part is the worst. The wind is stronger, and we can expect torrential rain. Are you up to protecting the house for another round?"

"Why don't we use the link to loan him some strength?" Pax suggests. I wonder why we haven't thought of it before.

"It could work," Wolf says, giving me a quick hug. "We used it to amplify Sequoia's call to the Allarans before we knew it would work. We can certainly try to amplify your gift. Are you willing to open your mind to us?"

I think about it for a moment. Do I want Sky in my head? Won't everyone know what I've tried so hard to hide? They'd read my feelings for Sky and the rage I keep caged. Still, if they don't help, I don't think I can hold it together for the second, harder half.

"Let's do it," I say. "If we don't, we might not make it out of this alive. Do you want Lucaya to know about the link? Donny already suspects something. He was watching when we tapped the wristbands at the blue hole, and I could see suspicion written all over his face."

"Did he say anything?" Wolf asks. I shake my head.

"Unless he does, we'll keep it to ourselves. Lucaya can be trusted, but an eight-year old boy might not keep such a secret."

We've had our break and the women arrive just as the wind begins to pick up again. Wolf takes Charles aside to explain what we plan to do, and Charles whispers it to his wife as they're getting settled. I tap my wristband and find everyone already there in the link. I'm overwhelmed by their love and realize it doesn't matter what they learn about me. They are my family.

We settle in our circles and get the pillows ready for the piercing sounds. A wall of wind slams the house from the land side. Hopefully, it'll push the surging water back out to sea.

It's all I can do to keep the house on the pylons. Pax's face is showing the strain. I can only imagine what the open link is doing to everyone else. Along with the force of the waves slapping the floor underneath us, torrential rain slashes against the roof and side, threatening to wash us into the ocean. Trickles of water coming down the walls of the safe room quickly become rivulets. I wonder how long it will take this room to fill with water, and whether we'd survive if we leave it.

Hold on, son. Wolf's voice, sounding tight with strain in my head, loans me courage. *Some of us will focus your ability on the roof. The rest will help you keep the building together. You can do this.*

Tension lifts, as if someone else is exercising my telekinesis. I gladly let them help and renew my focus on the pylons.

Who knew wind can be a hammer? I thought sustained wind meant a steady blow, but within the more than hundred mile-per-hour stream, huge gusts, much faster, slam the house over and over. Each hit is like a body blow as I push back with my mind. Thank God for the extra help from the others.

Sky suddenly sits straight, increased anxiety in her mental voice. *What's that?*

Pax straightens and says, *I hear it, too.*

I don't know how we can hear anything over the howling wind, but a low thrumming hum fills the air and presses down like a weight. It grows in volume, drowning the noise of the wind and rain.

Is the hurricane dying down? Sequoia asks.

It's too soon, Dylan replies. *We should have another hour of this, at least.*

The pressure on the house eases, and the noise quickly grows quieter, while the hum grows into a moan vibrating in my chest.

It's the dragon! Sky's excitement shoots through me, and, I suspect, everyone else. Our link is the strongest we've ever accomplished.

Then I see them, the pictures Sky described. The waves calm and the wind dissipates. Sun breaks through black swirling clouds that turn into mist and disappear. All three of our houses are still standing, one with some roof damage and the others intact. Sky appears like a bright swirling glow of gold, yellow, purple and indigo in his mind. Is this the aura Jewel sees? I'm overwhelmed with Sky's inner beauty. Then she responds, shocking the dragon.

He stills and waits, mind edged with interest and ready to receive from her. We loan her our linked minds and allow her to formulate images to send him. She weaves the love we all have for Jewel and sends him a picture of her face, with sparkling aqua eyes. I can't help the flash of rage lashing out at the memory of the Dracan who abducted her. The dragon recoils and sends back an image of a city full of life.

Then she shows him the artifact and what we did to save it, and I watch the scenes unfold like a movie. When she concludes with the Dracans taking Jewel and the artifact, Titan roars. The sound reverberates in our heads, even as we cover our ears against it. The grief hits then, pounding like hurricane-force wind against our minds and sinking deep in our guts. We're sucked into a black hole of despair while he shows us his dying egg.

We clearly see the "egg" is an artifact. Sky quickly sends an image of the four of us cradling it, touching and healing it. The pain ebbs and the darkness fades. She follows the image with a close-up of each of our faces, shaped and colored with her love for us. Pax is outlined in blue with both hard and soft accents. Jewel is a brilliant gem with a funny sweet quality. Sky's face is what she must see in the mirror and her compassionate warmth reaches out to him. My face is dark, strong, and heroic. Is that how she sees me?

Don't forget stupid, her thought follows the picture, and although I know she meant it just for me, everyone got the message, judging by the grin on her brother's face.

Concentrate, Sequoia admonishes.

Sky sends another image of the four of us with the healthy egg. Then a Dracan tears Jewel away and the egg gets sick again. Through the link, we see the dragon rescue Jewel from the city and bring her to us, careful to protect her from the ocean. Is that his thought, or Sky's? The exchange becomes fluid between them. He finally breaks it off and Sky collapses in a heap.

I think I know why our attempt to communicate with the dragon at the blue hole didn't work. He's as much an empath as Sky, and it was emotion that broke through, not simply the pictures.

I'm beat, and from the looks of them, so are the others. I tap the wristband and break the link. In my exhaustion, I don't even notice the silence. I close my eyes and drift off to sleep.

52
JEWEL

Juliana wasn't kidding when she said there will be more problems. They keep piling up. Marla and I head to Avery's rooms for lunch.

"Does anyone know what damage the hurricane left on the islands? My friends and family are there. Are they safe?" Tears, never far from spilling over these days, burn my eyes. I dab at them with an edge of my tunic.

"Murphrid says it moved through quickly, so there wasn't much flooding. I can't imagine your friends just sitting there, doing nothing. You know they're working hard to find you, and Storm would have held their homes together." Marla is doing her best to reassure me, but it doesn't help. I don't say anything.

"I hope Mom has some answers," she says. My stomach growls loudly, and she laughs. "And some food for you."

"It's been two days, Marla, and we're running out of time."

"I know," she answers. "But what can we do? Mom called us for a reason. Maybe they've worked something out."

Avery welcomes us into her beautiful sitting room, and I wonder if I'll ever see it again after I finally make my escape. I'm surprised I'll miss Atlantis. Is this what the Stockholm Syndrome is like? I've certainly developed affection for my captors, and I'm thinking of returning even after I've escaped. Maybe I understand more about them and their history and that they have positive relationships with other humans. Maybe I'm really growing to like these Dracans. I wonder how Storm would react. No, I don't. He'd hate it.

After we eat, Juliana joins us in one of the seating areas for tea and some of the delicious Dracan pastries. "The suits are ready," she says. "Murphrid has scheduled a fishing trip with three unnamed companions. All we'll have to do is wear the suits into the ship, pretend to be Dracans, and eject when they open the hatch. The problem is, everyone puts the suits on there, in the presence of the helpful crew."

Juliana sips from her teacup. "They keep their equipment on board all the time, so we'd have to smuggle them on board, overpower the crew somehow and get out of the ship in the exact location where the sea people will be waiting for us."

"What if Marla and I are two of the companions?" Avery asks. "Ashley could be the third. When the time comes to get the suits on, we can ask for privacy and the three of you will be waiting, ready to go. Then we'd only have to smuggle you on board before they take off and hide you in our cabin. Is that doable?"

"Wait a minute," I say. "Who, exactly, is going with me?"

"I am," Juliana answers. "Max and Murphrid are coming, too. Our suits have been altered for humans. Murphrid will use one of theirs."

Marla can tell I want to ask why she isn't coming and shakes her head. We'll talk about it later.

I ask instead, "Didn't he say their suits wouldn't get him to the surface?"

Avery answers, "Cruiser says they can move him quickly enough. The suits compensate for decompression, but humans would still have to move more slowly for the suits to work properly. Dracans don't have that problem."

Marla's eyes go wide in surprise. "Mom, how do you know about Cruiser?"

"I tortured it out of Dr. Jenkins," she says, and takes a sip of tea. The blood drains from my face.

Marla laughs. "Don't tease her."

"I walked in on Ashley talking to him," Avery explains, with a little smile on her face for me. "He fed me some pictures of the rescue his people are planning. It can work, but it must happen quickly. Murphrid scheduled the fishing trip for tomorrow."

"Why the rush?" Marla asks.

"Four wormholes were spotted before the hurricane hit the islands above us. Two ships disappeared, one of them carrying Shaula. The other was chasing him. At this point, both are lost. Our main concern now is how the wormholes might distort time. If we speed up, then earth time slows, and conversely, if we slow down, then time speeds up where the artifact is. We have no way of predicting it, nor will we know its effects. We are, quite literally, out of time."

"How will the sea people know where we are when we drop into the ocean?" Marla asks. "They can't swim as fast as the ships."

"No." Avery's voice drops, and we strain to hear her. "But Triton can get them there swiftly."

"What does Triton have to do with our escape?" I ask. The dragon is going to help us. How? Why?

"Cruiser can stay in mental touch with Ashley. He and Triton will follow the ship, and when Ashley gives him the signal, his team will be there," she explains. She pauses and I watch her eyes crinkle with humor.

"Simply think of Triton as a very fast, beautifully sleek bus."

All I can picture is a bunch of mermen riding a dragon through the sea. We are living in a fairy tale.

53
SKY

"They're back!" Mom's unusually chipper voice wakes me up as she pulls the curtains aside and bright sunshine floods the room. It feels wonderful after our horrific night. Shutters hit the deck with metallic thunks. The boys have been busy this morning.

"Who's back?" I mumble while I stretch the kinks out of my back.

"Dr. Emery and the Proteus, and this time they've brought a six-man sub with them. Gabe and Izzy can't wait to take you kids down, and there's room for Jewel when you find her."

When we find her. I like Mom's enthusiasm, and, frankly, I need it today. It's looking more and more hopeless as time goes on. We're no closer to rescuing Jewel than we were when she was first abducted last October. Granted, we know approximately where she is, but how do we get to her, or better yet, how does she get to us?

"That's wonderful, Mom," I reply. "I'd love to explore in a sub, and Storm will make sure nothing bad happens to us. When do we go?"

"This afternoon," she says, "after the windows are uncovered and the area around the houses is cleaned up a bit. The roads might be full of debris, but Storm can get you around it."

"You? Aren't you coming?"

"The men will go with you. We'll stay here with Sequoia." Peace and joy emanate from her and I'm happy they'll be here, out of harm's way.

I dress quickly and head out to the sand under the house where Pax hands me a garbage bag.

"We're making piles, so you can pick one type of item to put into the bag and dump on its pile. Under our house we're collecting driftwood and anything natural that's washed up. Anything that might belong to someone or be a part of something goes under Wolf's house. Trash, which is most of what we're finding, like cans and unidentifiable stuff, goes under Charles's house."

"I'll decide when I know what's around," I say, and set my mind to sifting through rubble while Storm moves big items into piles farther inland. I find enough debris to make a substantial trash pile.

After lunch, we take off to the docks. We've each packed for an overnight stay. Mom insisted we include swimsuits and towels in our backpacks, but there's little chance we'll need them. Who wears swimsuits in a submarine?

Dr. Emery waves from the deck of Proteus, and the men go up to meet him while Gabe and Izzy hurry down the gangplank to welcome us with handshakes and hugs.

"Where've you been?" I ask Gabe, smiling at Storm's annoyance. Good.

"Back to New England to pick up Namor. She's a six-person submarine we'll take down this time, so you can join us." He winks, teasing me to bait Storm. I hope it works.

"Namor, as in the submariner in the comics?" Pax asks, while Storm glowers at Gabe.

"Exactly," Izzy chimes in. Her musical voice grates on my nerves. I don't like the way she's checking Storm out, and it doesn't matter that she's inspecting Pax the same way. I know I'm overreacting when he touches my arm and sends me peace. I send it on to Izzy, which also calms me down. We have a job to do, and I'm eager to get going.

When the ship leaves the sheltered bay, I understand why people get seasick. I've been on ships in rough seas, but cruise ships are much bigger than Proteus, and their stabilizers keep them relatively steady. Not so with this research vessel. Hurricane Beth left some rough waters behind.

We meet Dr. Emery and our folks in the library conference room, armed with motion sickness patches handed to us by the ship's doctor. The patch works for me, and I send out feelers to see if anyone else is in distress. Thankfully, we're all stable.

"We're heading to the coordinates of the dragon sighting," Dr. Emery explains. "We'll launch Namor from there, with Izzy, Gabe, and the kids inside. Do you think you can call the dragon, Sky? Maybe you can convince it to lead you to Jewel, then to the artifact you need to fix."

"It's a long-shot," Dad says. "The dragon has always initiated contact. We don't know if he'll respond to a call from Sky."

"All you can do is try," he acknowledges. "We should be there in a couple of hours. You kids go along with Izzy and familiarize yourselves with Namor. Let her know if there's anything you need to take with you."

Gabe stays behind with the men and Izzy leads us below decks to the bay where Namor is being readied for the dive. I laugh. The sub is bright yellow, with two rows of portholes, one along the upper rim and the other below it. My parents are fans of the Beatles, and this is right off their Yellow Submarine album cover. I've heard them play the song enough to have it running through my mind now. Pax grins at me and taps his wristband.

You hear it too, don't you?

I'll never un-hear it again. We get to ride in a yellow submarine. I wonder if the Beatles had a vision or something.

Storm's voice joins us. *Let's hope this adventure leads us to Jewel and the artifact. If we're successful, I'll make it my theme song.*

I'll have it played at my wedding, I say, teasing him. He grunts and Pax's grin widens. We turn our attention to Izzy, who's pointing out where we'll sit and what we'll do with the instruments in front of the seats. I'm happy to see we each have at least two portholes, the one on top, at eye-level, and the one below it to expand our field of vision.

We join the others in the dining room. I have no appetite, but the trip will take hours, and I know I need to eat. I spot Gabe sitting with Charles and Wolf and join them at their table.

"What if we get hungry while we're down there? My stomach doesn't like this motion, and even with the medication, I'm not hungry now."

Gabe answers, "We have sandwiches, snacks and drinks on the sub. It'll be much calmer underwater. Your appetite will recover down below."

I nod and return to the deck outside. I take deep breaths of fresh salt air. It may be my last fresh air if this goes wrong. We could get killed, or even captured when we find the artifact. Won't the Dracans come after Jewel when we rescue her? Will Triton incinerate us once his egg is repaired?

It's time, and the submarine seems a lot smaller as we climb inside and take our places. Gabe and Izzy go through the checklist until we're finally lowered into the water. We bob like a cork in a boiling pot for a few minutes, but once we dive, everything stills. The vibration of the engines soon becomes white noise and I no longer hear it. I watch as the blue darkens to black and the lights surrounding the sub come on. I'm privileged to see this strange, largely unexplored undersea world.

Gabe was right. My appetite returns with a vengeance.

"What kind of sandwiches did we bring along?" I ask. Izzy reaches into a cooler and pulls out a tuna fish sandwich on wheat bread.

"Fish, of course," she says with a grin. I dig in hungrily and watch the ocean, hoping for a glimpse of some of the creatures from their first trip below. Giant squid. Now, that I'd like to see.

This is too easy. I'm waiting for the other shoe to drop, even as Max, Juliana, and I climb aboard the Dracan ship with no opposition. Where are the guards? Why is the gangway standing open? My skin crawls. I'm afraid the trap will shut as soon as we're inside.

We find the room assigned to Avery, where she and Murphrid have stowed the dive suits, and crouch in the corner between the door and the bunk. If anyone opens the door, they won't immediately see us, but there's no good place to hide in here.

"We'd better get ready before anyone gets here," Max says. He pulls a trunk out from under the bed and opens it. The suits aren't as bulky as I'd imagined them. In fact, they seem too thin to me. Even the helmets seem flimsy. The biggest parts of the suit are the attached flippers.

"How are these supposed to protect us from the pressure out there? Where are the oxygen tanks?" I wipe my sweat-slick palms on my tunic.

"It's the same material that covers the dome," Juliana explains.

"It's like cephalopod skin," Max adds, "which takes on the shape and color of everything it covers. In here, we might match the wall or the furniture, and once we're in the water, we'll be hard to spot." I can't tell if he's teasing or not.

We're wearing swimsuits under our clothes, and I watch as Max removes his top and pants and pulls the bottom of the suit up over his trunks. It fits loosely, and once he has the top on, I agree it makes a good disguise. With the helmet, he might pass for a small Dracan. It still seems too thin to me.

He turns around while we pull on the leggings. The top fits close to the skin, but not tightly. I'm surprised at how it moves with me. I'd always thought deep sea suits were stiff, like spacesuits. Even the attached gloves are supple, almost as if we have no gloves on at all.

"Try the helmets," Max insists, and pulls his down over his head. "We'll need to check each other's connections." His voice sounds tinny until I put my own helmet on my head. I expect claustrophobia, but, like the suit, it's a comfortable fit. I'm glad we can hear each other through speakers.

"One of you check mine," he says. I find three small levers along the edge where the back of it connects to the suit.

"Those levers close and seal the helmet. The one that activates the breather is on the back of your hand, where you can reach it. Do you see it?"

Juliana and I both find it. "What do we do with it?" Juliana asks.

"Turn it to the left when we're ready to leave. Once we've reached the surface, you'll need to turn it back to the right."

I ask, "How are we breathing now, with our helmets sealed?"

"The seal itself activates compressed air, which is fine when you're inside a pressurized space, like the ship. There are no tanks. All the components are built into the suit.

"The lever on your hand equalizes your pressure and delivers the gas mixture you'll need to survive at these depths. As we ascend, it will automatically adjust the mixture. Shouldn't have a problem depressurizing."

We hear a thump from outside the ship and Max goes to the door while Juliana lays our clothes in the trunk and pushes it back under the bed. "I have to get to Murphrid's room. Stay here and stay down." He slips out and leaves Juliana and me alone.

A noise outside the door alerts us someone else is in the ship. We duck down in our semi-exposed spot behind the door, helmets still on, and wait as the door opens.

"Marla and I will change in here," Avery says to someone in the corridor, who answers in the Dracan language.

She replies in English, "We'll check each other's connections. We know how they work."

I'm happy to see them, even though the room is awfully tight with the four of us in here. Avery lays the suits she's holding on the bed and Marla leans her forehead against my helmet and says, "Ashley and Murphrid are in the other cabin. She'll stay behind while Max goes with you. We're ready to take off and should be at our dive spot in fifteen minutes. Can you hold out that long?"

"Of course. Marla, why aren't you coming with us? Why is Max going without you?"

"His father needs closure. He won't stay, but he wants to say good-bye, and explain about us and our city."

I can understand that. It's hard to lose someone, especially when you can't say the things you need to or say goodbye. My heart aches for Storm. He was so young when his parents died. I'm glad Max cares enough to go back for his dad.

"How will he get back to you?"

"I'll pick him up, of course. I wish we could simply drop you off the same way. I'm sorry it has to be so complicated."

I nod, unable to speak. I hope I'll see her again someday.

The knock on the door comes too quickly. I give her a quick hug before she ducks behind the door. Then a tall Dracan leads Juliana and me down the corridor to the portal room. Two figures dressed like us stand next to another one. They nod at us, but I can't see their faces clearly through the face plates. I hope the Dracans can't see any better than I can.

One of the Dracans suddenly stiffens, and the other turns to us and says something in his language.

"Stand back against the wall," Murphrid says through the helmet link. "Something has happened, and we have to stay out of the way."

The wall is lined with bins recessed into alcoves. Murphrid reaches back and draws a handful of cords out of the bin he's leaning against.

The Dracan speaks again and the grin on his reptilian face turns my guts to jelly. The scientist translates, "We've caught a very big fish in the tractor beam. Back to the rooms, please. This fishing trip is over."

They shoo us back toward the corridor. Murphrid starts back, but before he reaches the hall, Max suddenly swivels and drops to the floor, sweeping his leg out and tripping the nearest Dracan. I don't wait to see what happens next but copy the maneuver while the second one turns to help his friend. I catch him completely off guard and he crashes to the floor. Juliana grabs one of his arms and flips him on his stomach. I grab the other and hold him down while she ties him with a cord Murphrid tosses at her.

She plants her knee in his back and yells at Max. "Need help?"

Max's captive is face down, hogtied with some of the same cord. As soon as they're secured, Murphrid does something with controls on the wall, and a section of the floor slides open to reveal a small chamber.

"Do not put us in there," the taller Dracan pleads. "We mean you no harm."

"It's not for you," Max assures him. "We're going fishing."

We drop into the opening and Murphrid presses a panel on the wall. The floor slides shut again, and the chamber fills with sea water. As soon as it's full, the bottom slides open and we float out into total blackness.

"Lights," Max says. "They're located on your other wrist. Sorry I forgot to show you."

My fingers find the button and I breathe a sigh of relief when the area around us lights up and we see the fish caught in the tractor beam.

"Is that for real?" Max's voice has gone up an octave.

"What is it?" Murphrid and Juliana ask at the same time.

"That, my friends, is a yellow submarine."

PAX

"I s everyone all right?" Gabe calls out. I can't see anything in this pitch darkness. What the heck happened?

"Criminy! My head hurts," Sky says, both fearful and extremely annoyed. I push back with calm and hear her sigh. She's right to be afraid. We have no power. How long will our air hold out? How long before the pressure crushes us?

"I'm fine," I assure him, rubbing my head where it hit something in the sudden stop.

Izzy's face lights up in the glow of a flashlight. "Here," she says, and sweeps the light over the rest of us. Sky is slumped over the console in front of her, holding her head in her hands. Gabe rubs his head, staring out at the black sea.

"Storm?" she asks, shaking him.

"I'm okay," he says. "I'm concentrating."

Once she's sure everyone is still alive, Izzy plays the light over the cabin. Since most of the equipment is bolted to the submarine, only a few sandwich wrappers and a spilled bottle of water on the floor indicate something catastrophic just happened. Did we run into a wall?

"I don't believe it," Gabe's voice sounds strained. A light reflects off his face through the porthole. I rush to his side. Four divers, floating in a pool of light, are staring at us. At these depths? How is that possible? Then I look up. We didn't run into a wall. We've been captured by a Dracan ship.

I tap my wristband, relieved when the link opens. The sub must be shielding us from the alien tech. *I don't think you need to hold us together. Check out what's above us.*

His anger nearly knocks me over, while Sky asks, *Are we prisoners?*

I'll kill them, he says, glaring at the divers.

Hold on, Ryder, we should find out who they are and what they want before you crush them. Sky sends him peace while I try to reason with him. He takes deep breaths, and the anger ebbs.

The divers have approached the sub. "What are they?" Izzy asks. "Are these the aliens you've told us about?"

"They aren't armed," Gabe says, and it's true they have nothing in their hands. "They seemed as surprised to see us as I was to see them."

"The battery back-up lights should have come on by now," Izzy mumbles while she pulls several levers and tries pushing buttons. "At least we know the emergency beacon has been activated, unless they have a way of disabling it. We know nothing about their technology."

She fumbles with a loose cable, attaches it to something, and a soft blue glow fills the cabin. It's good to have light again. I turn my attention to the divers outside, and it takes a moment for my eyes to adjust.

One of them suddenly waves its arms and swims toward my porthole. The others follow, and I know I've been seen. I'm curious to see what they look like and hold my ground. Its helmet seems small for a deep-sea diver, and I can't find any oxygen tanks. Can they breathe underwater? The blue glow behind me combined with the lights from their suits makes a glare on the faceplate of the helmet. I can't see them, after all.

The one in the lead presses its face to the porthole and startles me, causing me to step back.

My sister gasps loudly, *It's Jewel!*

I crowd her away from the small window and stare into the face of the most beautiful girl in the world, and tears burn my eyes. I want to punch Storm when he pushes me aside. He holds up his hand and points to his wrist. *Jewel, can you use your wristband?*

She shakes her head and points up at the ship.

"Do you know who that is?" Gabe asks. I understand his confusion. We're pushing and shoving each other to get to one small porthole and gesticulating without words. He and Izzy must think we've gone insane.

"It's Jewel," Sky tells them. "I don't know how she's here, or how we can rescue her, but it's definitely our friend. Is there any way to get her into the sub?"

"Not at this depth, I'm afraid," Gabe says. He pulls his eyebrows together in concentration. "We have an airlock, but if we open it now, we can't equalize the pressure."

I push Storm aside and place my hand on the window. She turns and pulls someone up next to her, then moves out of the way. I step back when Max's grinning face fills the porthole. The sub won't hold more than six people. We'll have to find another way to retrieve them. And who are the other two? Marla? Who else?

Sky and Jewel are staring at each other through another porthole when Max suddenly spins around, grabs her hand, and pulls her away from the submarine. A familiar low thrumming sound vibrates through the hull and penetrates my bones.

"It's Triton," Sky announces unnecessarily.

"The dragon?" Izzy's voice comes out as a squeak, and even in this low light I can see she's gone pale.

"I've got to see this," Gabe's voice is up an octave, too, but he sounds more excited than afraid. He glues his face to one of the portholes, and I help Izzy move next to him. He wraps an arm around her and pulls her close to share the window. I wonder if we'll tilt the sub with all of us crowding on one side.

"There," Storm points to a dizzying river of scales sliding by, close enough to reflect the light from the divers' suits. Dark forms drop off the undulating mass, and a sea dweller carrying a barbed spear approaches Jewel.

"No!" Storm and I shout in unison. The spear flies from the

merman's hand and he whirls toward us with a menacing grimace on his face. Jewel gestures for us to stop, swims to the creature and throws her arm over his shoulder.

Wait, Sky says. *She knows him.*

"Wow," Gabe says, several times in a row.

Izzy mumbles, "I can't believe what I'm seeing."

Can you let Triton know we're here? Storm asks. *Pax and I will amplify your thoughts, if you need our help.*

Yes, please, she says. *We need to deepen the link.*

A picture of the yellow submarine forms in my mind, and I realize she's already projecting to the dragon. Our faces are in the window and Jewel's face is in a figure outside of the sub, complete with her love for us. Triton might not recognize the faces, but he'll remember the emotions.

He sends back a picture of a triangle with an egg hanging from beneath it. I sense his question through the link.

Sky places us inside the "egg" and again shows Jewel in the water outside it.

He shows us the mermen escorting the four divers to the surface. Then he roars.

We slap our hands over our ears and double up in shock. Vibrations threaten to tear us apart even as the volume is about to burst our eardrums. Is he trying to kill us? Have we failed?

The shaking increases and we fall to the floor, writhing. Pain shoots through every nerve in my body. My joints feel like they're coming apart. Being crushed like a soda can would at least be instantaneous death. I wish for it as the agony goes on. Darkness pushes in and my vision narrows. Please, let this be the end.

A DIFFERENT VIBRATION wakes me up and I realize what Triton has done. He shook us free from the tractor beam and our engines are back on. Gabe struggles to his feet and staggers to the helm.

"Amazing," he says, while a grin stretches across his face. After I help Sky and check on Storm and Izzy, who are securely in their seats, I go see what he's so happy about.

During our blackout, we've ascended to a level where the sun penetrates the ocean just enough to see our surroundings. The dragon, a darker shadow in the dim water, undulates in the distance, swimming circles around us. The small dark shapes of fish-tailed men, some holding three of the four divers close to their sides, keep pace with us. Where's the fourth? Did they lose someone? Jewel?

"Proteus, come in, come in," Izzy taps the radio, but there's only static.

Our folks must be frantic. I try to open the link to Dad, but something is blocking it. Is the Dracan ship nearby? Could it be blocking the connection to the folks on the surface? I expect we'll be on the surface soon, judging by the lightened ocean.

"What is that?" Gabe asks.

I'm beginning to hate that question. Nothing unusual is visible from my porthole, but Sky, sitting on the other side, says, *it looks like a wall. We must be approaching an island.*

An island? We left the Proteus out in the middle of the Tongue of the Ocean, and I assume they're still there, trying to contact us and waiting for us to surface. Where is Triton taking us?

"There's an opening," Izzy says. "A large one. Could this be the dragon's lair?"

"Triton is taking us to his egg," Sky says. Her voice grows thick with tears. "He understood me. He's taking us to fix the artifact."

Storm leaves his seat to stand behind her, pulling her back to rest her head against his chest. I turn away. We're going to see Jewel, and I cannot wait to hold her in my arms.

56

JEWEL

Ashley Jenkins failed to tell me Cruiser is so talkative. He keeps me entertained with stories of his people, all in pictures, like a movie in my head. I barely notice how much time is passing on our way to the surface. The suit, as promised, keeps me breathing and surprisingly warm. I glance at Max, who waves at me, then find Juliana with her escort. Murphrid's escort has taken him ahead of us, before he runs out of air. His suit hasn't been altered like ours. The yellow submarine sends vibrations through the water, and its hum relaxes me. I can imagine how the others must have joked about its color.

My heart speeds up and Cruiser squeezes me in alarm. I shake my head, sending him pictures of Sky and Storm with their auras. He twitters when I show him Pax. He understands I'm excited to see them. I show him my memories of the colors of home, and of those I love. He expresses amazement and turns me toward him. His fishy grin tickles me and I laugh. Whatever happens, I will treasure these people along with my Dracan friends. I pray we get to the artifact in time.

Triton circles us, keeping dangerous sea creatures far away from us. He's a better protector than my Sentinel, at least in this environment. I can't wait to take the helmet off and see him in his true colors. My heart beats faster. I'm going to see again. Really see.

A dark shadow looms ahead and resolves into a rough wall as we draw closer. An opening appears, and I know where we're going. Please, God, let us be in time.

Triton disappears into the entrance, and as we follow, I marvel at its sheer magnitude. The tunnel is large enough for a Dracan ship to float through without touching any of the sheer walls. It reminds me of their tunnels in Blue Mountain, laser-bored and smooth. We wind through a series of curves deep into the island. Then we surface in an enormous cavern.

Cruiser pulls me into a hug, then pushes me toward a narrow beach, where Murphrid is waiting. As I approach, Max crawls out and sits, while Juliana bends to help him remove his helmet. I watch him take a deep breath and smile. At least I know the air is breathable. I stagger out, my legs unwilling to hold me up. I'm heavy and clumsy. Then Murphrid lifts the helmet off my head, and I'm nearly blinded by the shimmer of aqua, green, yellow and blue bouncing off the walls. Max's head is ringed in yellow with red streaks, a far cry from the dull brown of his aura before all this. Blue and magenta emanate from Juliana's head. We peel off our gloves and the bottom of the suits with the attached flippers. I'm glad we have swimsuits on, but I wonder how we'll manage with bare feet. Thankfully, the fine sand seems to extend throughout the cave and into the next tunnel.

The submarine surfaces and, while the sea dwellers push it to the beach, I spot the dragon still deep in the water, heading back out to sea. The hatch flies open, and Pax climbs out and jumps to the beach, ignoring the ladder. He runs to me and I melt in his tight hug, my tears mingling with his.

"Move over and give us a chance," Sky cries out, pushing him aside. My best friend and I cry together, unable to contain our joy. Storm wraps his arms around both of us.

"I've missed you all desperately," I say. "I have so much to tell you."

"Okay, break it up," Juliana says. "Let's go, Jewel. We have to hurry."

I'm about to introduce Juliana and Murphrid to my friends and find out who the man and woman with them are, when Murphrid lifts off the ground and flies toward a rock jutting out from the wall.

"Storm, stop!" I shout, grabbing his arm. "Don't hurt him."

Murphrid stops in midair, his eyes like saucers and his jaw hanging open, exposing rows of pointed teeth. Storm's expression scares me. I tap my wristband and nearly dissolve in tears again when he responds.

Give me one good reason not to kill him. His jaw clenches and unclenches while his narrowed eyes focus on my friend, and I know I'm the only reason Murphrid is still alive.

He saved my life. I wouldn't be here without him.

The Dracan lowers slowly to the ground and collapses in a heap. I should have warned him about Storm's rage. Sky sends him soothing waves and his aura changes from angry black and red streaks to magenta and gray. What's this?

Sky introduces me to Gabe and Izzy, and I introduce Murphrid and Juliana to my friends.

Where have I seen her before? Sky asks. Suddenly, her eyes widen, moving from Juliana to Storm. Before she can say anything, a low growl fills the cavern and we freeze.

A Dracan ship rises out of the depths, held in the powerful jaws of the most magnificent creature I've ever imagined. Triton lowers the ship to the sand and rears.

"Please don't roar," Sky shouts, sending him a picture of lifeless bodies scattered over the sand, and a wobbling artifact. The dragon's mouth snaps shut, and in my mind, an egg sits in a chamber with the four of us surrounding it. He understands her. Now my mouth is hanging open.

I can barely see the dragon's face beneath the rainbows of unimaginable colors swirling and dancing around him. His eyes snap and spark gold and blue over black streaks whirling in their depths. I wonder at the despair and grief in his eyes.

Wisps of smoke curl from his large nostrils. A fire-breather? Ears that seem too small for his head sit behind appendages that extend above his eye ridges like the furry antennae of some moths. Similar antennae hang beneath his chin like a beard. I can't get the image of his open mouth lined with sharp teeth out of my head. His scales are every bit as beautiful as I'd imagined them to be when I handled them in Ashley's lab. He's more like the Chinese renderings of dragons than ones in the story books I read as a child. I can't believe he's allowed us to get this close to him.

He swims to the beach and extends powerful legs, pulling himself out of the water with webbed claws. We crowd against one side of the chamber while he crawls out of the water and lumbers through a second opening. As soon as his back legs reach land, I pull my attention away from him and to the ship he's brought in.

Thuban, Avery and Ashley stand silently on shore. How did Thuban get here? Was he already in the ship? If he was in on our escape, it explains why it all seemed too easy, but why would the king of Atlantis go along with the subterfuge? I'm confused.

Marla holds her mother's hand and the two Dracans we overcame are now guarding their king. I'm afraid of Storm's reaction when he sees them, and I touch his arm.

Storm, please don't react. Please trust me. The Dracans in the ship are on our side.

He whirls around and stares at them. Max, who was as mesmerized as the rest of us, sees his movement, and runs to Marla when he spots her. He grabs her in his arms and turns to glare at Storm.

"If you hurt any of them, I promise I'll kill you."

Storm's eyes narrow, and Sky says, *Don't. We'll hear them out, but right now, we need to follow Triton. Pray we're not too late.*

5 7

STORM

The artifact wobbles much like the first one did, in the center of a circular cave covered in sand. From the grooves around the perimeter, I'm guessing Triton sleeps curled around his egg.

Sky sends him a picture of us walking close to the egg, and the dragon rumbles. I hope it means he approves.

All the others, lizards included, gather along the opposite side of the perimeter. My rage is caged for the moment, but at this point, anything can set it loose. I can't imagine why Jewel trusts them. Who is the girl with her? She seems familiar, but I know I've never seen her before. What is Marla doing here? Later. I need to concentrate.

Like the last time, Pax sniffs as we circle the artifact. Sky sends out feelers, and Jewel looks it over carefully. We'd found a crack in the force field the first artifact had spun around itself, and I'd been able to get in and break it open using telekinesis.

I get nothing, Sky says, discouraged. *Anyone else?*

No leaking colors, Jewel adds.

I don't smell anything. How are we supposed to get at it? The energy field is impenetrable.

Sky, I suggest. *Why don't you ask the dragon if there's a way in?*

Her smile warms me while she forms a picture to show the dragon.

She shows us breaking the egg, and Triton rears up and opens his mouth.

She quickly shows him the tetrahedron inside the energy field, and how we touched it and sent it love. At the same time, she sends love to the dragon and he settles back to the sand. She completes the picture with an image of the artifact spinning its egg back into shape.

The dragon's enormous eyes focus on us while he shows us how he plans to break the egg. My legs turn to jelly and I urgently need to run for my life.

She sends an image of cooked bodies smoking in the sand, and he rears up again while we see a picture of how we can protect ourselves. I'm not excited about it.

"Everyone, run! We need to get between the dragon and the wall. Now," Pax shouts and points to the narrow opening between Triton's monstrous body and the wall. It'll be tight. The largest Dracan hesitates, then herds Marla and her mother to the dragon, followed by the other woman and the rest of the lizards. Jewel, Sky, Pax, and I are the last ones in because we'll need to be the first ones out if this works. I'm surprised at how smooth Triton's scales are pressed against my face.

The rumble shivers his scales before we hear it. Then the chamber fills with a sound like a freight train, and the heat nearly knocks me out. Triton's grief and anguish almost finishes me until I realize it means the loud crack followed by an explosion was the force field breaking. I can't see it yet, but I send out a cushion so the artifact doesn't fall to the sand. Then I run out from behind the dragon.

Heat from the blistering sand burns my feet through my shoes. Jewel is barefoot. "Hold on," I shout. "Wait for me to lift you."

One by one, I float my friends out from behind the dragon and hold them with me in a ball of air. We hover over the artifact, and I reach down and lift it into the bubble with us, still spinning, still alive.

It feels us, Sky says, with wonder in her mental voice.

It needs us, Jewel adds. *Let's each take a side, like the last time.*

I slow its spin and notice it has the same symbols as the other. When the spinning stops, Sky is once again in front of the carving of the four figures surrounded by Terra and the love sign. The side facing Jewel has a coyote, a star, and a butterfly. Pax's side has a vertical moon with an arrow underneath it and a dragon on the bottom. The sun, which Wolf says stands for hope, is on my side. I can sure use some hope right now.

I focus on holding us and the artifact off the hot cavern floor. Just as we're about to touch it, it begins to shake, and we hear the first rumblings of a sound we never want to hear again. The dragon growls in alarm and leaps to his feet as the ground underneath us shakes. We hear the cries of the others as they're knocked to the sand behind him.

My concentration broken, the artifact wobbles and starts to sink while we try to regain our balance on air that's quickly dissipating. We'll cook on the hot sand, and I can't get control. Is this it?

We start to fall, then we're floating again. The artifact steadies in front of us, but I'm not doing it.

"Hurry," Jewel says, her eyes wide with shock and fear. She reaches for my hand and holds it on the sun symbol. I grab Sky's hand and together we touch the love symbol. She and Pax join hands over the dragon and moon, and he completes the circle with Jewel over the coyote and butterfly.

"Do it now," Sky says, and with our link, we send Sky's huge love into the artifact. Warmth spreads from the tetrahedron into us, and the sun symbol glows brightly in front of me. The dragon rumbles, but the artifact is silent. It sends gratitude and suddenly, it wants us to step away. We let go, and we're drawn away from it. How?

Once we've reached the cooler sand by the dragon, we're lowered gently to the ground. I turn back and watch the artifact happily spinning its protective shield, while I lean against the dragon's leg without thinking. The scales are vibrating. Is the dragon purring? He doesn't seem to mind my touching him, so I rest there until he shakes me off to move closer to the egg, where he circles it and settles in the sand.

Someone in this room can do what I do. Someone has as strong a gift of telekinesis as I do. How is that possible?

Exhausted, I press the wristband to turn off the link and make my way back down the tunnel to the first cave, where I sit on the beach, sifting sand through my fingers. Juliana sinks down next to me.

"That was insane back there," she says. I nod, too tired to speak. "I didn't know I could do that." Okay. That snaps me out of it.

"You? That was you? How?" I can barely get the words out in my rush to get answers.

"I don't know. It's the first time I've done anything like that. It does make sense though."

"What do you mean?" Something about the way she said it makes me uneasy. How does it make sense?

"When I was fourteen, Mom and Dad told me I had a brother who could make things fly with his mind. It made them sad to talk about him. He died before I was born."

"How old are you now?" I ask. She seems to be close to my age.

"I'll be seventeen soon," she answers. A year younger than me.

"I'm sorry." I don't know her, but I'm sad for her parents. I know what it's like to lose someone you love. "What was his name?"

"Darrock," she says, sending a lightning bolt of shock through me. It's impossible. My parents called me by that name. There must be another Darrock. My parents have been dead eight years, not seventeen.

"What's your last name?" I ask, afraid of her answer.

"Ryder," she says. "I'm Juliana Ryder. What's yours?"

Pax, Jewel, and I lead the way, staggering and shuffling through the thick sand to the cave where our submarine waits. We've cut the link off, each lost in our own thoughts. Gabe and Izzy follow, eager to get to the sub and back to Proteus.

The others come along, leaving Triton to guard his now-healthy egg. A shockwave knocks me off my feet.

"Sky? What is it?" My brother reaches down to lift me up.

"Didn't you feel that? The shockwave?" By the bewilderment in his eyes, I realize I was the only one who felt it. It must have come from Storm. I run, and nearly crash into my brother, who's passed me, and come to a sudden stop in the cavern. Juliana is hanging in the air over the water, and Storm's fury rips into my heart.

"No. Storm, stop!" Jewel screams as soon as she sees what he's doing. Why has he attacked Juliana?

"He didn't do anything," Juliana says. "I'm fine. I thought it prudent to distance myself from my brother."

Brother? No wonder she resembles him, but how is this possible? How can he not know about her?

"Please allow me to explain." The deep grating voice raises goose-bumps on my arms. I turn to see the largest of the Dracans standing close to the wall with his arm around a woman who resembles Marla. If this is her mother, she's vastly improved since the last time we saw her. The two guards stand ready to defend him if Storm tries anything. The smaller Dracan stands protectively behind a blond woman who grins at Jewel as if they're good friends. His teeth are bared, but I can't tell if he's grimacing in rage or smiling.

Marla's mother isn't disturbed, and neither is Max, standing beside her. In fact, everyone feels content. I glance at Jewel, who's smiling at the one who is obviously the leader.

"I am Thuban, King of Atlantis," he announces. "Avery is my mate. This is Dr. Ashley Jenkins and her son Murphrid." He waves toward the two.

"Jewel has been our honored guest, although she came to us reluctantly, as did Salali and Tom Ryder eight of your years ago."

The ground shakes with Storm's barely suppressed rage. I concentrate on calming him, but I can't reach him. Pax grabs his arm and activates both of their links. I do the same and see Jewel tap her band.

If you want answers, you'll have to calm down. Let him speak, he says, always the peacemaker.

I promise he's not the enemy. Let's hear him out. I knew nothing about this, Jewel says.

I'm not surprised they kept secrets from her. Does the Dracan mean 'prisoner' when he says, 'honored guest'?

The ground steadies and Storm nods.

"Shaula, who was once my trusted advisor, took your parents. He claimed they knew too much and were planning to reveal Dracan technology to the Allarans. I believed him and confined them to secure quarters. You should ask Jewel about her quarters. They were treated well.

"When I interviewed them and discovered they are scientists, I gave them access to our labs, knowing they would not escape. They made their home among us, thinking you, Storm, had been killed in their capture, as Shaula had led us all to believe. Since I did not know you were alive, be assured neither I nor those loyal to me had any part in the attacks against you.

"Two years later, Juliana was born."

Juliana sinks to the sand next to me, keeping her distance from her brother, but full of curiosity and wonder. Since I can feel her, I know she isn't a Dracan hybrid.

When the realization hits, I'm left breathless. I can feel Sequoia's baby. She can't be a hybrid, either.

Before I can share my discovery with the others, Storm shouts, "They were taken eight years ago. If what you say is true, then she'd only be six years old, not sixteen."

"Allaran wormholes have become unstable and have often caused time distortions. We were caught in one when your parents were taken, and it lasted until a few months ago. For every year you have experienced, your parents have lived approximately two and a half years. My own daughter would be just over seven years old had she been born on land. Instead, she is nearly eighteen, the same age as you."

"So, she's really my sister? My parents are alive? Where are they? I need to see them." A ray of hope breaks through the darkness of his rage. Could this be true?

"Yes, they are alive, and Juliana is your sister. Unfortunately, I do not know where they are. When Shaula betrayed me, he took them. My informants traced them to Superstition Mountain, and we tried to find them when we rescued Jewel, Max, and our daughter from their queen. They had already been moved elsewhere. A few days ago, we discovered Shaula had them on his ship, and I sent one of mine in pursuit. Both ships disappeared into an Allaran wormhole."

My heart skips a beat and Storm goes pale. He's afraid, but I can't help him. Those ships flew into the waterspout before the hurricane. I'm shocked one of them had his parents on board. Dark rage once again takes him over. He tries to contain it, and I loan him what little strength I have left.

Jewel suddenly speaks up, "King Thuban, were you on board the fishing vessel when we made our escape? Did you know about our plan?"

"I did, Jewel Adams. It was time to return you to your family, but it had to seem like an escape. I am still embroiled in the controversy over the artifacts, although I am convinced our scientists cannot do what you four do. I prefer to avoid an all-out war with my fellow rulers and believe those who agree with me will win with diplomacy. They cannot know I aided your escape."

"How will we get everybody to the surface?" Gabe pipes in. "Namor will only hold six. I know there are more of you coming along."

"It is late at night on the surface," Thuban says. I can't imagine how he knows that. "We will take them in my ship and drop them off on the research vessel."

"I'll go with Izzy and Gabe," Storm says. "The rest of you ride with the Dracans."

I'll come with you, I tell him.

No. Go with Jewel. I need to be alone. I'll see you on the Proteus.

I try to comfort him, but his wall is up again, thicker than ever. He climbs into the submarine after Gabe. Izzy checks the exterior and enters as soon as she's satisfied. The Dracans push the sub back into the water, and I watch it sink. My heart sinks with it.

SKY

Thuban boards his ship and the rest of us follow. I hang back with Jewel as the others enter one by one.

What about returning the artifact? I ask Jewel. *Doesn't Thuban have it?*

I thought he did, she answers. *He didn't mention it, though. I wonder if Shaula took it.*

Who is coming with us? I'm surprised when Jewel includes Murphrid and says Marla is not coming. Why the Dracan? Why not Marla? Before I can ask, we're inside, and I'm struck by how different it is from the Sentinels. This is built for efficiency rather than luxury. I go with Jewel and Juliana to retrieve their clothes and wait while they change.

"Juliana, have you ever been on the surface?"

"No, and I'm eager to see how you live there."

Jewel shakes her head. "It's much different than Atlantis. Prepare yourself to be disappointed."

I try the link, but it doesn't work in here. "Jewel, were you able to use your gift in Atlantis? Did you see all your colors?"

She shakes her head and pulls on a soft blue tunic. "The boys were right about the tunnels. Dracan technology blocks our gifts, and besides you and my friends and family, it was the one thing I missed the most."

"Is that why I didn't know I could do what Storm does?" Juliana asks. "I had no idea I could make things move with my mind."

"How did you save us back there if you've never practiced using your gift before?" Jewel always seems to ask the right questions, and a lot of them.

"It was instinctive, I guess. You were floating there when you suddenly dropped. I reached out and lifted you back up again. It seemed simple at the time, but I don't know if I can do it again."

"He'll help you learn," I assure her, hoping I'm right. "It will take him some time to get used to having a sister. You will stay, won't you?"

"If his family will have me, and only until they find my parents."

We leave the cabin and join the others in a room like the portal room in the Allaran vessel. Jewel's Dracan friend Murphrid is there, along with Max, Jewel, Juliana, Pax, and me.

"Are we the only ones going to the ship?" I ask. Jewel nods and grabs my hand.

"They're about to beam us down," she says. "We'll have to go one at a time."

The portal opens revealing our research vessel below. A spotlight comes on and a sailor points a handgun at us.

"Hold on," Pax shouts. "It's us. Don't shoot."

Light from our portal drops to the deck, and he steps off into the air. This, at least, is just like the Allaran ships. He floats down, hands up, until his feet are on the boat, and other hands reach into the light to pull him aside. I go next, landing safely, and find my dad already hugging him.

Max follows and Dad hugs him, too. "I can't tell you how happy I am to see you, Max," he says. "Your father has been terribly worried about you."

Suddenly, Charles calls out, "Jewel!" His voice grows thick with tears as she floats down and he cries, "Jewel, my baby," and reaches for her when she lands. He buries his face in her hair and she clings to him, both sobbing.

Wolf is astonished as Juliana descends. "Salali?" he whispers, reaching for her.

"Her daughter," she says. His joy and incredulity mix in a wave that makes my heart leap. I send him assurance and comfort.

Dr. Emery stares at the huge triangle blocking out the stars. "Who is that?" he asks, as a young man steps into the light and floats down to the deck. "How many people are they keeping down there?"

Pax taps his wristband. *Who the heck is this guy? I've never seen him before.*

It's Murphrid, Jewel responds. *He must be in his human form.*

And what a delicious form it is, I say, admiring the way his jeans and tight-fitting blue t-shirt show off muscular legs and arms. No wonder I didn't sense his emotions as he descended to the deck. His short sandy hair, dark brown eyes and a dazzling movie-star smile would make any female heart flutter. He's perfect, and I remember what the Watchers said about the Allarans and Dracans mating with human women. Now I understand how that happened.

Pax greets Murphrid as he lands on the deck and takes him over to Dr. Emery.

"This is our friend Murphy, Dr. Emery." I'm proud of him for his quick action and quicker thinking. People would question the origin of a name like Murphrid.

"Murphy Jenkins," the Dracan says, holding his hand out to the scientist who shakes it politely. He isn't smiling. "It is an honor to meet you, Dr. Emery. I have studied your work. You and your team have made many fascinating discoveries."

The beam suddenly goes dark, and the soundless triangle pulls away. The crewmen rush to the rails and watch it slice into the sea just beyond the vessel's spotlight, without a splash and leaving no trace. I tune out their excited chatter.

"Where are my scientists? My sub? And aren't you missing someone?" Dr. Emery's anger rises. Pax assures him of their safety.

"The radio wasn't working earlier," he explains. "They're on their way and should be here in the next hour or so. We'll explain everything as soon as they arrive."

He's still angry, afraid for his people, but he graciously leads us to the library and instructs a crewman to find us some food. It's no easy task at four in the morning, if the wall clock is correct. While we eat, we tell him what Gabe and Izzy already know about the dragon and the artifact and how we fixed this one. Jewel elects to wait until everyone is on board before she shares her story of Atlantis.

"You know you'll have to repeat everything when we're home with your mom and the others," her dad says.

"Of course," she answers. "With pleasure."

The yellow submarine surfaces as the sun rises. Jewel stands at the rail, with Pax's arm around her. I quickly suppress a stab of jealousy and join them. Why doesn't Storm see me the way my brother sees Jewel?

"I'd forgotten how brilliant the colors are," she says, swiping at a tear rolling down her cheek. Even to my eyes, the pink, yellow, and orange clouds in the east are magnificent. I can't imagine how colorful they are to her.

We watch the crane at the stern clamp onto the bobbing sub. It lifts the Namor effortlessly and sets it down in a cradle on the deck, designed to hold it snugly. The hatch opens, and Storm is the first one out.

.

6 0

JEWEL

From what Sky told me, the Allarans have only been good for transport during my captivity. At least we can count on them for that, now that we're leaving Andros to go back home. I watch Juliana's eyes widen as she's lifted into Vega's ship. Max, too. This is their first time meeting the aliens my friends have been most familiar with.

"Will you help her adjust?" I ask Storm.

"Do I have a choice?" he answers. He isn't happy about it. His aura is as wild with reds and blacks as it was when I first met him. His parents are alive, and he has a sister. Shouldn't he be a little bit happy? He disappears into the ship.

Sky grabs my hand, her anger and frustration mixed with joy. It's an odd sensation, but I understand it. She's happy I'm back but would love to dunk Storm's head in a bucket. I don't understand how he can be such an idiot.

Pax wraps his arm around my waist. "Ready?" he asks. I nod, enjoying the thrill of being close to him. His aura is as calm as ever, but now there are magenta swirls where before it was mainly blue and yellow. Am I causing them? He smiles down at me and I want to lose myself in his magnificent green eyes.

He lets go when Mom comes over, radiating joy and love in the rainbow colors of her aura. At least that's how I interpret them.

"You don't have my brother or sister lurking in the shadows somewhere, do you, Mom?" I ask, teasing her. She laughs and gives my arm a little push.

"I wish. I'd love to have more kids like you." Mom is coming with us in Vega's ship. She doesn't want to leave my side. I hope we aren't too crowded in the observation room. Murphrid, or Murphy as he's now called, has gone ahead with Dylan, Coral, Wolf, Sequoia, and Dad. I got a kick out of the way his scales flashed in excitement. He reminds me of an alien version of Pax, with his blue and yellow scales and his ability to remain calm. He couldn't wait to be lifted into Baran's ship. It still surprises me everyone else sees him as human, and a gorgeous one at that. When we get home, I'll put on the glasses Dad made for me to suppress my vision, just so I can see him that way, too.

I can't see colors in Murphrid's energy field, but I'm learning Dracan scales say a lot about their temperament. They change according to emotion, much like human auras do. Marla is the only one I've seen in human form, but with my vision back, I'll only see her as Dracan without my glasses.

Storm, Max, and Juliana are seated in their bubbles when Mom and I enter the room. We're surrounded by fish, eels, and even a lobster crawling along the reef on the screens. Max is fascinated with the chair, bending to examine it from different angles. Juliana relaxes with her eyes closed. Storm's wistful eyes stare at the screen. His aura has calmed a bit. He must be thinking about his dives. I've missed so much.

Mom knows me well. "We're coming back when Sequoia is close to her time. She wants her baby to be born on Andros with Lucaya in attendance. You'll have time to experience the islands and the reef, and maybe you'll even see Marla there." How would she know I miss my friend?

Vega enters the room, and the atmosphere instantly electrifies. The men's auras change, with streaks of dark red and black shooting through their normal colors. Even Storm's is more agitated than usual. A magenta glow overtakes the normal shades of the women.

"Star Children and others, welcome to my ship. Understandably, you have many questions, and I will attempt to answer some of them.

"Storm, we have only now discovered your parents were not killed in the Dracan attack on your family. We cannot know everything that goes on in their cities, and they've kept your parents a secret. I am deeply grieved at the years of anguish you have experienced as a result. Please accept my apologies and assurance we will help you find them."

"The way you helped us find Jewel?" Pax asks, his voice strained with the effort to refrain from killing the Allaran. "The way you helped us rescue her?"

"We regret the constraints put upon us where Jewel was concerned. Creator's plan did not allow for our active assistance. We must obey his directives. Jewel, please accept our apologies."

"Of course," I say, trying unsuccessfully to harden my voice so I sound more grown-up and less like a love-sick panting puppy. I hate reacting this way to the Allaran. "But, if Creator tells you not to rescue Salali and Tom, then how can you assure us you will?"

"We have received no such communication."

"Where are they?" Max asks, and I'm surprised to see his chair has wrapped around him, pinning his arms, as if it senses his volatile anger. He grunts as he struggles to pull his arms free, and his face is as red as the angry streaks in his aura. Amazing technology.

"Baran will answer when we've all gathered again. You must be wondering how Juliana has the same gift as her brother when we had nothing to do with her DNA. Juliana graciously allowed us to take a sample of her hair when she entered the ship, and I wish you to meet the scientist who has found the answer."

61

JEWEL

M y hackles rise, a growl starting low in my throat, when a stunning woman with golden skin and long white hair enters. She's dressed like Vega, in a silver jumpsuit, but everything about her is different, menacing. Pax's wide eyes follow her every move and his aura is now glowing magenta. I focus on Vega and it dawns on me, either this is an Allaran trick, or it's the way humans normally react to the species.

"I am Maia, scientist assigned to the ship that will guard our new Star Child," she says, her voice like nails on a chalkboard. I cringe. "Juliana, you received your Allaran DNA directly from your mother. We did not anticipate her cells would mutate in this fashion. This is an exciting discovery."

Juliana is not excited. She's furious, her teeth bared like an angry Dracan. At this moment, she reminds me of Shaula, and I shudder.

"Why hasn't she noticed her gifts until now?" my mother asks. Her trembling hands betray the effort it costs her to remain civil.

"The Dracans have a barrier that prevents us from using our gifts," I explain. "It covers everything, and I'm beginning to think it's more a molecular covering than the material protecting Atlantis, which is more like cephalopod skin. It must not cling to humans, since our gifts come back as soon as we're outside their enclosures. It may also be the reason I can't see Dracan auras."

"Very astute, Jewel," Vega says, and his approval warms me all over. "We have arrived. We will take our leave after we speak with the rest of you."

I watch as Max's chair releases him and Maia touches his shoulder. The way he leans toward her as she leads him to the portal reminds me of cartoons where aromatic wisps tease and draw the hapless character toward certain doom. He's the first one down, and the rest of us quickly follow.

I zip my jacket closed at the blast of cold air outside the ship, thankful Mom and Dad had the foresight to pack winter clothes for me. I was surprised to find out it's only February. So much has happened in these few months. Juliana shivers in a blanket Sky grabbed when we left Andros. Murphrid hurries to put an arm around her.

His grin and flashing scales lift my spirits. Juliana's aura shows magenta. Since I can't see his, I can only guess how he feels about her.

Baran waits as we gather on my meadow.

I have never seen my father scowl like he's doing right now. Wolf scowls as if he wishes he had a spear to run through the Allaran. Sequoia, in contrast, is warm and peaceful. I understand why Creator wanted to keep us away from them after the Great War. We have enough problems between men and women without them.

"Where are they?" Wolf asks, his voice tight with tension.

Baran answers, "They have been taken through a compromised wormhole. It is remotely possible it linked to Allara, but they are most likely somewhere on Terra. We will, of course, explore every possibility."

"How will you get to Allara to check?" my father asks.

"We closely guard the one open passage to our planet. The others are as capricious on Allara as they are on Terra. We never know when or where they will open, nor where they might lead."

Dad's eyebrows crunch together and he huffs. "You couldn't rescue our daughter. In fact you didn't know where to find the city of Atlantis. How will you find them if they're in a Dracan stronghold?"

"We now have more Dracan allies," Baran answers, glancing at Murphrid. "Thuban, who sheltered Storm's parents, not knowing how Shaula had abducted them, is determined to aid us. For the first time since the Great War, we will work together."

"Have your Dracan allies told you where our artifact is?" Wolf asks.

"The King of Atlantis has arranged to have the artifact returned to the cavern where the Star Children found it. The tunnel will then be filled, and we have assigned Watchers to protect it once again."

It seems like we've come full circle, Pax says. *Thank God we don't have to go back and rescue the artifact.*

I agree. Thank God.

Baran walks back to the portal beam of his ship, and Vega and Maia rise into theirs. Maia waves and smiles, and I'm glad to see them go.

Juliana copies Storm as he lifts some of the luggage. They float the bags between the two of them. It's good to see how quickly she's learning.

The windows of our house glow with a soft light. Home has never been more inviting. An SUV drives up and parks behind the jumble of cars already filling the driveway. This must have been where the Allarans picked everyone up for the trip to Andros. Sheriff Green exits and stands next to his car for a moment, before heading toward us. He seems hesitant, as if afraid his son might not be among us.

"Dad!" Max shouts, and both he and the sheriff take off running to meet in a bear hug.

My heart is happy. I'm home. Pax cares for me and I have my best friend Sky back.

Storm's parents are alive and the Allarans have promised to locate them. He has a sister now, not to mention a baby cousin on the way. I knew by Sequoia's golden aura she was different, but I didn't expect this. A baby! He doesn't know how good his life is. I wish he'd wise up about Sky. I hate seeing her sad.

We have a new half-Dracan friend who most people will only know as a human, and Dad has a science buddy to take to the observatory with him. I wonder how he'll explain Murphy to the other scientists. We've fixed two artifacts, and even though the one that belongs here hasn't yet been returned, the world is still alive and well.

Hopefully, everything is finally calming down and we can get back to life as usual.

We say goodnight to the other families and settle in to watch some news before bed. Mom and I cuddle and sip tea, but when the news comes on, I sit on the edge of my seat.

BREAKING NEWS: A third volcano in the last two weeks exploded in a fiery plume of ash and lava early this morning in Ecuador. Tungurahua, also known as the Throat of Fire, located ninety miles south of Quito, sent ash rocketing 20,000 feet in a matter of moments. Warned of an imminent eruption by the rumbling mountain, most residents had time to flee. It is unknown how many were not able to escape.

MAIPO, a volcano near Santiago, Chile, erupted nine days ago, destroying two nearby villages in a devastating iconoclastic flow. Hawaii's Mauna Loa, which hasn't erupted since 1985, became active in a dramatic display of ash and fire on Monday last week.

SCIENTISTS AGREE the Ring of Fire, a zone of volcanic and seismic activity that rings the Pacific and includes the entire west coast of the United States, is roaring to life. They are investigating the cause.

IN OTHER NEWS, people from southern California all the way up to Oregon are reporting strange moaning noises in the atmosphere. Some observers say they sound like trumpet blasts and fill the air with no discernible place of origin. Scientists are baffled at this ongoing mystery.

Cayla Knox reporting for News Channel Twelve."

∽

IT SEEMS we may not have as much time to recover as I'd hoped. Our next artifact is somewhere in the Ring of Fire.

∽

～

Thank you, dear Reader, for reading this second book in the Tetrasphere series. If you enjoyed it, please leave a review on Amazon, or where you bought the book. Your positive energy could be just what our planet needs.

By now, you'll want to know what happens next! Continue the story in **Voice of Viracocha, Tetrasphere Book 3**.

Just for you, I've included Chapter One. Read on and enjoy!

～

VOICE OF VIRACOCHA

TETRASPHERE – BOOK 3

One - Jewel Amaryllis Adams

The problem with the ancient Cherokee prophecy isn't that it foretold my friends and I were chosen to save the world. No, the problem is, it didn't predict whether we'd succeed or not.

What if we fail? What if two planets die and it's our fault?

My eyes follow a shaft of moonlight creeping across the ceiling, casting soft rainbows, each one an endless blend of subtle hues. Even the return of my enhanced vision doesn't soothe the jumbled nerves tying knots in my gut. I can't shake the feeling something is terribly wrong. It's been with me, a constant gnawing presence, since we returned from the Bahamas.

A strange vibration in the bed quickly grows into a ground-shaking earthquake, rattling the pictures on the wall. I hold tightly to the bed frame with one hand while I reach out to save the lamp on my nightstand from crashing to the floor. It isn't as strong as the earthquakes last fall, caused by Dracans digging tunnels, but someone will undoubtedly report it.

The Dracans have kept their promise. They've returned the artifact and sealed the passageway. It should give me some measure of peace. It doesn't. I watch the light for a while longer, then get up and dress to greet the dawn, grabbing my favorite blanket on the way out.

～

Spring comes early in the North Carolina mountains. It's only the beginning of March and already warming up. I sit in the swing on the porch, wrap my blanket around me and glance up at two alien discs reflecting the colors of the rising sun. Allaran ships. Invisible to everyone else, they're a common sight to me, the only human who can see through their cloaking ability. Before I met my three friends, I only saw one and called it my Sentinel. As a child I thought it was my guardian angel. Not anymore. Now I know we each have one assigned to us, and the aliens occupying them are not angels.

The Allarans have as much to lose as we do if we fail. The fate of their planet is directly tied to ours. The wormholes they created to travel between the planets have formed a permanent connection, and the tetrahedra keeping our Earth in balance are directly linked to the ones on Allara. You'd think they'd be more helpful.

I turn away to watch two does and their tiny fawns at the edge of the forest, each one outlined by bright light in the early morning dark. One fawn frantically butts his mother's tummy, then stills as he nurses. The other stays close to her mother, investigating the busy forest floor nearby. Although I can't tell their gender from here, my imagination takes over and gives them identity.

"The Dracans returned the artifact this morning. Did you feel the quake?" My best friend Sky pushes the door open with her hip, carefully holding a mug of steaming coffee in each hand. She settles next to me on the porch swing and hands me one, prepared just the way I like it, with cream and plenty of sugar.

"Is it glad to be back home?" It's still chilly out and she isn't wearing a jacket, so I offer to share my blanket.

"Very much," she answers, pulling her corner over her shoulders. "I felt its joy before they closed the tunnel." We discovered the artifacts are sentient when we fixed this one last fall.

"Sky, do you think we'll find them all?"

"I wish I knew," she replies, taking a sip of her coffee. "While you were living it up in Atlantis with your Dracan friends," she teases, "and the rest of us frantically searched for you, we all wondered what would happen if we fail. Will we end our planet? Would it be our fault? Anyone could break under that weight of responsibility. The stress is getting to all of us." The concern in her eyes is something I've seen far too often lately.

I jab her with my elbow, and she yelps when hot coffee sloshes out of her mug. I'd been abducted by the reptilian Dracans, imprisoned, half-blinded when they blocked my ability, and cut off from communicating with my friends and family. Their frantic search included diving the stunning barrier reef and exploring underwater caverns. Most importantly, they had each other and could use their gifts freely.

Not that living with the Dracans was a bad life. I learned to care deeply for them and their hybrids, especially Marla Snow. As much as I didn't like her during my short stint in high school, she proved to be a great friend when I needed one.

In the end, we fixed the second artifact. It was the first time I'd been able to see normally in months and the colors of my friends' auras fed my starving soul.

I force back tears. They come too easily these days. Sky is as puzzled as I am, and we're not the only ones. My mother took several vials of my blood to identify anything that might be causing my emotional roller-coaster ride. She does genetic research in her lab below our house. If anyone can spot an anomaly, it's my mom.

Sky nudges the porch with her toe, and the motion of the swing soothes me as we stare out at the field. "Do you believe everything the watchers told us?" she asks.

"Not really. They were mistaken about the Dracans' motives for wanting the artifact. They could have been wrong about other things, too."

We grow quiet as we remember the little aliens who'd died leading us to the tetrahedron under Clingman's Dome. If not for them, we would have been killed, too.

Sky breaks the silence. "We almost died getting to the first two artifacts. How often can we do that? How long can we keep it up? It's crazy that we're the only four people on Earth who can save the entire planet."

∼

~

Don't stop now! Want to know why Jewel's emotions are all over the place? Order your copy of **Voice of Viracocha** today!

If you enjoyed **Triton's Call**, please leave a review on Amazon, or where you bought the book. Your positive energy might help find and fix another artifact.

Visit my website www.ptlperrin.org for this and other books by P.T.L. Perrin. Or pick up **Voice of Viracocha: Tetrasphere Book 3** at your favorite online retailer.

I love hearing from you! Please connect with me!

Amazon: www.amazon.com/author/ptlperrin
Facebook author page: www.facebook.com/PTLPerrin
Facebook page: www.facebook.com/AuthorPattyPerrin
Facebook Group: Patty's Book Pals
Email: ptlperrin8@gmail.com

~

ABOUT THE AUTHOR

Patty Perrin, (P.T.L. Perrin), grew up in Europe as a military brat, with no television and a huge imagination. Books were her entertainment and augmented her education in German, Italian and American schools overseas. She speaks several languages and enjoys the diversity of people and cultures.

She wrote the Teen/YA Scifi **TETRASPHERE** series as pure entertainment and to answer some of the unanswerable questions about our amazing universe. Why would the Creator of this vast universe limit intelligent life to one tiny speck of a planet? What if other inhabited planets are interacting with Earth?

Terra's Call, the first book of the tetralogy, was a finalist in the Royal Palm Literary Awards. *Triton's Call*, the second book, won third place.

Patty and her tennis-pro husband Bill are parents and grandparents of a fluid, constantly growing family. Happily married, they live in south Florida where they exercise bragging rights in the winter, and enjoy the long summers, and where Patty is writing books she would have enjoyed reading back when she didn't have television.

ALSO BY P.T.L. PERRIN

∿

TETRASPHERE Series

Terra's Call - Book 1

∿